Maisey Yates is a *New York Times* bestselling author of more than seventy-five romance novels. She has a coffee habit she has no interest in kicking, and a slight Pinterest addiction. She lives with her husband and children in the Pacific Northwest. When Maisey isn't writing she can be found singing in the grocery store, shopping for shoes online and probably not doing dishes. Check out her website, maiseyyates.com.

THE SPANIARD'S UNTOUCHED BRIDE

MAISEY YATES

MILLS & BOON

First Published in Great Britain 2018
by Mills & Boon, an imprint of HarperCollins*Publishers*
1 London Bridge Street, London, SE1 9GF

© 2018 Maisey Yates

ISBN: 978-0-263-27023-5

MIX
Paper from
responsible sources
FSC® C007454

Printed and bound in Spain
by CPI, Barcelona

To romance novels.
Which have been my inspiration as a writer,
and my comfort as a reader.
I'm grateful there's an entire genre devoted to love.

PROLOGUE

HE DOESN'T HIRE WOMEN.

Camilla Alvarez looked into the mirror at her decidedly plain reflection. She was a woman, that much was true. Though, she had never been considered a beauty. Even so, she imagined that as far as Matías Navarro was concerned, she was a woman.

Her cheeks were still wet with tears, her eyes glittering with more. It was unthinkable. Losing her father suddenly as she had to a heart attack, and then losing the ranch, as well. And all the horses...

It was her heart. And, shattered though it was, fractured as it was now, she couldn't lose it. She could not.

But the horses, the *rancho*, everything was being sold to cover her father's debts. Everything was going to Matías Navarro.

He had been one of her father's fiercest competitors. His racehorses were the only steeds that could compete with those of Cesar Alvarez.

And now Matías owned them.

Because apparently, their *rancho* had been in debt, the supposed millions of dollars that her family possessed nothing more than smoke and mirrors. All mortgaged to extremes and behind on every payment.

Her father had been an idealist. A man completely

laser-focused on his ranch, his animals, his workers. With little time or thought given to anything else. She didn't even have to ask herself how it had happened. She knew. Her father hadn't liked the situation, and so he had ignored it.

Collectors had been hounding Camilla ever since Cesar's death. And her mother—predictably—had gone off to France, taking shelter under the wing of one of her many lovers.

She had always flaunted them in the face of her husband, but Camilla supposed that now that Cesar was dead, her mother felt it was all justified seeing as she clearly had an insurance policy.

Camilla had nothing. Nothing but the *rancho*. The place she had grown up in, grown wild in. Her mother had rarely been in residence, and for most of Camilla's life, it had simply been her and her father.

And he had allowed her to do whatever she wanted. To run barefoot. To ride until she reached the end of the property, and then beyond. Roaming all over the Spanish countryside as she pleased.

Her mother, an American heiress who had never settled well into the rural country life, had seen it all as beneath her.

Camilla had seen it as everything. And now it was gone.

She had begged, pleaded, as her horses had been led away from the property by members of Matías's staff for them to let her go, too. If she was going to lose the *rancho*, as long as she could be with the horses, as long as she could be with Fuego, she could survive it.

She had told them she would do anything, any job. But the stone-faced man guiding her favorite black stallion into the trailer had simply shaken his head and told her that Matías Navarro did not hire women.

And indeed, the evidence had been all around her that it was the truth. There was not a single woman among Matías's staff present at the *rancho*.

Her father was gone. Her horses were gone. Soon, she would be evicted from the *rancho*, with nowhere to go. There were no provisions made for her. She had nothing. Nothing and no one. She had never been able to count on her mother during good times, she had no illusions that she would be able to count on the woman now that things were difficult.

Camilla knew one thing. She knew horses.

She knew *those* horses. She loved *those* horses.

Fuego was going to be the next champion on the European racing circuit, she was confident in that. But no one else could handle him. No one else could ride him, and he had some way to go before he was ready for anyone else to try.

Matías Navarro would find out soon enough that his new acquisition was essentially useless to him. If the horse could not be broken, then he was worthless.

And without the horses… Her life felt worthless.

She looked back in the mirror, examining her face. She was not classically beautiful. Her mother had always despaired of her heavy bone structure, the angular nature of her jaw and chin. Not feminine, her rather spindly mother had declared.

For the first time, though, Camilla was completely pleased with this assessment of her looks. Because it was going to be an asset to her now.

She opened up the drawer in the vanity and pulled out a pair of scissors. Then she touched a lock of glossy, black hair, and ruthlessly stretched it tight, cutting it close to her ears.

Yes, she had found her solution.

Matías Navarro did not hire women. But perhaps he would hire a new stable boy.

CHAPTER ONE

CAMILLA STRAIGHTENED AND wiped her brow, looking out over the now familiar fields of the Navarro *rancho*. In the two months since she had come into Matías's employ, the place had become close to home. Of course, it couldn't compare to the Alvarez *rancho*. She had lived there for twenty-two years, and she couldn't imagine anywhere feeling like home the way that it had.

Sometimes she ached with the desire to walk through that familiar front door, to feel the red stone floor beneath her feet, the places where it was imperfect. Where it bowed and cracked from years of wear. It was like a familiar friend, and it was gone. She could never have it again.

But at least she had the horses.

It was a tricky thing, though, getting access to Fuego. Matías had refused to allow anyone but his most trusted handler and himself to get anywhere near him. Of course, he was proving to be difficult. Camilla had known he would be. Because he was a difficult animal.

But she had opted to keep herself mostly out of Matías's vision. She had not seen the point in drawing attention to herself, but it was becoming clear that if she wanted to have anything to do with Fuego she was going to have to assert herself.

A difficult thing, since the assumption was that she was a fourteen-year-old boy, simply doing work in exchange for board on the property.

Very few questions had been asked, and for that she was grateful. She had done a bit more digging about Matías and had discovered that he was generous with his employees. That he had a soft spot for troubled youth and made putting them to work something of a mission.

In spite of his family's difficult reputation, Matías himself seemed to be a good man. When she ignored that little *doesn't hire women* thing.

But she had found a workaround. She had decided to play the part of a troubled youth, fallen through the cracks and likely to end up sleeping on the streets if not for the kindness of the Navarro estate.

It was true enough. She had very few options available to her at the moment. She had no money.

And she was, in fact, qualified for the job she had been hired to do.

All in all, her solution was a reasonable one. So, perhaps concealing her gender might be considered less than reasonable.

But with her hair cut short, and baggy clothes over her rather straight up and down figure, no one questioned it.

In part, she imagined, because very few people looked directly at her. Much less Matías Navarro.

Or his beautiful, birdlike fiancée, who had come to live at the estate just last month. She was a lovely creature and reminded Camilla very much of her mother. She had cascading waves of curling blond hair, pale blue eyes and alabaster skin. Anytime she went out onto the *rancho* she took extensive breaks to stand in the shade and slather her body with sunscreen.

Matías seemed solicitous of her, often putting his hand on her lower back, or taking hold of her arm, as if the woman would fall onto her face on the uneven terrain if he did not hold on to her in some fashion.

Camilla wondered what it might be like to have someone treat her like that. No one had ever been gentle with her. Her father had treated her as though she were the son he didn't have. Had allowed her freedom, had encouraged hard labor. Her mother had treated her like an irritation. She had preferred the former.

But no one had ever made her feel precious. No one had ever made her feel fragile.

She sniffed and shrugged her shoulders upward, going back to the task of shoveling manure.

She would rather have this than be cloistered away in that giant manor house. Would rather be out in the sun, out where it smelled like hay and horse and grass.

She looked up and squinted. Judging by the position of the sun, it was about time for Matías to make his rounds. That meant he would be coming out to the stables, likely attempting to take Fuego into the arena to be lunged.

Historically, that had not gone well.

Camilla had watched through a crack in the door of the stable, whenever she had the opportunity. Whenever she wouldn't get caught by the foreman and scolded for being idle. She wouldn't do well at all to get fired.

She scampered over to the end of the stable and took her typical position. And then her breath caught.

There was Matías, walking into the arena with Fuego on a lead. Fuego was as beautiful as ever, his coat glossy beneath the late-afternoon sun. He tossed his head, already telegraphing his irritation with the situation, his ears listing backward.

Then her eyes slid to Matías. And everything inside her seemed to freeze.

He was stunning in his own right and reminded her in many ways of the animal he was attempting to tame. His black hair was pushed back off his forehead, his skin bronzed and gleaming. His chest was broad, his white shirt unbuttoned down to the center of his chest, the sleeves pushed up past powerful forearms. He was wearing tan breeches that molded to lean hips and powerful thighs, to say nothing of…other parts of him.

Camilla had been around jockeys her entire life. Typically, they were slightly built, all the better to ride quickly. And she knew that Matías did not race for that very reason. It wasn't practical. A man well over six feet tall with such a heavy build could never compete with other racers.

No, Matías was not a jockey. Therefore, the sight of him in those breeches was…a different experience. And one she was not accustomed to, no matter that she had grown up at a stable.

Matías and his foreman switched out the horse's lead for a lunging rope, and Matías stepped backward, moving to the edge of the arena, a whip in his hands, which would be used, not to harm the animal, but to signal changes in what he desired Fuego to do. When he wanted him to change his gait, when he wanted him to stop, or turn.

But, as had happened every time in the past couple of months, Fuego balked. He more than balked. He reared, nearly turning himself over onto his back. Camilla felt a spike of rage, and before she knew what she was doing she was tearing out of the stable and heading toward the arena.

Her face was on fire, her heart beating quickly, and this time it had nothing to do with Matías's breeches.

"Tonto!" she shouted. "You know he doesn't like it. And you insist on doing it. He's going to injure himself."

It took her a moment to realize what she had just done. That she had just shouted at the master of the domain, while in his domain. That she had just undone two months of attempting to go unnoticed by rendering herself as conspicuous as possible.

"I see," Matías said, taking too long strides across the arena and heading toward her. "You fancy yourself a great trainer, do you?"

Those dark eyes pinned her to the spot, her feet nearly growing down into the grass as he moved to the edge of the fence. She took a step backward, with great effort, trying to put some distance between herself and her formidable boss.

"Not great, perhaps," she said, attempting to keep her voice low and steady. "But I know the horse."

"What do you mean?"

"When I came here…" She desperately tried to improvise. "I did not lie when I said that I would have no home if I wasn't hired." She cast a look at the *rancho* foreman just to be sure that he was listening. So that he could corroborate at least that part of her tale. "I came from the Alvarez *rancho*. I'm familiar with Fuego. I can work with him."

"You're only just now telling us this?" Matías asked, shooting his foreman an appointed glare.

"Don't blame Juan. I didn't tell him. I was afraid to draw attention to myself. But now I see that Fuego is not going to acclimate to this new environment. Or to new trainers. I could ride him."

Matías leaned over, resting those strong forearms

over the top rail of the fence. "I am to believe that Cesar Alvarez allowed a scrawny boy to ride one of his most prized horses? That this beast responds to you?"

"That's right," she said, tilting her chin upward. "I have a way with him."

She had always had a way with difficult horses, just like her father had. It was a gift. One that Cesar Alvarez had believed you either had or didn't. He had told her it was in her DNA, as it was in his.

It had been their sole point of connection. Her father had been entirely invested in the *rancho*, and anyone who loved him had to love that place just as much. And she did. She very much did.

"I'm not letting you anywhere near that animal."

"Why not?" she asked. "What do you have to lose?"

"It's not so much what I stand to lose as what I don't want to have to cope with. I would rather not have to respond to an inquiry over a foolish boy breaking his neck on my *rancho*."

"I'm not going to break my neck," Camilla said. "But Fuego might snap a limb if you continue to handle him like this. I hear that you're very good with horses, Señor Navarro, but I have not yet seen it."

"You think insulting your boss is the way to long-term employment?"

"I assume that you are a man who would appreciate honesty. You are allowing your pride to get in the way of making the most of your animal, and I daresay I have seen it many times before."

One of Matías's dark brows shot upward. "Many times?"

"Yes. During the year I was employed with Cesar Alvarez. There were a lot of rich men with animals they could not handle."

"I'm a horseman," Matías said. "Not simply a rich man."

"You are a businessman primarily. That is nothing to be ashamed of, but it does mean that your focus is split."

Then Matías did something she did not expect. He laughed.

"All right then, boy. Come into the arena and show me what you can do."

Matías could not believe the unmitigated gall of the youth standing rooted in the grass only a few feet away from him. He could not be older than fourteen, and he spoke with the kind of boldness that grown men did not have in his presence. Although, in many ways that made sense.

Fourteen was that sort of age. When a boy could have all the bravado in the world, and not be aware of what consequences might befall him.

Matías was certain he had been similarly brash at that age. In all actuality at thirty-three he was still as brash, it was just that when you were a billionaire with limitless funds and no small amount of power, it was not considered brashness. It was simply considered reasonable.

He was a man of responsibility also, and one who— unlike the rest of the men in his family—cared about doing what was right. He cared about the ranch. About the village the ranch supported.

His *abuelo* was currently playing games with it. But Matías wasn't to be trifled with. The old man had pitted Matías and his older brother Diego against each other, saying they had to comply with specific terms, and whichever of them managed in an allotted time frame would get their share of the ranch and the family assets upon the old man's death.

If they both complied, they would get half each.

But if only one did…to the victor went the spoils.

Matías had no doubt he would be the one to win. Marriage was one of his grandfather's stipulations, and Matías had secured his union to Liliana Hart a couple of months earlier. He had known her casually for years. Had seen her at various functions with her parents, and her father had indicated he wouldn't be opposed to the union and Matías had seen it as an opportunity.

That was the sort of man he was. Decisive. Not opportunistic in the way his grandfather or brother were. He did things right.

And he reaped rewards for it.

He had expected the youth to back down the moment he had realized the manner of the man he was coming at. But he had not. Which Matías could only grudgingly admire.

The boy followed his command, moving closer to the arena, a scowl on his face.

Matías looked over at Fuego, his tempestuous new acquisition. The horse possessed the ability to be great. Matías knew it. He was an excellent judge of horseflesh. He was also an extremely skilled trainer. But the animal had refused to come to heel, no matter how long and hard Matías worked with him.

Though it galled him to admit the boy was correct, he was. Matías was also a businessman, and his work often demanded that he spend time away from the *rancho*. That meant having others work with the horses in his stead.

His family was an old one in Spain, and had been breeding champions for generations. But it had long ceased to be their primary source of income. And Matías was involved in various retail conglomerates across the world, his business centered in London, not in Spain.

Though he had achieved a level of status that allowed him to work from wherever he wanted, as various other business associates and dignitaries would meet with him wherever he chose, it still required a fair amount of travel.

So yes, in that way, this urchin boy was correct. The fact that Matías was a businessman did keep him from dedicating everything he had to the animals.

Matías regarded the boy as he walked over to the animal, who immediately seemed to still in his presence. If he had not, Matías would never have allowed the boy to get any closer. He hadn't lied when he said he was not going to subject himself to an inquiry over a teenage boy's stupidity.

Completely unafraid, the boy lifted his hand and brought it to Fuego's nose. The horse sniffed his hand and seemed to find him familiar. For he stilled, almost immediately. The boy grabbed the rope, close to the bridle, and then looked over at Matías, nodding his head once, in a clear bid for Matías to drop his end.

Matías complied.

The boy leaned into the horse, pressing his face against the horse's nose, stroking him gently and speaking to him in soft tones that Matías could not readily understand.

As if by magic, the horse quieted.

Then the boy turned to look at Matías. "I didn't lie to you. Fuego knows me. Now, he's not going to perform perfectly right away. He didn't always obey me. But I can ride him. I can work with him. And I can make it so that someone else can ride him, as well. Which is what you need if you want him to be able to race. As it is, his temperament is too hot. And the fact that no one can manage it makes it impossible. I can make him manageable. I will never make him well behaved, but manageable I can accomplish. And I assume your jockeys are strong enough riders to go from there."

"This is unprecedented," Matías said, looking over at Juan. "I do not allow children to train my animals."

"And yet," Juan responded, "clearly Cesar Alvarez did."

Matías looked back over at the boy, who was regarding him with rather hopeful eyes. "Fine. Whatever your duties are, you're relieved of them. Fuego is now your responsibility. Fernando Cortez is going to be the jockey that we use for him, so eventually you're going to be working with Fernando. But you may start by yourself."

"Good," the boy said, tilting his face upward.

He suddenly looked a bit older than Matías had thought originally. But perhaps that was the bravado again.

"Then it is good," he responded.

He moved over to the edge of the fence. Matías nodded once, signaling the boy to proceed.

The boy paused, then stared at him. "Don't you want to know my name?"

"If I know your name will you become a better horse trainer?" Matías asked.

"No," the boy said, blinking. "I don't suppose."

"Then I do not care to know your name."

The boy said nothing but set about silently moving Fuego through his paces. The horse was jumpy, skittish, but not completely immovable as he had been when Matías had attempted the same.

There was no denying that the boy had a way with the horse. And if Matías wanted him trained in time, he was going to have to allow the boy to step in. The last thing he wanted to do was mishandle such a magnificent creature.

Acquiring Cesar Alvarez's stock had been a boon for him, and he was not about to waste it.

"What about the other horses from the Alvarez *rancho*?" Matías called. "You are familiar with them, as well?"

"All of them," the boy said, not looking over at Matías. "I have worked with all of them."

"You will work with all of them here," he said, decisive now. "My trainers keep logs. Juan will show you the proper way to do this. That way I can read about your progress without having to speak to you. As I prefer it."

"Of course, *señor*," the boy said.

"It is because I'm a businessman, and not simply a horseman," Matías said.

He could have sworn he saw a smile curve the boy's lips. "Of course, *señor*."

Matías turned away, smiling. It was possible that now he had the break he needed to make this animal profitable for him. It seemed as though everything was finally going his way. His engagement to Liliana was cemented. Though she was staying in her own quarters, rather than coming into his.

She had found the transition in their relationship to be a fast one. From a business associate of her father's to his fiancée. And it was clear she required a bit of time to adjust.

He didn't mind. He was a patient man, in all things.

He began to walk back toward the ranch house.

He would fulfill his grandfather's requirements, and the control of the vast family estate would be his at last. A wife. A champion racehorse.

The old man should have known better than to challenge Matías Navarro. Because with him, challenges never went unanswered.

Matías would win this battle with the old man. He knew no other way.

CHAPTER TWO

CAMILLA COULDN'T REMEMBER the last time she'd had a chance to shower. It was an awful thing, but there was no shower in her personal quarters. She had to make do with the shared one in the stables, and it always felt a bigger risk than was strictly necessary.

Still, she was dying for one, especially after spending all day working in the intense heat. She had worked with Fuego until they were both nearly exhausted. But it was the happiest she had been since her father died. Being on the back of that horse again. Riding through the olive groves on the property, the hot, dry wind burning its way across her cheeks.

If her mother could see her now, she would truly despair of her. Reddish face, chapped lips, her hair cut close to her skull and just long enough now to stick up at strange angles when she ran her hands through it in frustration, from when the horses failed to do what she asked of them.

She did indeed look like a boy, and it was easy to feel fully immersed in the role. Until she needed something like a shower, in which case she became terribly aware of her body.

The other time she became terribly aware of her body was when Matías would stride across the grounds, wearing those problematic breeches. It made her feel hot, and it made her feel strange. And so much of the feeling centered on the parts of her body she tried to disguise, that it was impossible for her not to hyper-focus on them.

It was late, the sun having gone down a good half our earlier, a chill starting to wrap itself around her body. Hot days like that always left her skin feeling tight, as though there were an invisible layer of dust over every last inch of her.

Most of the staff had gone home, very few of them living in residence as she did, and the others either had private bathroom facilities or would be showering in the morning. At least that was what she was going to go ahead and bank on tonight.

She scampered into the stable, moving through to the tack room, and heading into the shower. She locked the door behind her and stripped her clothes off quickly, unwinding the precautionary medical wrap that she had around her chest.

It was such a slight chest, she probably didn't have to bind herself, not really. But it was a precaution that she took seriously. Along with these clandestine showers. Just in case. Just in case someone had a key to the room she was in. Just in case somehow, right after her shower, having just been naked, she looked somehow more female.

That was the one good thing about the dirt. It provided an extra layer of coverage. She smiled at that, stepping beneath the hot spray of water and scrubbing each inch of her body as quickly as possible.

That was one asset to short hair, as well. The fact that it took much less time to manage. To wash. And in the morning, she did nothing with it at all.

She hummed as she scrubbed and then shut the water off, much sooner than she would like. But really, she didn't have the luxury of lingering.

She dressed into the fresh clothes she had brought inside with her—nothing more than baggy sweat-pants—and was just about to pull her tank on when the doorknob rattled.

She froze, her heart fluttering like a frightened bird trapped in her chest.

"Occupied," she said, doing her best to keep her voice low and husky while panic raced through her.

The doorknob quit rattling. She wrapped her chest quickly with the bandage and then gathered up her dirty clothes, taking care to hide the old bandage that she had been wearing.

She unlocked the door, fortifying herself for who she might see on the other side, and stepped out. "I'm sorry," she said, the words dying on her lips as her eyes made contact with Matías Navarro's.

"Sorry," she said again, mumbling.

"I was taking a walk," he said, his voice hard. "And I saw that there were lights on in here and I came to check."

"I just needed a shower," she responded.

"There is no crime in that."

She shook her head and then attempted to scurry past him. But she ran into the edge of that heavily muscled arm, stumbling forward and dropping the armful of clothes in her hand.

"Easy," Matías said.

Then, much to her horror, before she could act he bent down and collected her clothing. And that pale, taupe-colored medical bandage had somehow risen to the top. Obvious, she thought.

Matías frowned. "Are you injured?"

"I…" She cleared her throat, her head spinning, her cheeks hot. She was grateful that he had supplied that question. Because of course that was the much more logical thought to have. Not that she had been binding her breasts for the past two and a half months to conceal her gender. "My wrist was feeling tender. Just… Fuego pulled a little bit harder and in the opposite direction than I expected when I was lunging him earlier." It was amazing how easy the lie came. Camilla had never been put in a position where she'd had to lie.

She had always done exactly what her father expected. Which had suited her just fine as it had all centered around the *rancho*.

Her mother had never required a lie. She was disinterested in her only child and did not care what Camilla was up to so long as it did not interfere with, or embarrass, her.

She had never known whether or not she was a good liar, because the opportunity had never presented itself. Apparently, she was proficient.

"The swelling has gone down now," she said. "And I'm feeling fine. I was afraid it might be sprained, but it is not."

"That's very interesting. Because I went over the logs earlier and did not see that in there."

"It didn't matter to me," she said, feeling the heat mounting her cheeks. "I mean, it didn't bear noting to me."

"Do not mistake me, boy. It is not your health that concerns me. If Fuego is not responding to training…"

"He is," Camilla said hurriedly.

Matías shifted, rubbing his thumb across the bandage. Something in her stomach grew tight, and then the whole thing flipped over. Her breasts suddenly felt heavy. Even bound beneath the fresh tape as they were.

"If he is a danger to you…"

"He isn't," she insisted, reaching out and snatching the clothing out of his hand. She couldn't bear him touching it. She didn't know why. It made her skin feel warm.

Idiot. That's because you just took a hot shower.

"As long as you're certain."

She nodded. "I am."

Matías nodded once in return, those well-sculpted lips turning down slightly. She felt…immobilized by them. Just for a moment. She didn't think she had ever seen such a handsome man. Not in her whole life. And here she was, dressed as a boy. And even if she wasn't, he would never look twice at her.

No man ever had. Matías Navarro would hardly have been the first. But even if there had been a possibility, it was rendered completely impossible by two things. He thought she was a boy, and he was engaged to his counterpart in beauty.

Liliana was the human version of a meringue. A confection of a woman. All light, airy and pastel. Sweet and beautiful.

Standing anywhere near her made Camilla's bones feel heavy. Made her shoulders feel broad, and her height absurd.

The sad thing was, she had a feeling that even if she was presenting as a woman she would show much the same way in the petite American's presence.

Her one consolation was that Liliana's Spanish was fairly atrocious.

Though, Matías never seemed to indicate that he thought so. And he often spoke to her in English, which

Camilla thought sounded lovely and cultured coming from his lips. She had grown up with both languages, because of her mother, and she was familiar with the way native speakers sounded.

She preferred it from Matías's lips.

"Be careful," Matías said before turning away.

And Camilla was left standing there, her heart thundering hard. And she knew that it was not beating quickly because of adrenaline anymore. That it was something else. Something impossible and terrible. Something that had to be ignored at all costs.

Fernando Cortez was going to have an introduction to Fuego today. Matías had arranged to watch the meeting, and he had also managed to get Liliana to agree to come watch, as well. They drove in an air-conditioned truck across the property to the arena, and then he set them both up in the shade at the edge of the arena.

Liliana's blond curls tumbled over her shoulders and down her back, half of her hair caught up in a row of pink flowers. Her cheeks were a pleasing, matching pink, as were her lips. She wore no makeup. Liliana often did that. He had a feeling it was, in many ways, to highlight just how beautiful she was.

She would make a beautiful wife. A very suitable wife. One that would make him the envy of many men. Certainly of his brother.

But Diego was disgraced, and he was on the verge of being disinherited. He would never marry in time to fulfill their grandfather's will, and, as a result, it would leave Matías in charge of everything. The whole of the Navarro *rancho*, and all the stock.

Plus, it would eliminate the opportunity for his brother to get his hands in Matías's business. That was actually his primary concern. That Diego would end up part owner of Matías's company, even if it was a minority share. Because when Matías had started his retail empire, it had been with money from the Navarro family trust. Which would technically be half Diego's were he to find a suitable bride.

But his brother was a villain. And out of the country after the death of his first wife, with rumors swirling around him.

He had gone on to amount to…nothing much. Gambling and whoring his way through Europe, managing to amass a fortune via misdeeds as far as Matías could see.

He and Diego had never been close, but after their mother's death they had only gotten more distant. His older brother, growing darker, had withdrawn into himself. He had begun to act out, destroying furniture and art pieces. Setting fire to a shed on the property. For his part, Matías had built a taller wall up around himself.

Their methods for surviving a childhood with a violent father who tended toward insanity had been vastly different. For his part, Matías had kept his head down. He had stayed the course that no one had set out for him. But one he had set out for himself.

Diego, meanwhile, had seemingly drunk his father's poison. He moved through life delighting in his wickedness. In his depravity.

Matías would not allow him to have control here. This land had seen enough suffering and cruelty.

Matías would marry Liliana and that would be the end of it all.

"He's a beautiful horse," Liliana said, leaning back in the cushioned chair that had been brought up to the arena for her comfort. She picked up the glass of lemonade that had been delivered for her, as well, and took a delicate sip, her pink lips on the straw captivating his attention.

He suspected his future bride was an innocent. Either that or she was quite good at acting the part of virginal maiden. It made no difference to him, in all honesty. But it was the reason he held himself back from her now.

"He is," Matías agreed. "But a temperamental one. So far, he only responds to that stable boy."

Liliana wrinkled her nose. "Well, that seems rather inconvenient, considering the stable boy can hardly compete in a race. Age limits, I should think."

"Yes. But that's why Fernando Cortez is coming today."

As if on cue the jockey strode out of the barn and into the arena. He had a brief exchange with the stable boy, who seemed somewhat agitated. But then, the boy was easily excitable when it came to the horse. In many ways, Matías appreciated that. The boy was passionate about the horses, it could not be denied, and while he found it somewhat unorthodox to have one who must be quite inexperienced handling such things, he could not deny that the horses responded to him.

Fernando took the lead rope out of the boy's hand, and Matías gripped the sides of his chair, sitting upright and leaning forward. "I hope he doesn't do anything stupid," Matías said.

"The boy or the jockey?" Liliana asked.

Matías glanced over at the boy, who was looking downright angry now. "Either one."

The boy crossed his arms and watched as Fernando approached Fuego, and abruptly swung himself up onto the horse's back.

Before Matías could react, the boy was crossing the

arena, flinging himself into the path of the horse, who was beginning to panic.

"Dios mio," Matías said, moving as quickly as he could.

The horse threw Fernando, and then his hoof clipped the boy in the side of the head. It opened up a gash on his forehead, and he went down to the dirt.

Liliana was standing, a look of horror etched across her lovely features, her pink lips gone waxen.

"Stay back!" he shouted back to his fiancée. The last thing he needed was for her to get in the path of that animal. It was certainly not good for a boy to be anywhere near that animal when it was in a rage. He was not going to allow a woman in there, as well.

Fernando was already standing, backing away from the angry horse. Matías was going to fire the man, and make sure everyone knew he was irresponsible. But first, he had to make sure his youngest employee was alive.

He bent down, holding his hand in front of the boy's nose. He was breathing. So there was that. But he was bleeding, and he was unconscious. Matías tore his shirt-sleeve and pressed the cloth up against the boy's forehead, lifting his slight form into his arms and carrying him toward the truck.

"Medico!" he shouted, putting the boy inside the truck.

Liliana had mobilized, and he knew that she was ensuring that a doctor was called.

Then he began to drive back to the house, hoping that his initial prediction of the horse killing the boy did not prove to be true.

CHAPTER THREE

CAMILLA FELT WOOZY, and when she came back to herself, she felt first a shot of anger, followed by one of pain. She groaned, putting her hand to her forehead. "What?"

"You were kicked," he said. "Not fully."

She opened her eyes and the light hurt. But she saw that she was in a truck, and Matías was driving. "Well, yes. I imagine my head would hurt even worse if the horse had gotten me directly."

"What's your name?" he asked, his tone infused with urgency.

She could hardly process the question. He had never asked her that before, and somehow it made her feel... warm. But then she realized he wasn't asking her.

At least, not her, Camilla Alvarez. He was asking his stable boy. And still, it felt significant. Even though he was only asking to make sure she didn't have a traumatic brain injury.

"Cam," she said, giving the name that she had given to everyone else here.

"Well, do your very best to stay awake, Cam. It won't do to have you falling asleep and not waking up, right?"

She tried to shake her head, but it hurt. "Yes," she said.

She tried to hold her eyes open for the rest of the

drive across the property, and then he put the truck in Park, getting out quickly and rounding to her side of the vehicle, opening the door and grabbing hold of her, pulling her into his strong arms. Holding her against his broad chest.

She suddenly felt weaker, but it wasn't because of the lack of blood, or from the hoof to the head. No, this weakness was squarely related to the fact that Matías Navarro was holding her close, like she mattered. Like she was special.

No, fool, he's holding you close like you're an injured child. Because that's what he thinks you are.

"I sent for a local doctor," he said, laying her down on the couch in the sitting room.

She took a moment to take in all of the details, as best she could. It was one way to try to keep her eyes open. One way to distract herself from the heat and strange tremors that were rolling over her.

Shock.

It had to be shock.

"Calling for emergency services would have taken too long. If we need to send you to a hospital, we can do that. But I would feel better if we brought someone directly to look at you now."

Just like that, she felt suddenly much more awake. Because being examined by a doctor would be problematic, all things considered. And going to a hospital, even more so.

But she couldn't say that. Anyway, she was in no fit condition to spring up off the couch and do anything. Much less run away and deny that she needed any medical attention.

She lay back, looking around the room. At the ornate scrollwork on the crown molding, at the way that it was mirrored in the wood carvings on the plush, pale blue upholstered chairs.

"Not my design choice," he said. "My flat in London and my penthouse in Barcelona look different."

"I… Nothing seems strange about it."

"Of course not," he said, his expression opaque. "Tell me, how long were you homeless?"

She shook her head. "I wasn't. I mean, I was certainly in danger of becoming homeless once Cesar died." Her heart clutched with grief. Because, after all, even though she was playing the part of a stable boy from her father's *rancho*, she was not. It was her father, and she still couldn't speak of him without feeling pain.

"And before you came to work for Cesar Alvarez?" he asked.

She bit her tongue. Because she was simply going to have to fabricate from here. They had a boy that had worked at the *rancho* for a while before her father had paid for him to go away to school. His parents had died, and he had fallen through the cracks of child welfare. It felt wrong to steal his story, but it was also the easiest thing to do under the circumstances.

"I never knew my father," she said, the line tasting like acid, particularly as she had just been thinking about the loss of her father. "My mother died when I was only nine. I was on my own for a while, but then I wandered onto Cesar Alvarez's ranch. He gave me work. He gave me purpose. Education. But horses are what I love. They're what I know. I followed the horses."

Matías nodded. "I love them, too. It is in my blood. My family has had this *rancho* for generations. It means a great deal to me."

"If this is your place, why don't you redecorate?"

Matías crossed to the armchair across from her, picking up a crystal decanter full of sherry. He poured some into a glass. He did not offer any to her. But then, that was because he thought she was fourteen.

Well, probably also because he didn't want her to fall asleep.

"It is not mine," he said, taking a sip of the liquid, then swirling it slightly. He set it down on the table with a decisive click. "It will be. But as it is now, my grandfather is very ill and he has laid out terms. Depending on what my brother and I do before he dies, that is how he will decide who gets what. If both of us comply, we will split it down the middle. If only one of us does, then to the victor goes the spoils."

"What are his terms?" she asked, blinking.

"It's good that I'm keeping you awake with my story, but it might be a little bit too much information. Suffice it to say, I have low expectations that my brother will be able to complete said terms. My brother is not a good man."

"They say..."

He tilted his head to the side, his expression no longer passive. "What do they say?"

Immediately, she regretted starting that line of conversation. "I know about your brother."

Everyone did.

"Of course."

"They say he was responsible for the death of his wife."

"Yes, they do."

She tried to straighten. "Do you believe it?"

"When it comes to Diego it is difficult for me to disbelieve much of anything. Except..." He frowned, hesitating for the space of a breath. "I don't believe he murdered Karina. I will not say he didn't have some level of responsibility for it. But he has also never tried to clear his name. Which is also just very like him. And difficult to apply a motive to."

"They talk about you, too," she said, realizing that this perhaps was not the best line of conversation. But she blamed her head injury. Also, the fact that when he was near it was difficult to breathe. And it made her feel dizzy.

"Do they?"

"They say you don't… That you don't hire women to work for you."

It was a deadly game that she was playing. At least, it felt that way to her. But Matías never looked at her closely. He looked at her the way he did the rest of his staff. Dismissively, though, not unkindly. He was energetic, and always seemed to be looking around, his focus never bound to one place for too long.

She had a feeling that if he was to ever truly look at her he would see much more than she wanted him to.

"It's true," he said, inclining his head, his arrogant mouth curving upward.

"Wh-why is that? You don't think women are good with horses?"

"Of course not," he said, waving his hand. "The problem is, they always fall in love with me."

The words hit Camilla in an uncomfortable space. Because she wasn't neutral to him. Of course, she wasn't in love. That was ludicrous. But she certainly wasn't immune to him, and she could see how it was possible that women might position themselves to get a job at the *rancho* simply to gain access to him.

"Perhaps," Matías said, "it is something you will understand when you're older."

Irritation prickled her face. "I understand it well enough now."

Matías chuckled. "Of course."

"That's very closed-minded of you, actually," she said.

Matías arched a brow. "Is it?"

"Yes," she insisted. "There are some men who might fall in love with you, as well."

He laughed at that. "I suppose that is a possibility, given that I am replete with charm. However, I have never gone up to my bedroom to find one of my male employees naked in residence."

Her mouth dropped open, her cheeks growing warm. "Oh."

"Indeed."

She was starting to feel dizzy, and she let her head fall back to the arm of the settee, staring up at the ornate ceiling. The room was beginning to swirl around her. A confection of gold, blue and white.

"Cam," Matías said. "Stay with me."

She jerked upward. "Stay with you?"

She was feeling confused again. The differences between Cam and Camilla beginning to seem fuzzy. The reason for him asking her to stay becoming ambiguous in her mind.

"Don't fall asleep," he said.

She blinked. Of course. Of course that was what he was asking her to do. He wasn't asking her to stay with him. As in...to stay in the house. As in, to be Camilla with him.

He didn't know who she was. And frankly, she didn't know who he was.

It had been much easier when he was nothing more than the faceless villain who had purchased her father's horses. Who had taken advantage of the state of the *rancho*, and of her father's debts.

He did not seem like a villain now. He was kind. And he cared about the horses. Also, surprisingly, he seemed to care whether or not she died. Though he had made it pretty clear that it was an investigation he wanted to avoid. But perhaps, he also cared whether or not she was dead.

It was strangely warming.

But then, that perhaps could also be the head injury.

Suddenly, the doors opened and the doctor and Juan came into the room. She was caught up in a flurry of being checked over, examined. But thank God, it seemed as though she wouldn't have to go to a hospital. The doctor looked into her eyes and deemed them clear.

And then he ushered Juan and Matías from the room. The older man looked at her with a strange glint in his eyes.

"Your name?"

"Cam," she responded.

"Age?"

She looked away. "Fourteen."

"Have you any parents?"

She shook her head. "No."

"Are you going to tell me the truth?" The older man looked at her with eyes that were far too piercing, far too knowing.

She shook her head, her throat growing dry. "That is as much of the truth as I can tell you."

"I must tell you," the doctor said. "I care a great deal for Matías. I treated him when he was a boy. When that father of his would injure him, give him a black eye, I was the one the staff would call to care for him, and I care for him still. I will not have him taken advantage of."

"I don't want to take advantage of him," she said.

"I believe you. I'm not sure why. Only that I spend a great deal of my time taking care of people. Looking at people. That is the only reason your ruse has worked so far. People like Matías… They train themselves to never look at anyone too closely. But that is what I do. Examine people."

"My head is all right?" she asked.

"Yes. Though I recommend you do not sleep outside. And that you don't work out in the sun for a few days. I will speak to Matías about this."

When the old doctor left the room her stomach twisted. What if he was lying? What if he was going to betray her? Tell her secret? Clearly, he had recognized that she was a woman and not a boy. He had no actual reason to trust her, no matter what he said. Except for some reason she also had a feeling that he would not lie when the truth would serve just as easily.

Because he'd had no reason to placate her. None at all. He could have raised the alarm immediately when he had realized that she was a woman, but instead he had sent Matías and Juan from the room.

Still, she picked at her fingernails, twisted her fingers, nerves overtaking her as she waited.

Matías came back in, his expression dark, stormy. "The doctor has recommended that I set up a room for you inside the house, at least for the next couple of nights. To make you more comfortable, and to ensure that you aren't by yourself."

"Thank you," she said, feeling guilty now. Because this was becoming more than simply taking care of the horses. This was becoming something more.

He was extending hospitality to her now, and she was lying to him.

But it wasn't to hurt him. It wasn't to take advantage of him. It was for Fuego.

Yes, for Fuego, but also for her own damaged heart. Because she had lost so much, and she hadn't been able to bear the idea of not having the horses, too.

She discovered fairly quickly that, in fact, a great many members of Matías's household staff were women.

She looked quizzically at the elderly woman who led her to the bedroom. "He told me he didn't hire women," she commented.

"He does not hire young women," she replied. "Particularly not to work with the horses. He is rarely home, but he is often out at the stables when he's here. So, those are the people he interacts with most often." She shook her head. "He had quite a few girls make appalling fools of themselves for him some years ago."

Camilla took some sense of relief in that assurance as she put on the sweats that had been brought to her from her quarters. At least she hadn't engaged in this ruse because of a false rumor.

That would have been truly untenable.

But she wasn't going to concern herself with that. Not now. She settled herself into the bed—the softest thing she had felt against her skin in months—and tried to stay awake, simply because she felt comfortable, truly comfortable, in the way she had grown up for the first time in so long she wanted to bask in it.

But she couldn't stay awake. And eventually, she gave in and let sleep pull her under.

CHAPTER FOUR

IT WAS THE screams that woke him up. Then at first, he was convinced that he was dreaming. Dreaming of that day that was buried back in his mind, so deep, so far, that his waking consciousness would never dare dredge it up. But in his dreams…his dreams were all women and horses screaming.

But it took only a few moments for him to realize that it wasn't screaming in his head. But in reality.

And he had one thought, only one thought, that the screams were coming from Liliana.

He tore himself out of bed and ran across the house, feeling a jumble of emotions, mixed memories combined with the reality of what was happening. Of course he should never have brought a woman here. Not one so delicate as she was.

Of course he should have known that the curse of the Navarro men—or rather, the women that they took as their own—would come to pass.

Ridiculous. She was having a nightmare, or, she had seen a spider. Something easily explainable. He was telling himself that as he made his way down the hall. But then he heard the screams of his housekeeper, and that was when true fear overtook him.

Heart raging, sweat beading on his back, he raced to

Liliana's room, only to discover that the door was flung open wide, as was the window, her lacy curtains blowing in the breeze. They were three floors up.

Surely, if Liliana wasn't happy she wouldn't resort to flinging herself out a window to escape him. All she would've had to do was ask.

That absurd thought wormed its way into his mind as he ran to the window and looked down below, half expecting to see her inert, white nightgown-clad form crumpled in the grass. But she was not there.

He looked across the broad expanse of lawn and saw her. That white, flowing figure—her nightgown and her pale blond hair—whipping in the breeze. But she was not alone. There was a black shadow that seemed to be consuming her, holding her fast.

Diego.

He knew it. Deep in his bones, he knew. His brother had stolen his bride.

And then, just like that, they were gone. Disappeared completely. Diego had Liliana.

He issued orders to his staff in rapid-fire Spanish, and only after a few moments did he see the boy standing there in the hall, his eyes wide, fear etched over his youthful face.

"Go back to bed," he commanded.

"What happened?" he asked.

"Liliana has been taken," he responded, not seeing any point in being dishonest.

The boy swore. "By who?"

"By my brother."

Camilla still wasn't allowed to go back to work because of her injury, and that meant that she was currently tied to the house, wandering the halls and feeling far too conspicuous.

But if anyone had been even close to looking at her before, they were not doing so now. Everyone was consumed with the search for Liliana Hart, who had been— it appeared—kidnapped out of her bedroom window by Matías's older brother.

Diego Navarro.

And as that search waged on, Camilla had far too much time to simply sit and think. To wonder about the manner of man Diego was, and to attempt to piece it together with what kind of information she had gotten from the doctor. About what kind of man Matías's father had been.

The old doctor had said that Matías had been injured by his father, and he had spoken of it as though it had been routine. Camilla could scarcely wrap her mind around that. Around such horror.

She tried to remember if she had ever heard anything about Matías's father, but she couldn't remember, as all of those rumors were obscured by those about his brother. People did talk about Diego. About how his pregnant wife had died, and how the circumstances had all seemed quite suspicious.

But of course, all of this had been done under the guise of saying prayers for the family, careful bits of gossip wrapped in concern.

Matías, for all that he had a reputation of being hard, also had a reputation for being good.

She had the feeling that none of the other Navarro men held such a claim.

She heard footsteps and scampered deeper into the library, where she was currently attempting to waste some hours. She settled into an armchair near the fireplace, grateful that the only light in the room came from the flames there and a small lamp positioned across the room.

Then she heard voices outside the door.

"Any word at all?" It was Matías's voice.

"None," came an unfamiliar response. "The grounds were searched thoroughly, but somehow, they seemed to have disappeared by the time we got to where the car was abandoned."

Matías let out a derisive snort. "I imagine, knowing my brother, a helicopter was involved."

Camilla raised her brows, putting her hand over her mouth to keep from making a sound that might give her away.

"You are certain it was your brother?"

"Oh, I am certain. There is little I would put beyond his boundaries."

"I am sorry," the other man said. "But if they are not in Spain any longer there isn't much we can do. We have no leads."

"And my brother has not resurfaced anywhere else in Europe yet," Matías said. "I've been keeping watch on his various haunts. Or rather, having certain people in my employ do so. Diego seems to have gone underground."

"We will do our very best. He will not be able to come back into the country without us knowing. That is certain."

She heard footsteps, then she heard Matías muttering about the fact that he had likely gained entry into the country without their knowing this time. She could see that he had little confidence in law enforcement at the moment.

The door opened a crack, and Camilla sank farther

back into the armchair, wishing that there was something she could hide behind. She didn't want to be alone in a room with Matías again. It had been confronting enough when she had been lying there with a head injury. At least then he had been concerned for her well-being and had likely only been looking at her to figure out how injured she was.

She just didn't want to encourage any more moments where he saw her clean, where he saw her in a domestic setting, without the sun in his eyes. Anything that might reveal her to him.

Plus, there was the simple fact that whenever she was in a room with him he made it feel so much smaller. And somehow he felt large. Something about that magnetism filling her chest, making her feel hollow, all at the same time.

She felt aches in places she was not normally conscious of, aches that she didn't know a remedy for.

He made her aware that she was a woman. Much more aware than she had ever been in her life, and certainly more aware than she wanted to be when trying to pass for a boy.

"Cam," Matías said, "I didn't expect anyone to be in here."

"Sorry," she said, starting to stand. "I can go somewhere else."

He waved a hand. "It doesn't matter."

"I am sorry," she said, "about Liliana."

She was sorry. Sorry that the other woman had been taken, that she was likely afraid. No matter what Matías said she supposed it was entirely possible that Diego actually was a killer, in which case Liliana might be in actual danger.

But in many ways she wasn't actually sorry that the

other woman was gone. Which was awful. Except that he made her feel funny. Made her feel light-headed. Made her bones feel heavy.

"So am I," he said, his tone fierce. "I must find her. There is no other option."

"You will," she said, "of course." She knew that it was an unearned confidence, but it was clearly what he needed to hear. She wanted to tell him what he needed to hear. Wanted to make that arrogant mouth curve up into a smile again. Wanted his dark eyes to look at her with approval. Even if it could never be the kind of approval or appreciation that part of her seemed to crave.

It was such a strange thing. Being caught between the urge to avoid him and to seek him out. To build a connection between the two of them and to keep their interactions limited. She wasn't sure that she would ever understand what she wanted from him.

"I'm certain this has to do with the estate. I should have known that if Diego had no intention of complying he would ensure that I could not."

"Surely your grandfather will…"

He shook his head. "My grandfather is not a nice man. You must understand…the men in my family believe in taking what they want without asking. I am from a long line of villains, Cam." He smiled, a dark, feral smile, highlighted by the flames in the fire. "No matter that I've tried to aim for something better. My grandfather doesn't care about scruples. I'm not sure that he will be impressed with my story. In fact, I suspect that he will take Diego's side. A man must take what he can. If he must take the *rancho* this way, I assume my *abuelo* will find this a creative solution."

"I don't see how that's possible," she said.

"Because you do not know my family. Truthfully,"

he said, "I should have seen this coming. Historically, women who marry Navarro men never come out of it well."

"You're speaking of your sister-in-law?"

He looked at her, clearly trying to decide how much to say. And then he surprised her by taking a seat. His large hands gripped the ends of the armrests, and she found herself fascinated by them. By their strength, their sheer masculinity. She had been around men all of her life, and yet somehow he was something separate. A different kind of creature. So much more than anyone else had ever been.

"I am speaking of my sister-in-law," he said, pausing for a moment. "And my mother." He shifted in his chair, those powerful legs spread wide. There was something gripping about that posture. It was casual, nearly lazy, and yet she knew that at a moment's notice he could spring into action. All of that leashed strength.

To say nothing of how boldly masculine it was. The way he spread his legs as if to draw attention to...

She blinked. There was no way she was looking there. She just wouldn't.

"My grandfather," he continued, his voice bringing her back into the present. Bringing her back to sanity. "Is...an eccentric. But my father... He had a dark soul. Always. If he was ever any different I certainly didn't know him to be. He was violent. He had periods of extended rage. He could never be pleased. And he took all of that out on Diego and myself. And our mother. Always our mother. Who was so pretty and delicate, a Spanish rose. She was miserable. All the years until she died. Until she fell off a horse and broke her neck." His eyes were blank, horribly flat and black, and she had a feeling that he was leaving out part of the story.

But she also knew that he was only saying these things for his own benefit. Here in the near dark library to a boy who didn't matter.

She was no one. He might as well be speaking to a mirror. And she understood that. At the moment she was grateful she could fulfill that for him.

She heard a buzzing sound, and then he reached for his pocket. He lifted his phone and frowned.

He answered it. "Hello?"

"Matías?" It was a woman's voice, clearly audible in the relative silence of the room, and Camilla recognized the American accent immediately. "I'm so glad that I reached you."

"Liliana? Where are you? Where has he taken you?"

"I can't say," came the reply, stilted, robotic.

"Why? Because you don't know? Are you injured?" He issued the questions rapid-fire.

"I'm not injured. I'm perfectly safe. In fact, I need for you to stop looking for me." The words were thick-sounding, sad. "I didn't mean to deceive you, and I never meant to hurt you in any way. But I cannot marry you because Diego is the man I really want. I left with him of my own free will. The only reason that I screamed is because he startled me. But it was always my intention to waste your time and make it difficult for you to complete your task, and then marry him. I was not kidnapped. You don't need to look for me."

"Liliana…"

"It's okay, Matías. Truly. I regret my behavior, but there is nothing to be done. Diego and I have already married. And that means… You know what that means. All of it will be his. If you fail to marry, then all of it will be his. It's too late. We have paperwork. Everything is legally binding. We're married. It's too late."

"Liliana…"

And then the phone line went dead, and Matías was left there glaring ferociously at the phone in his hand as if it were a snake.

"You can't possibly believe her," Camilla said. "She sounds as if she's in distress."

"She has married him," Matías said, the words falling heavily in the room. "My brother is a terrible villain, but what he is not is a monster. And what he is not capable of doing is forcing someone to say vows. Even he would not hold a gun to her head."

"He kidnapped her out of her bedroom window."

"Or not. If she is to be believed she went with him of her own volition." He threw his phone down onto the coffee table, the light from the fireplace reflecting off the planes and angles of his face. "I was fooled. I thought that my brother would fade into his own dissolute lifestyle. That he would not attempt to please my grandfather. But I was looking at it through my own eyes. I was going to engage in a real marriage. My brother would think nothing of taking a wife simply to fulfill the terms of the will. A wife he will probably casually discard in the end."

"But you were marrying her because of the will, weren't you?" she asked. She didn't know why she was asking that. Matías clearly cared about Liliana. If he didn't he wouldn't be so distressed. And something about that galled her. But she hoped that he didn't love her. Which was small, and terrible, and she had no right to think such a thing.

"But I intended to make it real," he said. "I'm not a man given to love. You must realize that. Or perhaps, at your age you do not. Love was never part of the equation for me. But a wife, children, all of that I would have.

Why not?" He shook his head. "It was all too easy, and that I should have realized."

"How long do you have?"

"Only a couple of weeks," he responded. "Diego is smart. Because by whatever means he accomplished it, he has married her."

"Perhaps he hasn't. Maybe all of it's a lie."

"No. He would have no reason to lie about that. Because he would know that it would only spur me into action. Better to keep quiet if he hadn't made arrangements to marry her."

For some reason, she didn't know what she was thinking, she reached out across the space between them and touched the top of his hand. And then she drew back as though she had been burned.

Scrambling out of her chair, she stepped toward the fireplace, trying to move herself into the darkness, as if that response wouldn't make all of this even more out of the ordinary.

That he wouldn't see the effect he had had on her. That was the last thing she needed. To introduce something so horrific into the equation. He was coping with the fact that his fiancée had been taken by another man—whether by force or by seduction, she felt at this point either was devastating—and eventually they would have a horse to train, to make it to the races.

If she ruined it now by being so stupid…

"Dios mio," he said, his voice harsh.

She looked over at him, and his face was frozen, a mask of rage, his dark eyes glittering in the firelight.

He stood, gripping her by the arms and drawing her close. "What is your part in this? All this time… Were you a part of this treachery that was committed against me?"

CHAPTER FIVE

Matías cursed himself. He called himself every kind of fool imaginable.

She was a woman.

It was so clear now that he was looking at her. Now that she was standing there, bathed in firelight.

How could he not have seen it? How could it have escaped his notice until now? It was all painfully clear, here in the firelight, in this quiet house with shock coursing through his veins. With that soft touch echoing over his skin, a ripple on the surface of the water that should not have been there.

Then Cam had taken a step backward, and something about the way the light had caught that stubborn face, that strong bone structure, had suddenly revealed what he had missed all this time.

His stable boy was not a boy at all.

And he had spoken to her so openly, freely. As though she were an extension of the wallpaper in the room, because to him she might as well have been. A boy who worked for him was beneath his notice. But this…a liar. A treacherous woman.

He would not have spoken to her so.

"Answer me," he said, tightening his hold on her arms. Definitely *her* arms.

It was so apparent now. She did not possess the frame of a young boy, not really. But of course, when he had held her yesterday after her injury he had been thinking only of her safety, not of the way that she was built.

She was strong. Of course she was. She had become so working with horses, he assumed, but it was not the strength of a rangy youth.

She was soft. And no amount of hard labor could disguise that.

He examined her face, and it struck him with full force. As though he had been looking at one of those trick images and had seen one version of it, only to be shown the other. And now he could not go back to seeing the first. Her face was square, her chin strong, her dark brows thick, and in a very basic sense those things lent her a masculine quality.

Combine that with baggy clothes and the disguised female figure, and he supposed at a glance anyone could be forgiven for mistaking her for a boy.

But not now that he was looking at her. *Really* looking.

Her cheekbones were too fine. That strong bone structure in her face the kind that supermodels would envy, the kind that with makeup would give a dramatic effect of hollows and angles.

It was not a soft beauty. And in many ways, perhaps it would not be considered beauty by most.

He had no idea what to think as he felt like she had just sprouted a second head. Anger. He felt anger. Because he could not cope with being tricked by two people, not in the same moment. Three, if he counted the treachery of his brother, who did not even have the *cojones* to make a phone call himself.

Of course, if anyone but Liliana had been on the other end of the line he simply wouldn't have believed it.

"Did you help my brother gain access to this place? Are you a spy? Is that why you were sent here?"

Suddenly, it all made more sense. The way the boy— no, she was not a boy—the way she had asked him questions. About why he didn't hire women. About why he needed to marry. She had been gauging the situation. Of course she had been.

He had been infiltrated. And everyone involved would pay.

"I was not," she said. Her eyes were glittering now, and he noted that she denied nothing. He had leveled no specific accusations against her beyond the possibility of her being a spy, had said nothing of her gender, but it fascinated him to see her nearly transform beneath his touch. It seemed as though her face had softened, her voice slightly higher now. "It had nothing to do with your brother or Liliana. I had nothing to do with that."

"If that is so, then why are you here?"

"I came because of the horses. That much was true." She swallowed hard, looking up at him, those dark eyes filled with unshed tears now. "I'm Cesar Alvarez's daughter. Those horses were mine, and I would do anything to be back with them. Surely you must understand that. It had nothing to do with you. It was all for them. All for me."

He wasn't sure if he believed her. If she was truly motivated by her love for the horses. Because what he knew about Cesar Alvarez was that the man had been in incredible debt.

His daughter would have no money to her name at all and would most definitely be susceptible to a man like his brother.

"I swear to you," she said, her expression getting desperate, "I had nothing to do with Liliana or Diego. I don't know your brother. I've never interacted with him. I came here for my own purposes. Because I would do anything for those horses. To make sure that Fuego's purpose isn't squandered. The horses are all I have left. My mother has gone off to Paris. You can check on that and see that it's true. You can check my phone records, anything that you want, and they will prove that I never spoke to your brother. I have been in contact with no one since I came here, and nobody knows that I'm here."

She seemed to regret making that admission to him. Seemed to regret letting him know that were she to disappear here on this mission, no one would be any the wiser as to where she had gone. He wondered then if he looked as frightening as his father used to look when he was in a rage.

That should make him back off. Should make him move away from her. And yet, he didn't.

"How old are you?" he demanded.

"Twenty-two," she responded, trembling in his arms now.

"A woman. Not a boy. And not a girl."

"No," she said.

"You want the horses. You want to train them."

"I *need* them," she insisted, "and they need me. You know that you can't handle Fuego without me. You know it. You have seen him, and you have seen what happens when others try to work with him. You're going to have that fool Fernando ride him?"

"Of course not. He was fired directly after what happened yesterday."

"You know that I'm the only one who can work with him right now."

"It is so important to you? Because if I don't manage to defeat my brother then all of this goes to him. Including your horses. That isn't what you want, is it?"

"No," she said.

"You have deceived me," he said, leaning closer to her, relishing the moment when she shrank away from him. Because dammit all, someone should be afraid of his wrath. His brother certainly should be, but the fool wasn't here.

"I'm sorry. It had nothing to do with you. Or rather, it did. If you would only hire women…"

"I have one use for a woman in my life at the moment. And now I wonder if you and I have a common enough purpose that you might serve me well."

She shrank back, her expression one of confusion. "I don't understand."

"I think you do." He released his hold on her and took a step back. "It is convenient, in many ways. As a boy you only served one purpose. But as a woman you can serve many. What is your name?" He felt a smile curve his lips. "Your real name."

"Camilla," she said. "Camilla Alvarez."

Camilla Alvarez. Of course. He'd heard about her, though he'd never met her. A spirited horsewoman said to have a near supernatural way with the animals, just as her father had.

A fine match for a man like him, in many ways. Though he had no intentions now of making a permanent arrangement. And yet…that did not negate his need for a bride.

He needed one, and he needed her quickly.

Camilla, it turned out, needed something, too.

That mutual need could be his salvation.

Holding the horses hostage didn't bother him in the least. He needed to gain control of the family *rancho*, of the family fortune. Diego had kidnapped his fian-cée, and there was no way in hell Matías was going to allow his brother to win.

His path was clear. And the solution to his problem was standing before him, delivered to him at just the appropriate moment.

"Well, Camilla Alvarez. If you want your horses, then I expect something in return. If you wish to re-main here, if you wish to train Fuego, then you will be my wife."

CHAPTER SIX

CAMILLA WAS IN a state of shock. One that superseded the *previous* shocked state that had accompanied being kicked by the horse.

Because somehow in the last moment her entire ruse had unraveled around her, one thread at a time. And not only had Matías discovered her identity, but he had also asked her to be his wife. His wife.

She, Camilla Alvarez, who had not done so much as kiss a man, who had never been held so close to a man as she was being held by Matías now—in anger, rather than in passion—was being proposed to by that same angry man.

"I don't understand…"

"I need a wife," he said, his voice hard as rock. "My brother has acquired a wife, and if I do not then the entirety of this estate goes to him. You are one with a stake in this, as well. Because the horses will go to him. You don't want that. Trust me. You think he's going to keep you on? You think he's going to care about the well-being of your beloved animals? Murderer or not, Diego is not a man given to caring."

"Not forever," she said. "I mean, I won't be your wife *forever.*"

He shrugged. "Of course, there will be no reason for

the marriage to be more than paper. But it must be legal. My grandfather will not live forever, and once ownership has been established, once everything has been settled, then you may have your divorce."

"An annulment," she said, "surely."

"No." He waved a hand decisively. "There will be nothing that shall call into question the validity of the union. I shall not take any chances of Diego contesting this in court. I put nothing past him, as I already stated. He stole my fiancée. He would think nothing of challenging the legality of this union, as he cannot take more than one wife. Otherwise, I feel he would steal you, as well."

Camilla felt edgy, unsettled, a raft of emotion and heat careening through her. "How would he set about stealing me?"

"I assume via seduction," Matías said. "As I assume this is what he did with Liliana, who had an extreme aversion to sharing my bed, and this makes it all the clearer."

Those words tangled up in her brain. "Liliana didn't…"

"I was not sleeping with her. Does that matter to you?"

"No," she said, shaking her head. "Only that you intended your marriage with her to be real. To be lasting, I mean. So, naturally I assumed…"

"Liliana presented herself as being quite the sheltered virgin," he said, his voice dripping with disdain. "She said she did not know me well enough."

"Oh."

"I suspect, however, that the real issue was that she had given herself to my brother already."

"Or," Camilla said softly, "she really might have been

taken, and he could have been forcing her to say those things."

"I suppose that's possible," he said. "But either way, I do not have the time to wait and find out. I have two weeks to marry. And if I engage in some kind of public national search for a wife, no doubt I will find one. However, I'm not sure my grandfather will find it compelling."

"But he'll appreciate your brother stooping to kidnapping and subterfuge?"

Matías chuckled. "Because that is Diego's way. He's the gambler. The black sheep. I… I am the *good* one, and I suspect my grandfather would like to see me accomplish his task while sticking to my personal code of honor. More to the point, I imagine he would find it amusing if I could not. Which is why I would have him believe this relationship is real."

"You have no trouble violating your code of honor so long as nobody knows?"

"Am I forcing you, Camilla?" he asked, her name dripping with disdain. "I believe that rather than force, what I have done is offer you a mutually beneficial deal. You want the horses, you want to be able to stay here and train them, and I will allow it, as long as you help me in this. I must be able to maintain control of the *rancho* in order for it to be so. I must be able to maintain control of my business. If Diego takes over the family assets in their entirety, then it is possible he will end up with a stake in the company I built myself. I will not allow that. However, if we are able to split the assets, then we can draw up an agreement that keeps him out of it. That means that half is mine. I feel very much that Diego wants to win more than he actually wants to control anything that happens here at the *rancho*. I, on the other hand, care very deeply about it. I am the one who has spent years here. I am the one who has cultivated a relationship with the animals, with the land. I should think that you of all people would understand that."

She did. His passion, his need for this place, resonated inside her. It reminded her of the way she felt about the place where she had grown up. The *rancho* that she missed with all her soul. Those familiar grounds, the worn entryway tiles, that she once again ached to feel beneath her feet.

"I agree," she said. "On one condition."

"And what is that?" he asked, his expression dark.

"When we divorce, return my father's *rancho* to me."

He said nothing for a moment. "That is a rather large ask."

She crossed her arms and gave him her fiercest glare. "As is demanding I marry you."

"You think you're worth millions?"

"Yes," she said, not blinking. "Or at least I think the demand that we marry is worth that."

He arched one dark brow. "You expect to be my wife in name only and come away with a grand estate?"

"And some of the horses. Not Fuego. I understand that you won't relinquish control of him. But the others. The ones that will never make champions for you. I want them."

"And additionally, you would like to continue to see Fuego. Am I right?"

"Of course. Do you have anyone else who can train him? Who can counsel a jockey on how best to handle him? No, I don't think you do."

"That is quite a hard bargain that you're driving, but I have to tell you that I'm inclined to refuse. You are not offering me enough in return."

"I am offering to be your wife for however long a term you need."

He appraised her slowly, and it felt like a flame held close to her skin and drawn over sensitive, vulnerable areas. A thorough burn that made her feel restless and helpless.

"If you were offering use of your body, then perhaps you would be in a greater position to demand such a thing."

Everything inside her recoiled, curled up into a ball, not out of disgust, but fear. That he had identified her shameful attraction to him, that he could see inside her. And that he was mocking her. Because surely, a man who had wanted to marry that birdlike blonde beauty would not find her attractive. Particularly not standing there in ragged boy's clothes, with her hair cut close to her skull and sticking up at odd angles.

"No. You need a wife. And that's all. If you want a prostitute, buy one." She tilted her chin upward, attempting to radiate defiance, attempting to radiate confidence.

She was banking on the fact that his options truly were limited or he never would have approached her with this in the first place.

If he was shocked by her words, he didn't show it.

"Fascinating," he said. "You truly do possess a remarkable amount of boldness. I assumed it was because of your youth, back when I thought that's what you were. Fourteen-year-old boys are often imbued with a sense of self-confidence that is undeserved. However, it is rare to find a woman who is the same."

"I cannot tell if you're flattering me or insulting me," she said.

"Neither," he said simply. "It is what you make of it.

I am merely observing. I find it inconvenient, as a great many people would be cowed by me, and you clearly are not. However, if you will agree to be my wife, then I will give you all that you have asked for."

Heart pounding, she stuck her hand out and met his gaze. "I agree," she said, "I will be your wife."

He looked down at her hand. "You expect to close this deal with a handshake?"

"Yes," she said. "As I see it as a business transaction, and nothing more. You're right. I am bold. And I'm feeling quite confident in my position."

She hoped she wasn't overplaying her hand. Because she had nothing. Nothing at all, except her person. Her gender had been the barrier to what she had wanted before, and now it was the key. She would not hesitate to use it. She could have her home back. Something she had never thought possible. All she would have to do was be his wife, and that was nothing. A simple legal matter. Then she would be free. She would be free to ride through the olive groves again, to run barefoot on hot, sundrenched grounds that spoke to her of happiness.

She had known, had felt driven and compelled to get work on this *rancho*, because she'd had nothing else, but she'd had no idea it might lead to this level of salvation. That it could well and truly solve all her problems.

"Then you have yourself a deal." He reached out, taking hold of her hand and shaking it hard, the strength and heat in his grip making something tremble deep inside her. But she ignored it.

She wanted the ranch. She wanted her freedom. Wanted something more than facing a life of potential homelessness should the whims of someone else dictate it.

"Perfect," he said. "Tomorrow I shall call my grandfather and explain there has been a change of bride. And then… We shall work at making you suitable."

Matías was still feeling the sharp, hot effects of rage as he picked up the phone the next morning to call his *abuelo*.

Liliana had been perfect. And now he was to be tasked with turning this…this *urchin* into a silk purse. Something he doubted was even possible. She was… He imagined in some ways she could be lovely. At least, he was hoping so.

But she was not Liliana. She would never be. Also, there would have to be a way to take the story and turn it into something that didn't sound salacious. That he had fallen for a woman dressed as a stable hand on his property during the course of his engagement to the lovely heiress would be a difficult one to spin, though not impossible.

Particularly given Liliana's defection.

The fact that she was now with Diego made that part easier, at least. In no way would he come out of it looking the cad. Not when she had been seduced away from him.

"*Hola*, Matías," came his grandfather's rough, cultured voice over the other end of the line. The man sounded yet more ancient with each passing day, and still, he spoke with an air of authority that made Matías grind his teeth.

The old man was a puppet master. Not overtly cruel in the ways his father had been, but he had been the creator of Matías's father, after all, and it was clear to see how a lifetime of those machinations had dulled Matías's father's senses to right and wrong. To any sense of human kindness.

The Navarro family had a legacy that seemed to be born of spite and nourished by blood. Matías wanted no part of it.

But his grandfather didn't want the *rancho*. And he didn't want to maintain control of his company.

"Hola," Matías responded. "I assume by now Diego has been in touch with you to inform you that he has taken a bride."

The old man chuckled. "Indeed. He has. Though I think in his case he has literally *taken* a bride. Your bride."

"Yes. However, it was convenient for me in many ways, as I did not have to shatter Liliana's heart," Matías said, each word decisive.

"Really, Matías," his grandfather said.

"Really. I have met someone else. Don't you see? I was trapped because I needed to honor my commitment to Liliana," he said, knowing he was spitting out a tale that gratified his grandfather's sense of what roles he and Diego played in their lives. Good and evil.

There was never a question as to how far Diego would go, because he lacked scruples, and it was well-known. But he knew that his grandfather would be incredibly amused to see how the scrupulous grandson dealt with this.

"Is that so?" his grandfather asked. "That seems a bit convenient."

"I suppose it is. But then things in life so seldom are, so it is nice when it all falls into place. There has been a girl working for me, taking care of the horses, and I found myself quite compelled by her skills with them. I find I had quite fallen for her before I realized what was happening. I never violated my commitment to Liliana, because of course I would never break my word. But things are clearly changed, and now Camilla Alvarez is going to become my wife. You may have heard of the Alvarez family. I know you knew Cesar Alvarez, from back in the days when you dealt in horses. From when you worked at the *rancho*."

His grandfather chuckled. "Yes. Cesar. Didn't he recently die?"

"Quite so. And I ended up taking in quite a few animals from his *rancho*. And that is how I met Camilla."

"A fascinating story. One I'm not entirely certain I believe."

"I do not require your belief. I simply wished to inform you that I am marrying Camilla within the time frame you have dictated. She will be the perfect wife for me. She will run the *rancho* with a great deal of skill, and with passion. She loves the horses."

"And you?" he asked. "Does she love you?"

"Perhaps not as much," he responded.

That made his grandfather laugh. "I do appreciate your honesty, Matías, as you are the only one of us who seems to feel bound by it at any given time. It is endlessly amusing."

"I do live to be a punchline, Grandfather. I'm glad that my engagement can provide you with some levity."

"You will have ample opportunity to present her to the world as your bride next week at the charity ball in Barcelona, will you not?"

"I suppose I will," Matías said, grinding his teeth together.

"Excellent. You know, because of my health I will not be able to attend, but I will look for the photographs in the paper."

"I should expect nothing less from you, *Abuelo*."

"I should hope not."

And with that, they ended the call. Matías felt a sense of triumph, in many ways, as he was certainly transcending the roadblocks that had been set out before him. He was not going to allow Diego to win. But at the same time, there was an element of manipulation he was having to capitulate to, and that, he would never find acceptable.

But he had work to do. A stylist to hire, a ring to procure, and he was not going to linger on anything unpleasant in view of that. There was far too much to be done.

And he would do what he always did. He would see it done.

CHAPTER SEVEN

WHEN CAMILLA WOKE UP, she was immediately yanked out of bed and into some kind of alternative reality.

She was sent straight into a lavish bedroom much different than the one she had been staying in when she had been Cam, the stable boy. This one was sumptuous, frilly and quite a bit more feminine than the one she had existed in back at home. It didn't take long for her to realize that she had been installed in Liliana's old room.

That she was being used as a direct replacement, even down to being sent to the same lacy surroundings full of flowing curtains and billowing canopies.

If the housekeeper found it strange that she was making this transition, she didn't say anything. If she found it strange when a rack filled with clothing was brought in, and a basket of lush toiletries was provided, she said nothing to that, either.

"You are to bathe," the woman said, her tone brisk. "Use the bath salts, and all of the scented washes. And then there is an appointment with a stylist later."

"Oh," Camilla said, feeling slightly dizzy. Reeling over how quickly things were changing.

"You want to know why I'm not surprised," the woman said. "It is because I knew the moment that I first saw you, that you were not a boy."

"But Matías…"

"If he truly did not see," the housekeeper said, "it is because he rarely pauses to look around him, not at the things he considers beneath his notice. It is why he hires people, you see. To deal with matters he finds unimportant."

"I see," she said.

"I'm not sure you do," she responded. "But I think you will."

After the other woman left, Camilla padded into the bathroom and took stock of all the finery there. The body washes, salts, soaps and scrubs. She opened the tops and smelled a few, setting aside some in lavender and some scented like warm brown sugar and honey.

Camilla stripped her clothes off slowly, relishing the lack of binding on her breasts. Enjoying the thought that she wouldn't be binding them again today, or ever.

The tub itself was pale blue with gold claw feet, deep enough to submerge in, she thought. She turned on the golden tap and poured some bath salts beneath the churning water, scent blooming upward, wrapping itself around her.

Then when it was full, she stepped inside. She sighed. She could be free to linger in the warmth, to sink in to the bottom of her chin and lie back, letting the lavender-scented water carry her to another moment in time altogether.

Letting it take the weight from her shoulders, if only for a moment. The months of grief and stress, the heavy cloak of sadness.

When she went back to reality she would have to face the fact her father was still gone. But at least her own fate was secure.

At least there was that.

When she finally got out, she wrapped herself in the softest towel she had ever felt in her life and padded out into the bedroom where there was silk underwear laid across the bed and a simple summer dress. She felt so strange putting them on. Stranger still, when she looked in the mirror and saw that billowing fabric resting gently over her curves.

She felt… Well, even there in the isolation of her bedroom she felt hideously self-conscious.

If Matías imagined that she was going to have some great transformation where she became even half the beauty that Liliana was with a little bit of polish and a pretty dress, he was going to be sorely disappointed.

Her hair was still short, and her face was still…well, her face.

Angles and hard lines much more suited to a man than a young woman, and no hair to disguise or soften it.

She didn't have time to ruminate on this, however, because shortly after, breakfast was brought to her room.

Coffee and homemade jam on fresh bread. *Huevos rancheros* and bacon.

Now, that made her feel spoiled beyond anything. She had been existing on much more meager offerings and it was wonderful to fill herself completely.

As soon as she had finished the last sip of her coffee, her room was invaded again by three different women all talking at once. There was much clucking over her hair, and discussion about color palettes and various other things.

One of the women took out a pair of scissors and Camilla was appalled when she approached her and began to run her fingers through her hair.

"There's not enough hair left to cut off!" Camilla protested.

"Trust me," the woman said, "you will want me to smooth out this hatchet job, and once I do it will look like there's more there."

She began snipping, shaping what remained of Camilla's dark hair. She left the top slightly longer, clipping the sides and the back shorter, and teasing it a little bit so that it looked much more like an artful, purposeful pixie cut then exactly what it was—exactly what the stylist had called it—a hatchet job. Something that Camilla had done to herself in a panicked rush with a pair of dull scissors.

Then the second woman began to get out various pots of makeup. An array of different colors that reminded Camilla of summer, sunsets and somehow, of candy.

Warm tones, golds and oranges were swept over her eyelids, her cheekbones, the hollows of her face, adding a sculpted look to her that she hadn't known was possible to achieve. By the time her eyes had been lined and mascara added to her lashes, she felt that even her mother would be hard-pressed to say she had a masculine appearance.

It was strong, certainly, quite a bit more angular, perhaps, than many women would consider ideal. But she was shocked to discover that she found the woman looking back at her in the mirror to be beautiful.

"The short hair is quite nice on you," the hairstylist said.

Camilla nodded, looking at herself, leaning in to try to get a better idea of everything. She was shocked.

"I didn't know I could look like this."

"It's all about finding what works for you," the woman said.

"I just… I was always told I wasn't…"

"What?" the makeup artist asked.

"I was told I wasn't beautiful," she responded. "Too dark. Not petite enough. In my figure…"

"Your skin is such a beautiful golden brown," the makeup artist said. "And you can wear gold tones that would make a paler woman look sallow. You have a strong beauty. Which means it will not always agree with everyone around you, but those who appreciate it will never find another woman to match you."

"And as for your figure," the woman who had done nothing yet, and therefore Camilla assumed was the stylist, "it is the kind many would envy. We simply need to find the right dress to show it off."

"But why do I need a dress?" She knew that she would need a wedding gown, and the very idea of that made her stomach turn over.

"Because," the woman said. "You have a ball to attend."

By dinner that night Matías was in a foul mood. He had not seen Camilla at all, and in many ways he supposed that was for the best. They were going to dine together tonight, but she was late. He didn't like tardiness. Not in the least.

He tapped his fingers on the table, still marveling at the changes that had occurred in his life in the past twenty-four hours. What had begun with a stable boy getting kicked in the head by a horse had ended with a kidnap, a shocking revelation and a marriage proposal.

Or more a marriage *demand*, he supposed.

But in the end, the semantics of it didn't matter. Not really.

The door to the dining room opened and he looked

up and was utterly stunned by what he saw. The woman walking in wearing a bright orange dress, her short, dark hair styled neatly, with the gold band around her head like a halo, looked like no one he had ever met before. And yet, at the same time, he recognized her.

There was no question that Cam was indeed a woman.

Her curves were slight, her body toned and athletic, but most definitely female. Her breasts were small and high, her waist slim, her hips sturdy, which was an odd descriptor, perhaps, but not a negative one.

It made a man want to test that strength. She was like a warrior goddess. All gold, bronze and a kind of glowing beauty that seemed nearly supernatural.

He curled his fingers into a fist and tried to gather his thoughts. She was a tool to be used to spite his grandfather, to thwart Diego. She was correct. If he wanted a woman for sex, he could easily acquire one. There were ways to go about keeping things discreet. He did consider himself a man of integrity, a man who would honor commitments once they were made. But so long as Camilla knew about the other women, as long as they were clear about the general state of their marriage, he saw no real issue with taking lovers. It was, indeed, a business transaction, sealed with a handshake as she had suggested. Then it shouldn't matter.

"Hello," she said, her shoulders slightly stiff, her expression difficult to read.

"So this is who you really are?" he asked.

"No," she said, making her way down the side of the table, her fingertips brushing against the glossy surface as she did so delicate. If he had ever truly looked at those hands he would have known immediately that she was all woman. "This is a very polished version of me. Though it is the one you will see for the duration of this ruse, I have no doubt, so long as I have that team readily available when needed. I cannot accomplish this on my own."

"Can you not? You are an heiress. I was under the impression that women like you learned these things from the womb. Isn't your mother a great socialite and beauty?"

"I am the heiress of nothing but debts, as I'm sure you're well aware. Meanwhile, my mother had little interest in a daughter, whether or not it was to raise her, or to teach her to use eyeliner. I was raised by my father."

She took a seat with two chair spaces between them. "I spent my life with horses. My father let me run wild, I think because he felt bad for the way my mother treated me. For her disinterest in me. Or perhaps, it was simply because he was lonely, as she was equally disinterested in him. Whatever the reason, it meant that I had a rather unconventional upbringing, as they go."

"He must have instilled a certain amount of boldness in you."

"Cesar Alvarez was nothing if not bold. A man who continued to run his empire as though he possessed millions when he was, in fact, in debt, that amount could be expected to be nothing less, I suppose."

"Did your father lie about a lot of things?"

She lifted a bare shoulder, and his eyes were drawn to that sleek, golden skin. She was a fascinating creature. To transform the way she had, from such a brown little sparrow beneath his notice, to this vision of gold and fire.

It didn't matter, of course, not really. He needed a wife to appease his grandfather, and he needed a woman on his arm for this gala because dammit all, he had his pride.

He might not have loved Liliana, but losing a fiancée to his brother was not acceptable, regardless.

Having another woman on his arm to replace the one he'd lost suited him. The fact that Camilla was a rare beauty was a bonus.

"Not that I knew. But then I had no idea about the state of his finances, so I suppose it's possible. I suppose it's possible that I never knew him. That he concealed a great many things from me. But I do think that I knew his heart. He loved me. And he loved his horses. It's why I feel so compelled to make sure that both are taken care of."

"And self-interest, I would imagine."

She nodded. "Self-interest certainly comes into it. I would like to not be homeless. And I miss the *rancho*. It was…in many ways my second parent. It raised me. The people on it raised me. It's part of who I am. In my blood. I would do…nearly anything to be restored to it."

"That, I think I can understand. I love this place," he said, looking around the ornate dining room.

"Did you have a happy childhood here?" She looked away from him when she asked that question, almost as if she already knew.

But then he wouldn't be surprised if she did. Rumors of his father's temper certainly weren't contained only to his village.

"I did not," he responded. "My mother died here. My father was a tyrant. My grandfather before him was no better. I suppose you could say what I love about this place is that it endured. That it remains beautiful in spite of the ugliness that has bled itself all over the grounds. There are very few honest things in this world, and I think you and I agree on what they are. Horses, and church. These things… They will not fail. I wish to make this place something it should have been all along. Something better. Something that is not about serving the egos of the men in control of it."

"And if Diego ends up with it..."

"He will be no different. He is not a man capable of love."

Her brows creased at the center. "And you?"

"There are things that I love. Or, if not love, then things that I feel a sense of obligation to. I have never understood the benefit of caring only for myself. I would rather invest in what is around me. Make no mistake, I am a difficult man, and I know you have seen this. My reputation speaks to that. But I consider myself a man of honor. Because I have seen what happens when a man turns away from it. When he has no code. No allegiance to anyone but himself. I will not be that man."

"Do you want to have a family here?"

He looked around, a strange tightness in his chest. "I had imagined I might. I felt it was the way to secure my hold on this place. Now I wonder if there is something else. It is perhaps best if I don't marry."

"You don't want children?"

The very idea of something so small and helpless in his care made him feel a sense of unease. "If I had a son," he said. "I believe he would spend most of the time in the company of his mother and also being raised away from me here on the *rancho*. I am here now because of the circumstances, but my primary obligations are in London."

"I understand," she said.

"But you do not approve."

"I know what it is," she said, raising her dark gaze to meet his, "to have a parent who's not at all interested in your existence."

"Sometimes that disinterest can be a kindness," he said. "What was your time spent with your mother like?"

She ducked her head. "Difficult. She did not... She didn't have the patience for me. And she despaired of my lack of beauty."

"The only thing, I think, worse than being neglected by her would have been to spend more of your time in her company."

She surprised him by laughing, her shoulders jolting forward as she lifted her hand to cover her mouth. "I suppose that's true. And a much more honest assessment of the situation than I have allowed myself to, given the past. She's terrible. And she's gone off to Paris to live with a lover, and I hope she stays there."

"She abandoned you? What were your prospects if you had not followed the horses here?"

"Homelessness. In that regard I did not lie to Juan when he hired me. I would have been tossed out onto the streets. There was no money. There was nowhere for me to go. No provision was made for me at all. I know that my father didn't expect to die so young. I know he thought that he was going to fix everything. That there was still time. And I think he didn't want me to know how difficult things were. How dire it had all become. He wanted to protect me."

"Sadly, his version of *protecting* you left you vulnerable," Matías said.

She nodded. "Yes."

They paused in their talking for a moment when his household staff came in and delivered large bowls of paella.

Then they ate in silence for a moment before Camilla lifted her head and treated him to another look from that luminous dark gaze. "What ball are we going to next week?"

"It is a charity gala," he responded. "It is where I will present you formally as my fiancée. Likely, it will be bigger than our actual wedding."

"Well, yes. I can see how difficult it might be to get together a large wedding ceremony in the amount of time we have."

"Well, the venue is already selected, and people have already been invited. It's just that the bride has changed."

She frowned. "That feels quite…reductive."

"Well, the bride is not important to me. Only the marriage."

She lifted a brow. "Well, in some ways I'm glad that Liliana escaped you in that case."

"Liliana did not love me, either. She would hardly have been heartbroken by this."

"I suppose she didn't," Camilla responded. "But she seemed… She seemed very sweet."

He bit back an acidic laugh. "Apparently not."

"Did she hurt you?" she asked.

"No," he said, then again, more definitively. "No." He had planned on marrying her, and he didn't like his plans being upended. But hurt? No. That would necessitate that he'd had feelings for Liliana that went beyond vague appreciation of her beauty. And he did not. "I felt…protective of her. As she did seem sweet. Sheltered. But it always made me feel as though I was trying to corral a baby chick. One that was fragile and delicate and might break at any moment."

Camilla squared her shoulders. "I am not so breakable."

He appraised her for a moment. "I did not think you were."

She lowered her head and he examined her features. Long, elegant neck, her strong jawline and the sweeping curve of her lips. She was actually quite the beauty. Her brows were dark and bold, her eyelashes no less so. She was the kind of woman a man would find himself hard-pressed to look away from once she had caught his attention.

The kind of woman who would stand out, a regal, steady creature in a room full of butterflies.

His gut tightened, and he had to acknowledge that he was beginning to find himself attracted to his fiancée.

"Do you know how to dance?" he asked, the question, and the need for an answer, suddenly occurring to him.

"A bit," she said, hesitating. "I mean, we would dance at *fiestas* at the *rancho*. Informal gatherings. Always attended by all members of the staff. My father was... generous. Egalitarian."

"You will find this gala to be anything but. It will be appallingly formal, and every woman in residence will be ready to pick you apart. Especially given the nature of our engagement. It would perhaps be best if you were as prepared as possible. I get the sense that while you grew up with a certain amount of privilege, it was not the same sort that Liliana possessed."

A challenge lit her eyes. "I would suggest that my upbringing produced a much stronger person. My father allowed me to work. He allowed me to fail. He taught me to take chances. And he allowed me to work with the horses. It's in our blood."

"Having seen you with the horses, I believe it. But that is not going to help you when it comes to fending off attacks of a rather more feminine nature."

"Why would these attacks be of a feminine nature?"

"Because jealousy is an ugly thing," he said.

She frowned. "You're quite obsessed with the idea that women are in love with you. Or, rather, on the verge of falling in love with you if the breeze blows in the wrong direction."

"It has nothing to do with me," he said. "Rather, my money, or the mystique of the Navarro family. The Navarro men."

"I was under the impression that the men in your family did not have the best reputations."

He shook his head. "That adds to it. Often. Good-looking men with dark pasts, desperately in need of reformation and something to spend their billions of dollars on."

"That's quite bleak."

"You consider yourself above that temptation. Obviously. And yet, here you are, prepared to marry me for your financial benefit."

She tilted her head to the side, her expression remaining steadfast. "And yet," she said, "I am not in love with you. And I think it would take quite a bit more than a breeze to propel me in that direction."

"Fair enough."

"Furthermore," she said, pressing her palms flat on the table and standing, "I do not want your money. Not in the generic sense. You know about my father's estate. You have ownership of the horses. You are the clearest path to having my family assets restored. I have a very specific need of you, not just some generic billionaire."

"Careful," he said. "I'm likely to fall in love with you. As that was a very specific bit of praise."

"I imagine you'll do just fine."

He stood then, closing the distance between them

and reaching out, grasping hold of her fingers, lacing his through them and pulling her forward. He had been correct in his assessment of her. She was strong. But he had caught her off guard. Her dark eyes widened, her full lips dropping into a rounded oh.

Heat flared in his gut, an intense, visceral need to draw her in to his body. To close all the space between them. "Perhaps not," he said, gripping her chin and tilting her face upward. He could see her pulse throbbing at the base of her throat, watched as her eyes grew even darker. As the slender brown rings around her pupils slimmed. He wanted to see if her mouth tasted as ripe and sweet as it looked like it might. *Dios*, how he wanted to sample that surprise that shaped her lips just so.

But he would not.

This was about the *rancho*, not about his own selfish desires. He did not use women. He never had. And he wouldn't start with her.

He straightened, bringing her into a close hold. "We shall see how the dance lesson goes."

CHAPTER EIGHT

CAMILLA HAD BEEN hoping for a nice slice of cake after the paella. Instead, she was ushered into the ballroom with the assurance that coffee would follow. She hoped there would be chocolate. For certain, there was going to be a dance, and she was not sure how she felt about that.

Her whole body still burned from when Matías had grabbed hold of her in the dining room.

He was teasing her. She knew that. He was not going to fall in love with her, and he was not so compelled to touch her that he had no choice but to take hold of her back there.

She had no idea what he thought about her. What he assumed in terms of her level of experience. Likely, he hadn't thought about it at all.

As he had said, the bride in this equation was completely interchangeable with the one that had been scheduled to appear before. So why would he give a single thought to whether or not she had ever been held in a man's arms before? Why would he care that she had never danced with a man, had never been held close, had never been kissed?

She felt restless and edgy, and she kept catching sight of herself in random mirrors and various reflective surfaces and getting a shock.

She didn't recognize the woman she saw there.

It was like she was inhabiting a stranger's body. Strange, because it had felt less like that when she had been masquerading as the stable boy. Plain. Nondescript. She was much more comfortable that way. Identified much more closely with those adjectives than bright or fiery or any of the other words that might be used to describe her as she looked now.

"Are you ready?" Matías asked, turning toward her and holding his hand out. She knew from experience that it was strong, hot and rough. That even though he was wearing a suit, looking every inch the businessman, he had the hands of a working man.

She admired that about him. Because for all that he might seem mercenary, for all that he was a hard taskmaster, he was not above doing the work himself. He held himself to the exact same standards that he held everyone around him to.

Her father had been like that. A man who had valued hard work and had also expected that he would partake in it, no matter how wealthy he became.

"There is no music," she said.

"It's all right. You won't need music. You're going to follow my lead, not a song."

She sniffed. "I think dancing without music would be quite boring. Whenever we dance at the *rancho* somebody plays guitar, and someone plays tambourine. And we all just…move. The way that it feels good to move."

"Yes. Because you are using dance as an expression of joy." He began to step toward her, his face that of a predator. "At a gala like this, dance will not be used in a similar fashion. It will be used to gauge relationships. Used as an opportunity to assess someone's upbringing. Their importance. Everyone will be watching. And they will wonder why your hands did or didn't linger when they touched my shoulder. Why I did not steal a kiss when the music slowed and I had ample opportunity. Why my hand was positioned just a bit too high at the center of your back, rather than taking the opportunity to flirt with impropriety by drawing it down just a bit lower."

Her face flushed, her entire body growing warm. "I don't think anyone will be watching us that closely."

"You mock me for saying that women fall in love with me, but I am a man of status, and I have recently been abandoned by my fiancée. No doubt my brother will arrange for there to be headlines about his recent nuptials as early as tomorrow. With plenty of time for rumors to be swirling by the evening of the gala. People will be watching to see—is our relationship real or are you simply a stand-in? Are you nothing more than a Band-Aid that I have put over my wound? A trick, a salve for my pride."

She looked away from him. "Well," she said, "aren't I?"

"I refuse to allow you to appear to be such. I refuse to allow Diego to control this, or for my grandfather to have his way in manipulating us."

"He is rather succeeding in manipulating you into marriage." That last word ended on a squeak as she found herself pulled back into his arms, his iron fingers wrapped around her own, his arm curved around her waist. Her breasts were pressed up against the hard wall of his chest, and she tried so hard to keep her breathing regulated. To keep herself from panicking and taking in air so deeply that it forced those vulnerable parts of her into contact with him.

But she failed. Sensitive, aching breasts brushing

against him helplessly. She looked up at him, and their eyes clashed. Then she looked away, and regretted it immediately, because he must know she was only reacting that way because of the effect that he had on her. And she didn't want him to know that he affected her at all.

If she could only find a way to resemble the woman that she saw in the mirror. If she could only find a way to play the part of glorious sophisticate. Of course, it was probably difficult to convince anyone that you were a glorious sophisticate when they had originally seen you as a teenage boy.

Still. She wanted to try.

Because Matías Navarro was a whole lot more man than she had ever encountered in her life, and she was only just barely a woman by anyone's standards.

She had been cosseted in many ways. She would never have described herself as such before now. But though she hadn't been kept in an ivory tower, though she hadn't been pampered or treated like a princess, she had been held apart from the rest of the world.

Running around barefoot on the *rancho* had been like living in a fantasyland. It had had nothing to do with real life. Nothing to do with survival. And she had been placed in a survival situation after her father had died.

She hadn't known how to take care of herself. Hadn't known how to go out and get a job. Because she had never needed one.

And she did not know the ways in which women operated in this part of the world. She had very purposefully looked away from the way her mother moved through life, because it both enraged her and made her feel small. Inadequate.

Because truth be told, though she might like to pretend she didn't hold beauty in high regard, it had always felt futile to want to be beautiful when she was always destined to be outshone by her own mother.

But now she wished she had learned a little bit more of the world. Now she wished that she knew more about controlling her own body, her own femininity. At the moment she felt as though it was all controlling her. It felt as though she was at the mercy of all of this. Of him, of her own self.

That strange, glowing woman that she had seen in the mirror with a luminous face and an enticing figure wrapped tightly in an orange dress.

And then they began to move.

As he had said, he led, his confident steps somehow dictating her own. He made her feel like she was flying, floating, his strength the only thing keeping her from collapsing onto the high-gloss marble floor.

It was like magic. The closest thing to freedom she had felt that wasn't on the back of a horse.

She was lost. In the effortless way he manipulated her body, and that handsome face of his, all those glorious planes and angles.

He held her so tightly, and yet somehow she still felt like she was flying.

Her heart was beating so hard she thought it might burrow its way out of her chest, but it wasn't because of exertion, or because she was tired. It was a strange, exultant spike of adrenaline that was unlike anything she had ever experienced before.

The closest thing to it was the first moment she had seen him. The way her body had reacted that very first time she had spotted that strong, masculine form walking across the stables. And now he was holding her. Now he was going to be her husband.

That thought made her pounding heart jerk forward suddenly, slamming it against her breastbone.

Her eyes flew to his, and he looked down at her, clearly unaffected by this. Of course, for him, this was routine. For him, there was nothing different about dancing with a woman. For him, at this point, there wasn't even anything different about being engaged.

She was a replacement. That was all. A tool that was being used to aid him in acquiring this estate.

She meant nothing to him. Less than nothing. If she left him tonight he would have her replaced tomorrow by an unwitting maid.

And for her, this would always be dangerous. Because for her, this was singular. This experience of being held by a man. This experience of wanting. To touch him. To kiss him.

That thought took root in her mind, skittered down her spine like an electric shock.

Kiss him. Did she really want to kiss him?

She looked at that dangerous, sculpted mouth and imagined what it might be like to press her own against it. To test the shape of it. To test its strength.

It made her melt, dissolve at her core, and when he tried to sweep her into the next step, she stumbled, and found herself pressed yet more tightly against him. She had to wonder if this had been a bit of calculation on the part of her body.

If this was some kind of latent feminine instinct propelling her toward the things she desired.

It was certainly not a decision she would have made consciously. She would be too frightened to do it. Too timid. She was bold in so many ways, but not in this.

The fear of rejection, of being told she wasn't enough, of him laughing at her even, asking why a woman such as herself would imagine she might have some impact on a man that women fell in love with every other day...

Yes, that would have held her back. But here she was, pressed tightly against him, her mouth but a whisper away from his.

The world seemed frozen, even though she knew they still moved.

But then they did stop. He lifted his hand, warm and rough against her cheek as he drew his forefinger along the edge of her jaw, down to the center of her lower lip. She felt her eyelids begin to flutter closed, helpless to do anything but lean into his touch.

His eyes were so intense as they looked into hers. So very purposeful. She could feel the tension between them like a physical band, drawing them together.

She waited. Waited for the press of that mouth against hers. But it didn't come. Instead, he released his hold on her and left her standing there, shivering in the sudden chill of his withdrawn heat.

"I have a ring for you," he said, walking across the room, his footsteps slow and steady, echoing in the vast, empty space.

It was so quiet in there. Then she realized that it had been silent except for their footsteps the entire time they were dancing. It had felt like there was music.

But there hadn't been.

Not ever.

It had all been in her head.

She looked at his dispassionate face and felt foolish. Felt as if a magical spell had been lifted and suddenly she could see clearly again. And it was clear that this was nothing to him.

He moved to an ornate side table and opened the drawer, producing a small, velvet box.

"Were you able to convince Diego to overnight your engagement ring?" she asked, feeling the arch, brittle tone in her words and not able to do anything to modify it.

She felt hideously exposed. As if he could read every last one of her insecurities. As if he could see her disappointment. The thwarted desire for a kiss that she should never have wanted.

"Liliana's ring would not have suited you," he said. "It was classic. Quite delicate."

She bristled. Of course she was not delicate. Of course she did not rate the sweet little antique design that his fragile American flower would have.

"For you," he continued, "I thought I might select something stronger."

She was awash in shame. In embarrassment. She felt as though he was just as likely to produce a ring made of Teflon as he was an actual engagement ring.

But then he opened the lid on the box and her breath caught. It was gold, and it was brilliant. The diamond in the center was yellow, and it glowed like the center of the sun.

"You are not a traditional woman," he said. "You are unique. And you are fiery. I thought you deserved a ring that reflected that."

She clenched her teeth tightly together, trying her best to look unaffected. "You think you know me?"

"You are bold. Bold enough to go undercover to gain a job here. To risk everything to be near the horses."

"It's easy to risk everything when you own nothing," she pointed out.

"Perhaps. But a great many people in your position would have simply sat down and bemoaned the unfairness of life. You were not prepared to cope with your loss. Not the loss of your father, not the loss of the *rancho*. And yet, you have done so admirably. And perhaps your actions were unorthodox, but I find that I respect that all the more. It is rare that someone is able to fool me, Camilla," he said. "I should be angry, but I find that I only respect what you have done."

He thrust the ring box toward her and she took it, still feeling slightly stunned.

"There," he said. "It is done."

"I haven't put it on yet," she said.

"But you will," he responded, his tone maddeningly certain.

"Perhaps," she said, snapping the box shut just to spite him. She had a feeling he'd expected her to go all silly over the piece of jewelry. She had a feeling he had expected her to slip it on her finger immediately. To see how it might fit.

Driven either by some magpie instinct he imagined all women must possess, or by some sense of avarice that someone like her—someone impoverished—might be expected to demonstrate.

The truth was, she felt both of those things stirring in her chest, but she would not give him the satisfaction of it.

She had expected a kiss. She had not received it.

She was not going to give him what he expected.

"Do you suppose my dancing will suffice?" she asked, letting her hands drop to her sides, her fingers curled around the ring box.

"So long as you don't trip over your feet," he returned.

She sniffed. "If you lead correctly, I don't suppose there is a danger of that."

A slow smile spread over his face, and he chuckled. "Then I will endeavor to lead, *mi tesoro*."

CHAPTER NINE

MATÍAS SPENT THE next few days avoiding Camilla. He told himself that was not what he was doing, because he was no coward. Particularly not where women were concerned. He was a man who'd had ample and early access to the female form, who had never much seen the point in denying himself physical feminine company when the need arose itself.

However, he felt it best not to engage himself physically with Camilla Alvarez. Their fates were too linked. Their lives far too intertwined at the moment for his peace of mind.

When all was said and done, he wished to part with her as business partners might.

But that did not stop the yawning ache in his gut from making itself known.

They would get through tonight. Through the public presentation of them as an engaged couple. And then he would find himself a woman to deal with his physical desires.

As he had suspected, his brother had ensured that his marriage to Liliana became a headline the world over. In the days since her defection, it had become headline news.

And so he had to replace it with the headline of his own, and he was determined to do so tonight.

Another reason he could not afford a distraction.

He had to maintain control of himself. Even though the attraction that sparked between himself and Camilla was convenient when it came to presenting a front as an engaged couple, he could not afford to be anything but in absolute control of himself and his body.

He thought of the way she had fallen against him a few days ago during their dance lesson. The way she had tilted her face up toward him, her eyes fluttering closed. And it irked him that he couldn't read her. That he could not tell whether it was innocent on her part, or whether she was, in fact, a skilled seductress.

That was the problem with her in general. The fact that she had tricked him as she had done when she had come to work for him meant he did not trust anything she did or said now. They were allied of a necessity, and he believed what it suited him to believe, but he also believed it entirely possible that she might have ulterior motives.

He was all right with that, as long as he was fully cognizant that it might be the case.

In order to be fully cognizant he had to keep his lower extremities out of the equation.

Everything was prepared for the trip down to the city. He had arranged to have his penthouse prepared, so the two of them could spend the night there after the ball ended.

He had asked that his staff arrange to have any personal items she might need brought there and installed for her.

He was now waiting in the antechamber of his family home, and she was late.

He looked down at his watch, then looked up at the stairs, filled with impatience. Surely, arriving at an appointed time was not difficult. Liliana certainly had never had any trouble with it.

But then Liliana was an accomplished socialite, and he knew that Camilla was not.

Still, he had an entire team of people aiding in her preparations. Surely, it could not be that difficult.

He heard footsteps and looked up, and was shocked by the level of intensity that hit him hard in the stomach.

Because there she was, bare-shouldered, wearing a strapless gown that conformed to her lithe figure, until it reached her hips, where it fanned out in a glorious blaze of glittering gold. Her short hair was adorned with a simple golden band that was fashioned to look like a vine.

That vision of her as a goddess of some sort was only cemented by this. And suddenly, he did not care if they were late.

Her brown eyes were wide, and he could not read the emotion in them as she descended the staircase, her gown swishing around her with each movement.

When she reached the bottom of the steps, she looked at him with deep uncertainty. "Do you like it?"

"The dress?"

"I suppose so." Though she was keeping her tone flat, even, he could sense a vulnerability to her in that moment. One he found quite surprising.

"I like it on you," he returned.

She looked down, and he took her arm, surprised by the softness of her skin. He examined her profile, the strong shape of her jaw, the sweet, supple curve of her lip.

She was a fascinating woman. And more and more he could not fathom he had ever believed her ruse.

He simply hadn't looked.

It made him wonder what else he didn't see. It made him wonder what else he had closed himself off to.

But then he supposed there was no real point in lingering on those thoughts.

It didn't matter. He had her now. And he was going to get his part of the family fortune. Even if he was not going to have it all in its entirety. He would not be made a fool of by Diego. He would not allow his brother to win.

He might not be able to ensure his loss, but he could ensure he did not take it all.

And with Camilla on his arm tonight, he was likely to paint a very convincing picture of the entire scenario. It would be clear to anyone with eyes why he would have been tempted away from that pale, fragile woman he had found himself engaged to, drawn to this bright, vibrant creature.

She might not have the fame of Liliana Hart, might not possess a newsworthy family, but any man would be able to see why she was a temptation.

"The car is waiting," he said, leading them both out of the house and toward the limousine that was waiting for them.

She stopped. "That seems a bit expected," she commented.

"Please forgive me my expected limousine," he said. "The sad thing about events like this is we must endeavor to be expected. We must fulfill the expectations of those in attendance. Otherwise, there is precious little point in attending at all."

His driver opened the door for both of them, and they slid inside. Then, when they were safely ensconced, on the road and headed toward the city, she turned to him.

"Did your father do as expected?"

"No, my family has always made it their mission to do as little that was expected of them as possible. I have tried to be different. I was not taught the difference between right and wrong. Nobody attempted to teach me the value of integrity, and yet because of the deficit of it in my life I figured it out all the same. A man cannot live by his own rules, Camilla. A man must answer to a higher power. It is simply the way of it. If not, then he is bound to the whims of his own heart, his own desires. That ends in bad places. Dark places."

"Your father was cruel to you..."

His chest tightened, the words screaming in his head, begging to be released while his whole body tensed for a battle to hold it back. There was something about her. Something that made it seem so easy to share things he had never told another soul.

Perhaps it was because when he'd first spoken freely to her he'd seen her as a boy. A member of his staff. He'd barely seen her at all.

In the darkness of the car, he physically couldn't see her, and perhaps that was why he wanted to speak to her now. It was like confession. Whether or not it would be good for his soul, he couldn't say.

"It is not that. Yes, my father was cruel to me. He was cruel to everyone he encountered. But my father killed my mother, Camilla." The next words were torn, from somewhere deep inside him, with a pain he had no idea he still possessed the ability to feel. "It was not an accident."

Camilla was frozen, her heart turning brittle in her chest, cracking from the inside out. His father had killed his mother? It seemed impossible. Impossible words issued from the most beautiful lips. He was every inch Prince Charming to her Cinderella tonight, and yet, she had not felt a sense of enchantment when she had descended down the stairs toward him.

Instead, she had only felt a sense of dread, a sense of being deficient. Because she could never be the woman he had chosen for himself in the first place. She could never be that kind of sweet, delicate beauty she knew that men like him—all men—preferred.

But now she questioned that feeling. She had assumed, of course, that she was the only one carrying around dark feelings. She was the only one beset by misgivings of any kind. Because how could a man who looked so sublime in a custom-made tux be carrying around any sort of weight in his chest?

And yet, his was the greatest of all.

"How do you know?" she asked, her words muted.

"I saw it," he said, the words rough. "I saw him with my own eyes. You wonder how I can be so certain that Diego did not kill his wife. Because I spent my childhood with a man capable of such a thing. And while I think my brother is morally bankrupt, not unaffected by the life we led here at the *rancho*, I don't believe he's a killer. I looked into the eyes of a man who would do such a thing. I had been left to live with that man in the aftermath, while the local government bent over backward to cover it up, corruption and payoffs raining while Justice died a sad, horrible death alongside my mother. Diego is a villain. But he is not a killer."

"Did Diego see…?"

"No," he said, the words sharp. Hard. "I was the only one who was there that day. My father did not see it, either. I was frozen, up in a tree. I was…eight years old, I suppose."

She could tell that he remembered everything. From his age to his exact position in the tree, his specific vantage point. But that he was going out of his way to keep it vague. To keep it easy.

That he was doing what he had to do to protect himself.

"I had been playing out in the olive groves, and I heard the sound of approaching horses. A chase. A game, I thought at first, except when I realized it was my father and my mother I knew it could not be. My father did not play games. At least, not the kind that anyone but himself could win."

"Matías…"

"He shot her." There was a very long silence after that. The only sound in the limo the tires on the road. She said nothing. Could do nothing but simply sit and wait. She was…horrorstruck. She wanted to hold him and she knew she could not. Should not. He wasn't hers. And of course he never could be. But she wanted him to be. Oh, she wanted him to be now.

"She fell off the horse," he said finally, his tone distant, pained, "or, the horse fell, and there was screaming. I do not think it was the gunshot that killed her, but the fall from the horse. When I said she broke her neck falling from a horse…that was in the official report, and I know they were covering up some of what happened. But I do think there was truth in it. The way that the horse toppled over after." His words were hard, flat. "And I could not move. I was afraid that if I did he would kill me, too. I did try to tell the police. But the police chief said I was not to repeat that story. It was an accident. A terrible riding accident, as to be expected when people spent so much time with horses. An acknowledged risk, you see."

Camilla pressed her hands against her chest, as if that might do something to calm her thundering heart.

As if it might do something to dampen the horror she felt. "I'm so sorry. How could they do that to you? How could they do that to a child?"

"I don't tell you this to make you sorry for me. It is done. There will be no justice for my mother, and there never can be. All the evidence is long gone and buried. Every police officer involved in the investigation moved on, retired. And my father is dead. My father is dead, so he cannot be arrested. I hope, very much, that he burns in hell for what he has done. As it is, he was killed by something so mundane as a stroke while he was in the company of no fewer than three prostitutes. If that end would have brought him shame, I would have considered it a partial form of justice, but the man had no shame at all. And so, I can only hope there is justice in the afterlife for him. For he did not suffer enough in this life."

Her thoughts jumbled together, her heart full of immense pain. It was all starting to make sense. His need to redeem the *rancho*.

This place, the place where his mother had been killed, was a place of ghosts and demons for him. And she imagined that he was on a quest for redemption.

"And Diego…"

"I believe one of the more commonly held rumors. Which is that his wife caught him out in an affair and killed herself as a result."

"He must feel…awful."

"I don't know that he possesses the capacity," Matías said. "He's a vain, selfish man. And while I don't believe he would ever physically harm someone…he does it every day by living only to please himself."

They made the rest of the drive in silence, and when the limo pulled up to the front of the well-lit hotel, the previous conversation from the car temporarily fled her mind as she felt a growing sense of nerves over what lay ahead.

Shallow, trivial in many ways in light of all that Matías had told her. But she was only human, a human who was about to be put on display in a room full of people, and then put on display yet again in the papers. Online. The world over. Not because of any interest in her, but because of the interest in Matías and the entire Navarro family.

Matías exited the car and she stayed in her seat, her eyes fixed upon the entry doors that were standing open, people filtering in and out wearing all manner of evening finery. Long gowns glittering beneath the spotlights.

She saw a beautiful blonde make her way down the stairs, a formfitting gown highlighting her voluptuous figure, her hair left loose and blowing in the warm evening breeze.

For the first time in quite a while, Camilla missed her hair. Wondered if Matías would find her more beautiful if she hadn't cut it all off.

Then she frowned. She wasn't supposed to care what Matías thought. This wasn't about him. It was a business deal. She was the one who had said that. The one who had shaken hands with him as though they were in a board room. As though they had not been sitting in his family library, he coping with the betrayal of a fiancée, and she dressed as a boy.

The limousine door opened and Matías stood there, looming over her, tall, dark and perfectly dressed.

The sight of him took her breath away, and she was reminded why it was so difficult for her to keep the nature of the arrangement straight in her mind.

Because he was beautiful. So very beautiful and it didn't matter that she was not a lovely enough woman to catch his attention. At least, it didn't matter to her body.

It was shameful. The fact that she was not immune to him. That she would like to be disdainful of all his egotistical assertions that all women fell at his feet the moment they set eyes on him.

But she could not be disdainful because she was not immune in the least. And she was perilously close to falling at his feet.

So don't.

She held on to that stern, internal admonishment as she reached out to take hold of his hand. She lifted her chin, meeting his gaze, doing her best to appear confident.

Mercifully, she was wearing flat shoes, the nature of her long dress making heels unnecessary. They had an elegant, pointed toe and glittered gold just like her gown, and were easy to walk in.

With each step they took toward the ballroom her stomach tied itself in a slightly tighter knot.

She took a breath and imagined that instead of approaching a ballroom, she was approaching a barn. That all she would have to do was wrangle a two-ton animal, rather than dance before an audience of people who would be judging her, assessing her value.

She found that settling.

Horses were her confidence.

This was not.

And so she reminded herself who she was. That she could outride anyone here. That she possessed skills they could not possibly imagine. That she might, in fact, have a misstep tonight, but it would not change the fact that when it came to doing what she loved, no one could best her.

Somehow, that helped. Somehow, it infused her with a sense of confidence she had not known she could find here.

These men, these women, might well be the rulers of this domain, and she most certainly was not. But she had dominion over what she loved. And once she had completed this ruse with Matías, no one would ever be able to take it from her again.

She could withstand anything in order to ensure that. Anything at all.

She found herself holding her head higher, carrying her shoulders a bit straighter.

Matías put his hand low on her back and ushered her inside, and she felt that touch like lightning. She turned to look at him, her heart racing. No man had ever made her feel like this before. And a moment ago it had made her feel ashamed. It had made her feel as though she was simply one of the scores of women who had fallen prey to his charms before.

An inadequate one, at that. One who could not measure up in terms of beauty or grace.

But none of the other women that he had ever been with before would have matched her for horsemanship. Of that, she was confident.

And perhaps, a man would not find that to be an asset in a lover.

Just thinking the word made her stomach turn over.

Perhaps *he* would not. She was strong, she was athletic. She knew what her body could do, knew how to test the limits of her physical abilities when it came to doing ranch work.

She would be more than able to do the same in bed with a man.

Her face grew hot, her throat tight and prickly.

That burst of confidence had pushed her mind into strange territory. Or perhaps it was that hand on her body. Perhaps it was simply prolonged exposure to him. Perhaps it was everything. All the changes that had occurred in her life over the past few months.

And perhaps more than anything that time spent dressed as a boy and working at his *rancho*.

Being so aware of the fact that she was a woman when no one saw her that way. Being so aware that she was a woman when she could not behave like one.

And now she was thrust into this. The spotlight where her beauty, her femininity, was being highlighted in a way it never had been before. Where she was experiencing forced proximity with a man in a way that she had never done before.

Perhaps that was why her thoughts had gone to lovers and bedrooms.

She didn't want them to go there again.

She simply had to get through the night.

Then tomorrow she would focus on getting through that day. And the next. And the wedding day. And all the days after that until this ended and she got what she truly desired. Which was not Matías, but the ownership of the family *rancho*. The horses.

She simply had to keep sight of that end goal. That was all.

Matías swept her inside the beautiful, glittering hotel, and she marveled at the surroundings. The marble pillars, the glittering chandelier at the center of the room. And all the people swirling beneath it. Women in swirling pastel dresses, men in sharply cut suits.

To her, all men's suits looked roughly the same, but no man looked the way Matías did. They all looked domesticated, and somehow, putting Matías in a tuxedo only made him look more dangerous. Only highlighted the fact that in many ways, though he could move in this world freely, it was not *his* world.

He was like her in that way. Although, her ability to move within this space was up for debate and would continue to be until the evening was finished.

His fingertips brushed her arm as he abandoned her for a moment to procure glasses of champagne for them. Rough hands.

Working man's hands.

Yes, he might look the part of sophisticated businessman in this environment, but in reality he was part of the ranch. And it was part of him.

It was in his soul, in his blood, for better or worse, and now that she knew so much of the worst, she appreciated it on an even deeper level. Appreciated him, and his drive to possess it. To bend it to his will.

And now she knew the weight of his burden. The trauma he'd experienced and he'd come out the other side so…he cared so very much about what was right.

No one else knew the whole story. No one but her.

It made her feel…so strongly linked to him. To this man who was so different from her. So much more experienced.

But also…so much the same. He loved his land. He loved the horses.

She didn't want to feel anything for him, but she did. Oh, she did.

He handed her the glass of champagne and she took it in her left hand, lifting it to her lips, and it was then she noticed how her ring sparkled in the light. Her engagement ring. And she was not the only one who noticed the way that it caught the lights.

Suddenly, she felt at least fifty sets of eyes on her, and the discomfort from that chased away some of the feelings that had been wrapping themselves around her heart.

And it was only a moment before a couple made their way to Matías and herself, led by the petite, blonde wife and her much older husband.

"Matías," the woman said. "I daresay we did not expect to see you here tonight. Not after news of your broken engagement had surfaced. But it appears that you're here after all. And with a woman. A woman with a ring."

She looked at Camilla with an expression of speculation, her hands clasped together tightly, reminding Camilla of a praying mantis.

"Yes," Matías said, his tone smooth. "This is my fiancée, Camilla Alvarez. Her father was the late celebrated trainer Cesar Alvarez. I met her during a business venture and had quite the immediate connection."

"But up until last week you were engaged to Liliana Hart," the woman said as though Matías might have forgotten.

"I was indeed. I can only say that Liliana and I were clearly not suited, and she was the one who was brave enough to break things off before they became more permanent. I am thankful that Liliana followed her heart so that I was free to follow mine."

Matías nodded definitively, clearly pleased to let the conversation end on that note, and swept her away from the couple, taking her champagne glass from her hand and depositing it—along with his—on a passing tray. "I say we take this opportunity to share our first dance," he whispered, his lips close to her ear, his breath playing havoc over her skin, sending heat rioting through her body.

"Okay," she said breathlessly, her hands feeling slightly clammy.

"Knowing Señora Gomez, what I said to her will make its way into the paper nearly verbatim. I thought that was a good quote to offer up to the press. And a good chance for us to have our photograph taken."

He swept her into his arms, and this time, when they began to move, it was in time with music. The strains of the live quartet's song wound its way around them, but it wasn't what moved her. It was Matías.

Suddenly, she wished, if only for a night, that this were real. That the words he had spoken to that woman, so greedy for gossip and scandal, were true in some regard.

You don't want that. You don't want your life controlled by a man. You don't want to be bound to someone forever.

She didn't. Truly. But just for a while, it would be nice to be wanted. To be found beautiful.

She had spent so long not particularly feeling like she was any of those things. And this game they were playing touched the edges of those wounds.

She felt a pull between those old insecurities and new confidence that she hadn't known she possessed the ability to feel.

He made her want to know things. To test these new discoveries she was making.

To find out just what her body was capable of, in all areas. To discover why it mattered that she was a woman, and he was a man.

She had simply never wanted it before. Had never thought of it.

It made her want to laugh, really. The idea that he had somehow made her into a woman. And it was all a little bit silly, considering the symbolism. Considering the fact that she had literally been masquerading as a boy prior to his discovery, and then given this incredible makeover that turned her into a version of herself she didn't recognize.

"You are very quiet," he said, the words soft.

Matías was never soft, and the fact that he was being soft in this moment was notable.

"We're dancing. Should I be...noisy?"

"How are you liking the ball, Cinderella?"

"It's very nice. Though strange."

She adjusted her hold on him, moving her fingers across his broad shoulders. She wondered what it would be like to touch him without these layers of fabric between them. And for some reason the thought didn't even shock her. Because she was too busy being wrapped up in this magic spell.

"Why is it strange?"

"I have never been the center of attention in my entire life. My father loved me, very much, but I was a part of his crew. I was a part of the staff at the *rancho*. I think, in many ways, I was the son that he never had, but I'm not sure that I was ever truly his daughter."

"And your mother didn't care at all."

She bit her lip. He'd confided in her. Perhaps it would be okay to confide in him. She had been lonely for a long time. She was tired of that. Tired of feeling alone. "My mother was...*is*...only able to love herself, I think. She fancies herself in love with a parade of different men, but in the end she is never changed by them. In the end none of them can entice her to be faithful."

"Usually that doesn't mean you love yourself an extraordinary amount," he said slowly. "I would suggest it means she does not love herself very much at all. And doesn't know how to allow anyone else to do it, either."

She blinked. "Oh. I never thought of it that way." It was easier to think of her mother as selfish, unfeeling. Not wounded in some way.

"It was not your job to think of her that way. Not your job to be sympathetic. She is your mother, and she should have taken better care of you."

"Still," she said softly. "I think you're right."

"Often, the great and terrible tyrants in our lives are just as great a tragedy to themselves as they are to us."

"Except that your father was a greater tragedy to your mother."

He nodded slowly. "Yes. The women who love the men in my family do not come to good ends." She could feel a warning implicit in those words, and if she had not been feeling so much, such a large weight sitting on her chest, she might have said something sharp to lighten the mood. Might have argued with him, called him out on his ego for suggesting that a woman might fall for him.

But things had changed too much between them since they had gotten in the car tonight. And she knew more about him than she had earlier. More than that, she felt...

Somehow, the idea of being without him did not feel like freedom anymore, and that frightened her very much.

"I think we're drawing a lot of attention," he said. "It is that dress of yours."

"It is the ring on my finger," she returned. "And the fact that I'm with you."

"You're the most beautiful woman in this room," he

said. "They're all flowers. Pale, lovely, but insipid. You are the sun itself."

She felt her face growing warm, her breasts getting heavy, aching. She didn't know what to make of that. Didn't even know what it meant. What it might be preparing her for. And yet, she knew that was what it was. A preparation of some kind. For something more. Something from him. Something she didn't even have a name for.

Sex.

She shifted uncomfortably in his arms, and suddenly was very aware of that space between her thighs, of the ache there. Of the fact that she was aroused, and that she wanted him. Wanted him to touch her there. More thoughts that should shock her, and yet didn't. None of this did. She couldn't account for that. Couldn't account for who she was when she was in his arms. But it was something different. Someone different. A different creature entirely than she had been when she had first arrived at his *rancho*.

"I've never been called beautiful before," she said, and then cringed as the words left her mouth, because it was such a vulnerable thing to admit. To a man who was beauty incarnate. Who had to keep women off his property so they would not make fools of themselves around him.

The look in his eyes was so hot, it melted her. And when he spoke it was slow, steady and with such grave purpose she could not doubt him. "Perhaps it is simply because no one has ever taken the time to look," he said. "When you first arrived at my *rancho* I didn't look at you. I looked through you. But I am looking now. And I see you, Camilla."

His tone was so grave, his eyes so serious, and resting on her with a kind of intensity that she wasn't sure he could manufacture. But surely, it was all for show. Surely, this conversation was simply so he could paint the appropriate picture to the people around them.

Surely, it wasn't because she was truly beautiful. Surely, that wasn't why he continued to look at her, why his hand suddenly drifted down, lower on her back, and why he suddenly released his hold on her, and reached out to cup her chin with his thumb and forefinger.

Her lips felt like they were on fire, and she was suddenly so acutely aware of them she could scarcely breathe. She had never felt so very conscious of her face before, of every minute thing her expression might be doing. And when she realized how dry her mouth had become, when she slipped her tongue out to moisten her lips, it felt like a sexual act. Like an invitation.

One she would have said only a moment ago she had not even known how to issue. And yet apparently, she did.

Apparently, she did, because only a breath later, he closed the space between them, and claimed her mouth with his own.

CHAPTER TEN

IT WAS FOR SHOW, of course. That was why Matías had leaned down and pressed a kiss to Camilla's mouth. Not because it was so full and edible he could no longer resist it. Not because keeping his hands off her had been an exercise in futility from the moment he had seen her earlier. Not because he would rather kiss her than continue their entirely too honest brand of conversation.

Not because he was beginning to feel an impossible, immeasurable shift happening inside his chest that seemed to uncover parts of him that he had thought long destroyed.

A part of his soul he thought had bled into the earth and soaked into the ground along with his mother's life's blood on that terrible day.

This was for show. It was for the cameras. For the pictures that his grandfather would expect to see in the papers tomorrow. To go with that perfect headline he had spoken to Señora Gomez earlier in the evening.

Yes, that was why he pressed his mouth to hers. That was why he parted those delicate, sweet lips with his tongue and thrust deep inside her mouth, gripping her chin hard as he angled her head so that he could taste her deeper, take greater advantage of her inexperience, of the involuntary gasp she made, so that he might gorge himself on her.

It was all to give the impression of a man consumed by passion. It was not because he was a man consumed by passion, that was impossible. He was Matías Navarro, and he was consumed by nothing. He controlled each and every impulse, had dominion over all that he was, all that he wanted.

He did nothing more than what he chose to do. He was not a man like his father, ruled by temper. Or like his brother, steeped in debauchery.

He was *not* seduced. He never had been. He had always done the seduction. And the fact that she was trembling beneath his touch indicated that he was doing the seducing yet again. And if he was shaking, as well, it was only because of adrenaline. Because of arousal. Because his body was readying itself for an intimate act that would never eventuate. Not with her.

Though, he was having difficulty remembering why now.

When he pulled away from her, he remembered. Her lips were flushed with her arousal, her eyes glassy, but it was the look of wonder in them that hit him square in the gut.

The innocence there.

If there was any part of him that was pretending she was not a virgin, he could no longer pretend. He was not a man who had ever allowed himself to entertain the idea of taking a woman's virginity. That was the territory of villains like his brother, and the fact he wanted Camilla, even though he did not intend to make their union permanent, appalled him. It had been different with Liliana. He had intended to offer her a commitment that would last. To do the honorable thing. To offer her his name, his protection. She was like a hothouse flower. She would not only require protection, require being coddled, but she would expect and demand it.

Camilla would never submit to such a thing. She was wild, untamable. She was nothing like Liliana and all her pale, quiet beauty. Camilla was the sun, but she was also a storm. Uncontrollable. Unmanageable. She would tear through the *rancho*, tear through his life and tear through her own with all that same vigor and carelessness that she had employed when she had cut off all her hair and posed as a boy to get hired on by him.

He would never be able to tame her, never be able to leash her, and of course, he didn't want to.

But she had all that reckless spirit and it was not compatible to his life. Still.

Right now he wanted to crush her beneath him, spread those thighs and bury himself inside her.

But he could not. He would not.

"Wow," she breathed, that sweet, innocent reaction touching him in places he should not allow.

"Do not look at me like that."

She blinked. "Look at you like what?"

"Like you're looking at me right now," he returned. "Like I have taught you something new. It will look strange in a picture."

He tacked that last part on quickly, and he felt guilty when she looked like she had been struck.

"Sorry."

"Don't be," he said. "You have done nothing wrong."

Except reached inside him and changed something around. Moved parts of himself so that sacred spaces that had long been covered were exposed.

It was only a kiss. There was no reason to apply so

much to it. One would be forgiven for thinking *he* was the virgin given that response.

"You said I did."

"I only meant…you cannot look at me as though that was your first kiss. We are supposed to be a couple."

"But it was," she said softly.

His groin tightened, his stomach tense. "Do not tell me things like that, Camilla."

"Why not? You told me all those dark things about your past. Surely, this isn't a deeper revelation than that."

Again, she produced a kind of clear, real honesty in him he could not fight. "When you tell me things like that I am tempted. Tempted to teach you everything those eyes tell me you do not know. Tempted to make sure that I am not only your first kiss but also your first lover. And the lover that you think about every time thereafter. The lover you compare all other men to."

He was certain that that would scare her. Certain that that was a bridge too far for his innocent beauty. She would not want those things. She was fearsome, a warrior, but she was not worldly. She had been protected from the advances of men like him. She didn't have to say that for him to know it was true. Had she not been, she would have been kissed many times already. Would have been far from untouched.

She deserved her first time to be with a nice man. A man who would honor that gift. A man who was careful with things, rather than breaking them.

"What if I want you to?" she said softly. "What if I want you to teach me those things?"

"You do not know what you ask for," he said.

"I do. I am not so sheltered that I don't understand the way things are between men and women. And I…

I will not fall in love with you. I'm independent. I was born with a fierce spirit. I'm like my father. I have the gift of speaking to horses. I have the gift of strength and solitude. I am not meant to be tied down. So you have no worries on that score. Not for me."

"Your father married your mother. He fell for someone who betrayed him immeasurably over the course of his life. Why do you assume that because you're like him you're immune?"

"My father was bound to my mother because of me. And he was bound to stay married because of his faith. He could have sought an annulment, I suppose, because of her behavior, but he did not. It suited him. To keep that marriage. I think, in the end, he knew that a real marriage was not for him anyway. He wanted to spend long hours out on the *rancho*. He did not want to throw dinner parties. He did not want to spend his time catering to a wife. Any more than I want to spend my time catering to a husband. Do you think that I want to get dressed up and go to parties like this all the time? No. I would rather wear jeans. And I would rather ride horses. I would rather wear boots than these glittering gold shoes, no matter how beautiful they are. But just because I want those things does not mean that I'm immune to the desires of a man's touch. And I want yours, Matías. I crave yours."

She was bold, even in this. He was reminded of that first meeting. When she had spoken to him with such force, and he had imagined that it had come from the brashness of youth. Now he knew. It was simply the fire inside her. Some might call it an unearned confidence. But he found it to be a singular, beautiful gift.

She was no seductress. She was looking at him with frankness, with open desire. She was not gazing at him through her veiled lashes, fluttering her eyes at him. No. There was no shame. If there was embarrassment, it was simply because she was afraid of rejection. But there was no game being played here. She wanted. And so she asked. It was a fascinating thing to see. And it was…

Intoxicating.

To have a woman look him in the eye and swear she would not fall in love with him. To have a woman ask for what she wanted.

To want this creature that could offer him nothing in terms of skill in the bedroom. Who could not do tricks and would likely have no idea of what to do with his body once he took his clothes off for her.

That novelty should not appeal to him, and yet it did. Just as he had said, the temptation to educate her was real. The temptation to brand her as his. To burn his mark into her skin.

Perhaps he should be appalled by such an impulse and yet he could no more fight against it than he could fight against her honest, open request.

"You must tell me," he said, "little one." He braced his hand on the back of her head, holding her steady as he looked into her dark eyes. "That you want me to take your virginity. That you want me to take you back to my penthouse here in Barcelona. You want me to taste you, touch you. That you want me inside your body. You must say those things to me, so that I know for sure you understand what you ask."

"Remember," she said, those pouty lips curving upward. "I am not fourteen. I am a woman."

"When it comes to experience with men, you are barely that. You must ask, *mi tesoro*, so that I know that this is what you want."

"I want to," she said. She swallowed hard, that fine

throat working as she did. "I want for you to make love to me. I want you to take my virginity." And then she did something he did not expect. She curved her fingers around the back of his head, holding him tight as he was holding her. "I want you inside me." And then she kissed him, with all the boldness of a harlot, licked his lips with the seductive attention of a Siren. Then when she drew back, she blushed like an innocent.

And he was lost.

"Very well," he rasped, his voice a stranger's. "I will give you what you desire. But we will finish tonight. We will finish this together, and when we leave, we will leave it behind."

"What do you mean?"

"Here," he said, looking around the room, "we are an engaged couple. Here, we are engaging in a performance. Once we are in my bedroom, it will simply be Camilla and Matías. There will be nothing outside of that. It will not be a business transaction. Do you understand?"

"Yes," she whispered.

"No," he said, "I don't think you do. I do not require you to be this glittering creature. I require nothing of you beyond yourself. That is who I want in my bed tonight."

She ducked her head. "I'm not sure that you've met her before."

"Then I feel, *mi amor*, this would be an excellent time for you to introduce me."

It was those words that stuck with her. Those words that propelled her through the evening. That empowered her as she danced with him, each song powerful and deep, like something more intimate than it was, because of the shared knowledge of what was going to take place later.

He wanted her. He had said so. Her as she was, not her as this elegant creature that had been fashioned by a team of people. Not her, the one who had come to him in disguise.

The her that perhaps not even she knew. That she had shown to no one.

And it terrified her. Because she was suddenly so certain that in many ways she had spent all of her life burying some desires of hers down deep.

Her father had given her a great many things. He had given her the freedom to do as she pleased as long as she stayed within the boundaries of the *rancho*. He had given her a kind of freedom from her mother's expectations by allowing her to be the opposite.

But there had been no place for her to explore that other part of herself. The part that was very much a woman and wanted to be with a man. The part that wanted to be beautiful. To feel lovely.

They managed to make it through the entire evening, and she marveled at the way that Matías dealt with the people around him. He was a chameleon. Able to be charming and firm in the same conversation. To speak hard truths, and then smooth them over with a smile.

He was not a man that anyone wanted to defy, and she had a feeling that it had nothing to do with his family name or their formidable reputation, but everything to do with the magnetism of the man himself.

He was unlike anyone she had ever known. And she had a feeling that would always be the case.

Had a feeling that after this was over she would remember him forever. She would carry a small piece of him with her.

It felt…romantic in many ways. At least the right kind of romance for a woman like her. A woman who wanted nothing more than her freedom. Who wanted nothing more than to feel desired when she wished to, and to have total agency in her life at other moments.

When he swept her out of the ballroom, and back into the limo, she was afraid she might have left her stomach behind. Her anticipation had been growing stronger with each passing moment, but now that it was time, she found herself getting nervous. Found herself feeling that confidence slipping away again.

The limo pulled up outside the penthouse, and she looked up, her heart pounding hard at the base of her throat. "I didn't bring anything with me," she said.

"I've taken care of everything," he said.

"Have you?" she asked.

"Yes. You do not have to fear anything. Just follow my lead."

"Will there be music?" she asked.

"You will not be following a song," he said, brushing his fingertips to her lips. "You will be following me."

It was such a strange assurance, quietly spoken, and should be dissonant from the mouth of a man who was just so very masculine and dangerous as Matías was, and yet she believed him.

That while she was with him, while she was his, he would care for her.

No one had ever assured her of such a thing before. She hadn't realized she had wanted it until now.

"Even a toothbrush?" she asked, not wanting to reveal the vulnerability that she felt.

"Oh, yes," he said, "everything has been provided for you."

"And a nightgown?"

He chuckled, then grabbed hold of her chin, holding her face steady. "You won't be needing one."

Then she found herself being swept out of the limo and into the antechamber of the lovely, antiquated apartment building. They swept through the lobby and down to an elevator at the very end of the marble-carved room.

He pulled out a key card and swiped it, then they stepped inside. "This only goes to my floor," he said.

"You have your own floor?"

He shrugged. "I'm a man with specific needs. Privacy is one of them."

"I see," she said, suddenly feeling a lead weight in her stomach. "For when you bring women here," she said.

"I never claimed to be a saint, Camilla," he said, leaning against the door of the elevator, those deft fingers working the knot on his bow tie, letting it fall loose. "I have had lovers. Many of them. Not when I was engaged to Liliana. And not since meeting you. But yes. It suits me to have luxury accommodation in various places in the world for that reason."

"Just very strange. To think about, I mean. I've never touched another man. And you've touched…"

"Trust me," he said, a smile tipping the corner of his lips. "You will benefit from my experience."

"I'm sure I will," she said.

But that didn't mean jealousy didn't burn hot and fierce in her stomach, like a particularly vicious acid.

She had never kissed another man. Never wanted another man. But this man wanted easily. He wanted for no other reason than a face was beautiful, or a body pleasingly shaped.

It wasn't a flaw, she supposed, but it was certainly something.

The elevator doors swept open when it reached the top floor, and he pushed away from the door, leading her out into an apartment that was shockingly modern against the ornate backdrop of the lift.

"This is what you were talking about," she said, thinking of what he had said about the decor at the *rancho*.

"Yes," he said. "Most of my properties look more like this." He indicated the stark black-and-white design, the touches of chrome and other sorts of things that screamed masculinity in a very basic way.

She squinted. "You didn't do the decor," she commented.

"No," he said. He began to undo the cuffs on his shirt. "How did you know?" He slipped his jacket off and let it slide down onto the sleek leather couch that was positioned at the center of the room. Then he began to work the buttons on his white shirt.

"It doesn't look particularly like you. It just looks like someone was told to design a room for a man. Any man. One who doesn't particularly like frills. It's very generic."

He laughed. "And you think, perhaps, the ornate florals and powder blues of the *rancho* are more to my taste?"

She laughed. "I do. Because they have history. Because they're part of you. Whether you wanted to be or not."

Something in his face went hard, his mouth setting into a grim line. "I think that's quite enough talking."

And then she found herself being caught up in his strong embrace, pulled forward, his mouth hard and hot on hers as he devastated her with a savage kiss.

When he moved away from her she was breathing

hard, and then he took a step back, unbuttoning his shirt the rest of the way.

His body was…well, it was as classically masculine as their surroundings. But much, much more compelling. All strong lines and incredible muscle, dark hair covering that taut, bronzed skin.

She had never seen a man who looked quite like him before.

"Yes?" he asked.

"I'm just…staring," she said.

"Why are you staring?"

"Because you're…you're beautiful," she said before she could stop herself.

It was an incredibly gauche thing to say, but at the moment she felt that she was incredibly gauche and there was no way around it. She was inexperienced. Nonexperienced.

Had never even kissed a man until tonight, and she was about to do everything with him. Let him see her, let him touch her. See him, touch him. It was intoxicating, exhilarating and terrifying.

She wanted it. And she wanted to remember what he had told her earlier. Wanted to embrace who she was. Not who she was pretending to be. Not who she had dressed up as, either to get hired at the *rancho* or to get ready for the ball tonight.

And that meant committing to not being embarrassed when she said things like that. That he was beautiful. She was going to enjoy this. All of this. Claim it for herself. Because she supposed, that was the flipside to all that experience. He had had this experience before. It was not foreign to him. It wasn't new. Which meant that it was so much more for her than for him. She wanted to embrace that. Relish it.

"You're beautiful," she said again. "Truly."

Then, bolstered by that thought, she took a step forward, and she pressed her palm flat against his chest. He was so warm. Hot. She could feel his heartbeat raging against her touch. And that bolstered her, too. The fact that he wasn't unmoved by this. The fact that she did tempt him. Did test him. The fact that she created the same response in him as he created in her.

And no matter that her mother had always told her men were led around by their members. She chose to believe that it mattered still.

Her mother had taught her very few things, but that was one of the things she remembered. And along with that, she remembered her saying that men wanted sex and women wanted attention. And so she had imagined that if she ever came to this moment she would be in a situation of unequal desires. That she would crave attention, and he would simply crave touch.

But she knew, standing there looking at him, looking at the fire in his eyes, listening to the desires of her own body, that their desires were one. That they were united in their need tonight.

She didn't simply want attention. She wanted him. Needed him.

"I don't know what I'm doing," she said softly.

"I do," he said. "You don't have to know the steps. You simply have to follow my lead. And I will not let you fall."

Her heart swelled, those words, that promise, echoing through her.

Then he reached around behind her and grabbed hold of her zipper tab, drawing it down the center of her back. The bodice fell loose, the dress falling around her hips. Then he grabbed her hand and pulled her forward, and she stepped away from the glittering fabric, standing before him wearing nothing but glimmering, lacy underwear that she knew did very little to cover her body. She was not wearing a bra, because the dress had possessed built-in support, and so her breasts were bare to him, her nipples tight beneath his inspection.

She knew that he could see her dark curls at the apex of her thighs through that flimsy, light-colored lace. She knew that she should be embarrassed, but she wasn't. Because he wanted her. He wanted this. And just like with the dancing he had promised to lead. Promised to help make sure her steps didn't falter. She trusted him. Trusted him to do what he said, even if she had no reason to. But he was Matías. He was everything. He was the fulfillment of fantasies she hadn't even known she possessed. He was every secret desire she had always been afraid to put words to. He was the man that made her feel happiest to be a woman.

And for however long she could have him, she would. Oh, she would.

"Beautiful," he said, his dark eyes sharp, intense, as they looked at her mostly naked form.

She didn't wish for her long hair then. She didn't even wish for the gown. She had never felt more wholly female, perfectly feminine, than she did in that moment.

He reached out, and he dragged one of those callous thumbs over her tightened nipple. She gasped, drawing away from him because it was so shocking, so sensational.

"Teach me," he said, his voice rough. "Teach me what you like. Tell me when something feels good to you. Though I might embarrass myself."

"How?"

He chuckled, shaking his head. "Such an innocent."

He reached out, wrapping his fingers around her wrist, and drawing her hand toward the front of his pants. She gasped when she felt him there, hard, masculine and much larger than she had expected him to be.

"When a man wants a woman very, very much it becomes difficult for him to control himself. I would like to stay hard for you. I need to last for you. So that you can have as many orgasms as you want. So that I can pleasure you, over and over again before I finally take my own pleasure. And if I do not maintain my control, that may be difficult."

"Because you can only…you can only…*once*?" Her lack of experience was slightly mortifying, but they were naked together so she supposed being coy now was just silly.

"I can only come once in a certain amount of time. You, on the other hand, will not be similarly limited."

"That's…very interesting."

He leaned in, the tendons in his neck standing out, tension clear in every line of his body. "How is it you don't know about this? Haven't you talked to friends? Overheard men talking at the *rancho*?"

"I was the boss's daughter. They were very careful around me. And as for friends… I have horses. Which is informative enough regarding procreation but not regarding um…sexual…pleasures."

"But you must be somewhat familiar with pleasure," he insisted. "Haven't you explored your body on your own?" She shook her head. "And I haven't… I don't think I've experienced the pleasure you're talking about before," she said, feeling her face growing hot.

"You don't think you've had an orgasm?"

"No."

"Then you haven't," he said firmly. "If you had, you would have known."

And then on a growl, he lifted her up off her feet and pressed her against his body, kissing her, hard and deep, one hand pressed firmly against the center of her shoulder blades, the other cupping the back of her head.

The hair on his chest was rough, and it abraded her nipples, but it was not an unpleasant sensation.

It was…well, it was perfect. It was everything that she loved about their contrast. He was so hot, so hard, rough and intense. He matched her softness. Her smoothness. In the tentative feeling inside her.

And he coaxed something else out of her. Her recklessness. A wildness that she had not known existed.

Everything she had felt when on the dance floor with him, that sense of flying, freedom, was amplified now. And there was an edge to it. Something sharp, something sweet. A sense of desperation, but also something leisurely. As if she could hold on to this desperate, building feeling forever and ever. Hold off whatever storm was encroaching.

Because those rough hands skating over every inch of her curves, that large palm coming down to cup her butt as he pulled her more firmly against his body, allowing her to feel his heart and arousal up against her stomach, was such a heady, magical thing that she never wanted it to end.

Then he moved both hands to her hips, drawing them down to her thighs, and he lifted her up off the ground completely, wrapping her legs around his waist, bringing the vulnerable center of her up against all that hardened masculinity.

She gasped, a burst of pleasure breaking inside her, a wave of sensation pulsing between her legs.

And she wondered if that was it.

"Not yet," he said as if reading her mind. He dragged his lips down her throat, kissing the tender skin there, before licking the edge of her collarbone, and down farther to her breast, drawing one nipple into his mouth as he rocked his hips forward, sending another shock of sensation through her.

He squeezed her bottom, pulling her forward as he arched his hips again, and she gripped his shoulders, her fingernails digging into his skin as that small, pulsing sensation bloomed, expanded and became a never-ending storm inside her. That earlier feeling had only been a preview. A small taste of what was to come. This was endless. It was incredible. She never wanted it to stop, and yet she wasn't afraid she could withstand much more. He wanted this to happen to her multiple times over the course of the evening? She would never survive. Ever. It would break her. Destroy her. She was certain.

She gasped, and then went limp in his arms, resting her head against his shoulder, and he held her fast, moving through the open floor plan toward a door off to the left. He kicked it open, and then deposited her on a large bed at the center of the room.

She was still feeling languid and boneless from the force of her release, far too aroused and satisfied to feel any nerves about what might come next.

When he lowered himself down onto the bed, her heart leaped into her throat, her entire body on edge.

But then he looked at her, and she remembered his promise. That he would not let her fall. That he wouldn't let her steps falter.

He hadn't promised not to hurt her. She imagined that even with all of her years of riding horses it was going to hurt a bit, but he had promised that in the end it would be right. And she clung to that. She didn't need for it to be painless. She just needed it to be.

He moved his rough hand down her stomach, beneath the waistband of her panties and down between her thighs where he found her aroused and ready for his touch.

She wasn't embarrassed for him to know. How much she desired him. How ready her body was for his invasion.

He pressed two fingers down tightly, bracketing that sensitive bundle of nerves there, making her shiver, making her shake. Making her long for another release, which she would have imagined impossible only a moment before.

She shivered. "I want you," she whispered.

"Do you want me?" he asked, his dark eyes burning intensely into her own. "Do you, Camilla? Or do you simply want the pleasure that you know I can give you?"

"I don't know," she said, her voice trembling. "The kind of pleasure you can give me, I mean. I don't know anything about it at all. But I knew the minute that I saw you that there was something about you. Something about you that called to something in me. I just knew that you changed something inside me. And I wanted so badly for that not to be true. I wanted so badly to want nothing more than to simply be there with the horses. To simply gain back what the family lost. It was all I was supposed to do. All I was supposed to care about. And then there was you. There was you and this need inside me. And it wasn't there before. So yes, Matías, I want you."

She felt incredibly vulnerable, more naked than she had a moment ago. Even with his hand between her legs, she had not felt this vulnerable. But now she had admitted that. That her desire had appeared, manifested itself in her life at the same time that he had exposed a level she had not known possible. And yet, it also felt worth it. It also felt real.

So much deeper, so much stronger, than any other relationship she'd had. Than that nonexistent one with her mother as long as she could be a cute accessory, and then thereafter had ceased to exist. And even to her father, who had loved her, but who had also molded her into the image of what he had wanted. A companion to stay with him on the *rancho*. A daughter who behaved more like a son. This thing with Matías was like none of that. It was stripped bare of any artifice. Of any kind of calculation or manipulation. It was simply about the two of them. And about desire.

She ignored the tightening around her heart, focused on the need in her stomach. Because that was simpler. She could still make that about him. That heaviness gathering between her thighs. She could still make it about him and be safe. But anything in her chest. No. She couldn't risk that.

"Tell me you want me," he said, moving his fingers up slightly, squeezing that sensitive bundle of nerves again, before sliding them back down, not allowing himself to delve into her crease, not allowing himself to touch where she ached for him the most.

She bucked her hips, trying to force his touch to become yet more intimate.

He chuckled, his hold remaining fast. "Be a good girl," he said. "And tell me that you want me." He leaned in, his lips nearly touching hers. "When you wish to break a horse, you must first show it who its master is.

And I think you will find that I am the master of your body, *mi amor*."

She shivered, trying to muster up some kind of rage at that statement. Wanting to tell him that she was the master of her own body, of her own future. Wanting to tell him that he could not play such games with her.

But instead, only a whimper came out of her lips, and she bucked her hips even more intently, desperate now. For more. For his touch. For his possession, whatever that might mean.

"Patience," he said. Then he nipped her bottom lip before kissing her deep, hard, and shifting his hand so that his thumb was pressed up against her, one finger plunging deep inside her.

She gasped. The invasion was both welcome and unfamiliar, and it took a moment for her body to acclimate. But then…she wanted more. Oh, how she wanted more. She wanted all of him. Every last bit. Every hard, breathless inch.

"Matías," she said, the words coming out choked, desperate.

But she had already purposed that there would be no place for pride here. Had already committed herself to honesty. And as he worked his finger in and out of her desperate body, as he slid his thumb over and over her body, she gave herself up to it. To him. Surrendered herself completely, pleasure finding her this time on a short, sharp scream. Her body pulsed around his finger, her release like a storm, no less powerful for the fact that she'd had her first one only moments before in his living room.

She had surrendered her pride to him. And she did not regret it. But she did want something in return. On trembling limbs she rose up to her knees and pushed her panties down her thighs, stripping them off and throwing them off the edge of the bed, so that she was completely naked before him. There really was no point in being shy when she'd come apart in his arms twice, not when he had already had his fingers buried inside her.

She pushed lightly at his shoulder, and he went down on his back, not resisting her touch. Then she bent down, pressing a kiss to his bare shoulder, to his chest, to that place where his heart raged beneath that solid wall of muscle. Then she kissed his stomach, that hard, ridged abdomen that made her body weak with need. She paused, appraising the bulge in his pants. That was uncharted territory. But she would never be able to reclaim anything if she lost her boldness now.

A smile curved her lips and she let her fingertips drift across that cloth-covered arousal. "I think that I know a great deal more about horses than you," she said, biting her lip as she squeezed him. "And perhaps a bit more about mastery."

"Do not challenge me, Camilla," he said. "You're playing with fire."

"Good. I've always liked to live dangerously."

"You might get burned."

"Perhaps," she said, moving both hands to his belt and beginning to work through the loops. "I want to be burned."

She worked his pants down his lean hips and exposed his arousal to her hungry gaze. He was gorgeous. Intimidating, certainly, but he made her mouth water. Made her body feel hollow, aching to be filled. And she knew exactly with what.

But first…

But first.

She leaned down, boldly sliding her tongue over his

hardened length. He swore, raising his hand and fisting her short hair. It hurt, but she pressed on. She tilted her head, taking him deep into her mouth, relishing that musky, masculine flavor on her tongue, his heat and hardness.

Everything.

She wrapped her fingers around his base and continued to move her tongue over him, savoring him as if he were a delicacy.

"Enough," he said roughly, reaching down and lifting her up by the waist, bringing her down so that she was straddling him as though she was about to ride, her center connecting with his body. "I need you," he said, his voice rough.

And that was enough. It was all she needed. She rocked backward slightly, holding on to his arousal and guiding it to the center of her body.

He swore, then reached over to his nightstand quickly. "Condom," he said through gritted teeth. He produced a plastic packet and held it out to her. "Put it on me."

Another challenge. She wasn't going to back down, either.

She tore the packet open with shaking fingers, and thence resituated herself, fumbling for a moment before rolling the latex down over his length. Then she moved back into her previous position, struggling slightly to find the angle, and then lowering herself down slowly, biting her lip to keep from crying out as he stretched her in new and unfamiliar ways, inch by tantalizing inch.

There was no dramatic tearing pain, and she credited her years as a horsewoman with that, but it was strange. New and different and not entirely pleasurable. But he was big, and she imagined that was difficult to get used to.

But then, as she seated herself fully onto him, a sensual thrill shot through her. Not just because of how it felt, but because the idea of getting used to him—to this—meant being with him…more.

She would have months with him. To do just this. To feel him deep inside her, to have him beneath her, naked and gorgeous. To explore his body, taste him, lick him wherever she wanted.

It made her feel powerful.

It made her feel free.

And then she began to ride him. She pressed her hands on his chest, her eyes meeting his as she rose up, and then went back down, as she explored that ancient rhythm, her body honed and fit from years of outdoor labor.

A ripple of pleasure worked its way through her body, that slight discomfort being replaced by a deep, intense satisfaction. And when her orgasm began to build inside her again, she knew what it was. She knew what to chase. She rolled her hips forward, seeking out that completion that she had already experienced twice before.

Then suddenly, she found their positions reversed, found herself on her back, Matías looming over her, dark and intense, his teeth gritted.

The air rushed from her body, and she felt…small. Fragile.

Completely out of control, as opposed to the way she had felt a moment before.

He captured her arms and lifted them up over her head, holding them tight with his hand, both wrists captured in his iron grip.

His thrusts were harder, setting a rhythm she could not anticipate or control. She was the one being written, and she had no experience of such a thing.

She also had no choice but to surrender to it.

She let her head fall back, and she allowed him to be her master.

The erotic thrill of such a thing shocked her. The joy in her helplessness something she had not anticipated.

She rocked against him, then wrapped her legs around his lean hips, moving along with his every thrust, meeting him each time.

And then he began to shake, then he began to tremble, and that mask of his, all that control, fell away and for one moment, one fleeting glance, she saw him as he was. Stripped completely bare of everything in its entirety as he shook and shuddered out his release.

But she only had a moment to watch, only a moment to enjoy before she gave herself up to her own pleasure, before she lost herself completely, clung to him as her internal muscles pulsed around him, as he shook in her arms and as she trembled in his. And when the storm passed, the only sound in the room was their labored breathing. It felt right. It felt like home. Like the wind through the olive groves. Familiar somehow, even though she had never experienced anything like it before.

Then he looked at her, like he might need her.

And it was no longer the pleasure in her body that commended her sole focus, but the pain in her heart.

She squeezed her eyes tightly shut and wished that it would go away.

CHAPTER ELEVEN

Matías watched Camilla sleep for a couple of hours before he went into the kitchen and rummaged around in the fridge for a tray of meat and cheese. He brought the charcuterie back into the bedroom and sat on the edge of the bed, waiting. She stirred, and then looked at him with sleepy eyes.

"Hello," he said, his voice roughened by the long hours spent in silence.

"Is it morning?" she asked, rolling onto her back, drawing her arm up above her head.

She was naked and making no move to cover herself. He didn't mind.

"Technically."

"It's still dark out," she said, pushing herself into a sitting position.

Her hair, artfully styled before he had taken her to bed, was now sticking straight up at the center, the golden crown she had been wearing discarded during their lovemaking. She looked like a beautiful, fallen fairy.

"Yes," he said, "it is. But I was hungry." He placed the food in front of her. "I thought you might be, too."

She eyed the cheese. "I suppose I am. But…"

"Don't worry about anything. We can stay here for

as long as we like tomorrow. Or today, as the case may be. There is nothing pressing for us to attend to. You should eat. Because I expect for you to build up your strength. Because I want you again."

He supposed he ought to feel guilt, perhaps. As he had defiled a virgin last night, something he had never done before, and he intended to do it again before the sun rose.

He did not feel guilt. It was blessedly absent. Possibly because of the color in her cheeks that spoke of her pleasure, or maybe because the sounds she had made as she had found her release still echoed in his ears. Whatever the reason, he felt surprisingly content, all things considered.

Considering that he would be getting married in a week's time. Considering that his original fiancée had been stolen and he disliked very much being manipulated in the way that he was, he felt very content indeed.

That could perhaps be because he had a warm and very willing woman in his bed. And he liked that very much indeed.

She drew her knees to her chest and picked up a piece of cheese, nibbling at it, and he watched the movements of her mouth, the very sensual slide of her tongue against the food. He wanted it against his skin again. But he would give her time.

"Tell me," he said, "about all of the plans that you have once we are finished here."

It would do him good to remember that there were plans for the end of all of this.

"My plans?" She swallowed the mouthful of cheese and looked at him quizzically. "Just…to go back to my *rancho*. To train my horses. I don't have any desire to compete. I would rather stay closer to home. But I should like to continue to train racehorses."

"That will put us in competition," he commented.

She tilted her head to the side. "I suppose it will. But then, our fathers always were."

"Yes. But I believe their relationship was a bit different."

Her cheeks turned a dusky rose color. "Perhaps."

"Do you have plans to expand the operation?"

She blinked. "I don't know. Right now I simply want to get back to what I know. It has been… It has been such a difficult few months. I can't even explain it. Or maybe I can. Just…feeling as though the rug was pulled out from under my life completely. As though I was left standing on nothing. Just falling, endlessly. My father died, and I have barely had a moment to grieve him properly. Because at the same time I lost my home. I lost my horses."

"And you did what you had to in order to keep them. To find them again."

She shrugged. "It was the only power I had. The only possible thing I could reclaim. There was nothing else. No way that I could get ownership of the ranch back on my own. No way that I could bring my father back from the dead. But I knew where you were. And I knew… I knew that you had the horses. I knew that you had Fuego. And I thought…if I could keep that connection maybe I could keep from going completely insane."

"You seem quite sane to me."

"That's up for debate, I suppose. Not very many women would chop off all of their hair on the spur of the moment and decide to try to get a job disguised as a boy."

"What made you think of that?" he asked. "It was quite inventive."

"I begged for a job. When your staff was there taking the horses away I begged to allow me to go with them. And the man who was leading Fuego away told me that you didn't hire women. So…it seemed the logical thing to do. At least, in my mind."

"I suppose there aren't very many people who would think to do that."

"Yes," she agreed. "Which is why it might be a stretch to call it *logical*."

"You're inventive. You're resourceful, and you're very brave." He pressed his thumb against her lower lip, looking at the longing in her eyes. It called to him. To a deep, empty place in his soul. "I know what it's like to feel alone, Camilla." Again, he found himself confessing to her. Only ever her. At first he had thought it was because she was unimportant. Because she wouldn't remain in his life, and so it didn't matter. But after what they'd shared, he could no longer pretend she didn't matter. "When my mother died the sense of isolation that followed was profound. I was the only one who knew that my father was responsible. No one else would believe me. My brother and I were never close, but that drove an even deeper wedge between us. We were just boys, but in many ways we had to become men far too soon."

"And you became a good man. While your brother…"

He swallowed hard. He thought of Diego as a child. All angry and defiant and impossible to talk to. He had been angry at him for a long time, because he'd imagined they'd shared the same upbringing, and that he'd had every chance to do the same with his life that Matías had. But Diego didn't know all of Matías's se-

crets. And it hit him then it was very likely he didn't
know the whole story of Diego. "I don't know that he
ever had a chance."

"But you did. And if you did, then I suppose he could
have, as well."

He hesitated, suddenly not so certain of that. Suddenly not so sure of anything. He didn't like that. Didn't
like relativism as a whole. He preferred things black-
and-white. It was how he lived his life. "Sometimes I
think people are put together differently," he said. "It
is the best explanation I have."

"Perhaps you have more of your mother in you," she
said softly.

"Perhaps," he said, the word rough, pulled from him.

"Is that the real reason you don't hire women?" she
asked softly. "Is it because of your mother? Is it because
you don't want women working on the *rancho*? Doing
that kind of work?"

"My mother wasn't killed by a horse," he said. "She
was killed by my father. The horse being spooked was
his fault."

"Still." She placed her soft hand on his forearm.
He felt something shift inside his chest, and he didn't
like it. Didn't like it at all. The ways in which she re-
arranged him. Things inside him that he had so carefully placed where he wanted them. "I think that might
be why."

"When I dream, it's all screaming. Horses and
women."

The words sounded black and blank, and hopelessly
pathetic. He didn't talk about this. Not to anyone. Not
ever.

"Matías," she said softly, wrapping her arms around
him, resting her cheek against his chest. "You had to

be strong and good, so much more than anyone else, because you were the only one who could be. It's not fair."

She was trying to…comfort him. He could not remember the last time anyone had done that. If they ever had. Probably, his mother had done it, but he couldn't remember. All he remembered was the fighting. All he remembered was his mother hiding from his father. All he remembered was hiding from all of it.

"When Fuego kicked you…" Those words broke off, and he found himself unable to speak. His throat was tight. His lungs burned. He waited. Waited for the wave to pass. For the pressure to release. "It reminded me of when she died," he choked out. "Even if they don't mean to, they're large animals, and they can cause so much harm."

She stroked his arm as though he were a pet and not a man and he couldn't even muster up any anger over it. "It's amazing to me that you want to continue working with horses. That you want to keep the *rancho*. All things considered. I know why. At least, I know what you told me. About wanting to be the one that controls it. About wanting to redeem it all. But…no one would blame you if you decided you didn't want any of it."

That had been his intention in his twenties. His fortune elsewhere. Why he had left Spain and centered his business in London. But he had found that there was no getting away from his past. And that the farther he got away from his home, the farther away he went from the *rancho*, the more his dreams plagued him.

"That place has become a mission," he admitted. "Unfinished business, in many ways. Once it's all settled, I don't intend to spend too much time there."

"You're so good at it, though," she said, continuing to caress him with those lovely fingers. "I can't imagine you simply disappearing into a desk job. It isn't you."

"Maybe it is," he said, reaching down and putting his finger beneath her chin, tilting her face upward. "Perhaps I prefer this," he said, looking around the penthouse. "Perhaps I prefer evenings spent at galas to quiet evenings in rural libraries. Perhaps I prefer spending my days in glass and steel skyscrapers to dusty arenas."

"You don't." She said those words with such confidence that he wanted to laugh at her, except he could not because her dark eyes were so serious. So sincere. She reached up, grabbing hold of the hand that was beneath her chin, and drawing it down. She smoothed her thumb over his palm, her eyes never leaving his. "I can tell, because of your hands. You don't have the hands of a man content to work at a computer. Content to work at a desk. These calluses are thick, worn in from years of work. It's your heart. Right here. This is what you choose to do when you're not doing the thing you must do to increase your fortune. A man who does ranch work in a casual capacity is not going to have hands like this." Then she shocked him, placed his hand against her breast, a slow smile curving her lips, deep satisfaction etched into her expression. "You have just the kind of hands that I like."

"Tell me, then," he said, feeling driven to know the answer all of a sudden. "If I am the kind of man you like, then why didn't you do this with any of the other men who worked on your father's *rancho*? Why didn't you end up with them when you could have?"

"Because they weren't you. That was the missing piece. Rough hands were never going to be enough."

He was so aroused he could hardly think anymore. But before he took her again, he needed to know something. "Tell me," he said, "your dream. Your biggest dream."

When all of this was over and he set her free again, he was determined to see it done. The Alvarez *rancho* would be returned to her ownership, and he would be sure that her mother had no claim on it. Would be sure that it was entirely for Camilla.

He was going to give her Fuego, as well, in addition to the rest of the horses. He was determined on that score, too. Yes, the horse would have been an amazing asset for his own ranch, but he knew now that the animal had to go with Camilla. There was no other option.

But anything else, whatever else she desired, he was determined to ensure she had it. He would not be a man who left a woman broken. Not as his father had done.

He would ensure that whatever he had taken from Camilla tonight, he would restore it as best he could.

She looked blindsided by that question, confused. "Just the *rancho*," she insisted.

"That is something you already had. Is there anything more you want? Anything?"

She looked down. "No. I can't think of anything else. All I want is my normal life back. I couldn't... I couldn't begin to want anything else."

He had a feeling that she was lying, but whether to him or to herself he didn't know. And he was past the point of talking. Because her skin was soft and sweet beneath his touch, because her nipple had grown hard beneath his palm and his own body was growing hard in response.

He took the plate of meat and cheese and set it aside

and pulled Camilla into his arms. "Whatever you want," he said, "I will see that it is yours. You have my word."

The word of a Navarro had never meant much. But Matías was determined to change that.

He was determined to change it for her.

CHAPTER TWELVE

THE DAY OF the wedding began like any other day, which surprised Camilla to a degree, as the entire thing loomed large in her mind. There was no reason to be nervous, and she knew that. She and Matías had been over this, and over it and over it. How it would all go, how long it was going to last.

It was not going to be a terribly formal affair.

She had been presented with a small selection of gowns earlier in the week, and she had chosen one that best suited the outdoor event.

She had a feeling it was very different to the dress that Liliana would have selected, but it was right for her. Simple, white and with clean, elegant lines.

Though, as Matías had pointed out, a bit wickedly—while holding her arms above her head, his hips locked against hers as his weight pressed her down into the mattress—she was no longer a virgin, and therefore, did not have to wear white.

She had scoffed at him and said that the symbolism of the white dress had long since gone out of fashion.

And then he had kissed her and done something with his tongue that had made it impossible to think. And after she'd had to concede—to herself—there was no point in pretending that she was anything near a virgin now. One week spent in his bed and he had introduced her to a great many sensual delights.

Just thinking about that made her face hot. But not from embarrassment. Nothing the two of them did together embarrassed her. And she wasn't anywhere near finished with him.

She was already weaving fantasies about how they might continue this once their *arrangement* was finished.

Their ranches were only a few hours apart. It would be possible for them to continue seeing one another while carrying on separate lives. He could see to his business, and then when he had the chance he could come and visit her. They could sleep together. She could show him the house that she loved so much. Take him out back to the gardens, to the fountains, show him all the beautiful mosaics there. Take him on a ride through the trees, to the base of the mountains.

These were foolish fantasies, and she'd never in her life been prone to such things. But then she'd never wanted a man before. Had never been so…consumed— obsessed even—with another person. His body. His mind. His soul.

They had so much in common.

Well, except for the whole playboy international billionaire thing. But his soul. His soul matched hers in so many ways. Fiercely independent. Wanting to make his own way.

Except, much more than she, Matías was driven by demons from his past. She knew it, even if she couldn't understand them all.

At night he slept fitfully. And she stayed by his side, her hand on his chest. Sometimes she stayed awake and simply watched him, as if somehow holding vigil beside him as he wrestled with his past pain even in his dreams, she could provide some kind of support.

He made her *want*.

It was an endless well of want, not one that simply began and ended in the bedroom, but one that seemed to go on and on. In the evenings, when she was sated in the physical sense, there was still something else that lingered. Something that gnawed at her, nagged at her. Something that tugged at her heart and made her physically ache.

She did her best to ignore it, because she felt that only insanity sat at the end of that path.

But now it was time for the wedding. And somehow, she had expected the sky to fall before then. But it had not. Instead, when she had woken early that morning, Matías was already gone. Probably off doing chores on the *rancho*, and there was nothing unusual about that, though often they woke together.

But then she set about to readying herself for the event. The wedding would take place in the late afternoon, followed by a dinner and dancing. Mostly, people from the village had been invited. Distant relatives. And of course, Matías's grandfather would be making the trip, even though his health made it very difficult.

That made Camilla feel as though a weight was settled on her chest. Matías's family was a source of such pain to him, she was angry that his grandfather was intruding on their day. Except, the day would not exist if not for his grandfather. Truly, he was the cause of it. It was more. He was the reason they were doing this.

And she knew that. Truly she did. But sometimes, that twinge around her heart made it difficult to fully internalize. To fully believe. Because it felt like more. Even though it shouldn't, it did.

There were things about it that felt so very real. So real they hurt.

She looked at her reflection in the mirror, now more used to this glossier version of herself.

She was wearing a veil that reached the ground, blended together with the soft, gauzy fabric of her dress. Her lipstick was dark, drawing attention to her mouth, matching the dramatic winged eyeliner that the stylist had put together for her.

She felt beautiful. But it had nothing to do with the makeup. Nothing to do with the dress. And everything to do with the past week spent in Matías's arms.

He never made her feel like he wished she were another woman.

She had worried for a time that he would prefer Liliana. Had worried that he was fantasizing about the petite blonde while they were in bed together. But it become clear quickly that he had a deep appreciation for her athletic body. And all the things she could do with it. She might be inexperienced, but she was physically able, and he took great advantage of that.

Much to both of their delight.

That made her smile. Smile as Maria, the housekeeper, handed her the simple, deep crimson bouquet. Continued smiling as she walked down the stairs of the house and into the foyer.

"Everything is set up outside," the older woman said. "And they will be ready for you in a moment. I will signal you when it is time."

She couldn't believe the moment had arrived. And yet, it seemed like an entire lifetime in the making. As if all of this, her relationship with Matías, had been destined to be from the beginning.

This wasn't real. It wasn't. What was real had been

that first time they had made love. That was Matías and Camilla.

This was for the audience. This was for his grandfather. And she had to remember that. Had to try to find the practical woman she was, buried underneath the makeup. Beneath the bridal gown that made all this feel like a beautiful waking dream when she knew full well it was a simple business transaction.

Maria rushed outside and Camilla took a deep breath, pressing her hands against her stomach.

"Well," came a voice from behind her. "Don't you make a radiant bride."

She turned, and her heart hit her sternum hard. For the man standing in front of her was not Matías. He was tall, darkly handsome and resembled her fiancée just enough that she knew exactly who he was.

He possessed the same sort of magnetism, the same height and breadth. But there was something menacing about him. Something that went beyond dangerous. Something deadly.

"Diego, I presume," she said.

"You make this sound very like an overdramatic soap opera," he drawled, moving closer to her. "I must say, I am impressed with my brother's resourcefulness. Often, his scruples prevent him from claiming certain victories. I myself have never understood why he'd limit himself the way he does."

"I'm not entirely sure what you're talking about," she said. "Matías is my lover. He has been. Liliana's defection was only a good thing for us."

She did not know where she was drawing the strength to come at him like this. Except, it was the story that she and Matías had agreed on, a distortion of the truth to show the world why he was choosing to marry her, and it was not his day to wed beautiful, pale Liliana.

Because if it was, her heart would have broken into a million pieces and shattered on the ground.

She would rather this—this temporary union that might turn to nothing in the end—than watch him marry another woman. A marriage he had meant to be forever, leaving no chance for them to have anything more later on.

"It is a very nice story," Diego said. "But I already read it in the paper. You know, my brother fancies himself a good man, but he is not so different from me. He simply draws lines around moral dilemmas as he sees fit. And I have never seen the point of doing so. He decides that certain actions are *right*, and certain actions are *wrong*. He has decided that his motivation for inheriting the *rancho* is higher than mine, and therefore, he must win at this game. I require no motivation of myself beyond my need to win. To be satisfied. I don't need to pretend I am being *good*."

"Is that why you took Liliana?"

A smile curved one side of his mouth upward. "She was simply a means to an end. Like everything else."

"Did she go with you of her own free will? Or did you kidnap her?"

He chuckled. "Oh, I kidnapped her. But she was convinced quickly enough to marry me. I just had to have her throw out that lie to Matías so he wouldn't come searching for her. He's not very trusting. He believed so quickly that she would betray him. It's a character flaw, for sure. If I were you, I would watch out for that later on. If he were to walk in now, I imagine he would have a lot of follow-up questions for you. Particularly if he were to walk in when you were in my embrace."

Diego took another step toward her, and Camilla took a step away. "Don't come anywhere near me," she said. "You're a villain."

He laughed. "To you. But a villain is his own hero. I read that somewhere once. I quite like it. Although, I am not overly concerned with being either. I'm simply concerned with winning."

"Well, Matías and I are getting married today. So you're not going to win."

"Am I not? Because I will get my share of the family fortune. If I choose to press the issue with my lawyer, I will probably end up with a stake in my brother's company." That dark gaze turned cruel. "And he has had to settle for second best when it comes to wives. Yes, I think my victory, while not total, was handily enough done."

The door to the house opened again, and Maria waved her on. "It is time," she said.

"I had better go take my place in the audience, then," Diego said. "But rest assured and remember this. My brother might talk about being good. He might talk about doing the right thing, and in the end he might do the right thing by you, whatever that means. If it looks like a permanent marriage, or an attempt at commitment. But he will not love you. That is something the men in our family are incapable of."

Then he left her standing there, feeling diminished. Her heart feeling torn in two. He had not said anything she hadn't already thought to be true. Hadn't dropped any grand revelations on her. And still, he had accomplished everything he had set out to do. He had sent her out into the blinding sunlight on shaking legs. Had planted doubts inside her when before she had been quite content walking toward that while knowing that in the end, this would end as nothing.

But now Diego's words were swirling inside her, painful, horrendous. And she realized it was reality. He had made it impossible to pretend that this was going to end as a fairy tale. He had made it impossible for her to cling to that last shred of fantasy, which she had to admit to herself as she made her way toward the site of the wedding, she had been doing.

But then she came to the head of the aisle, and all the guests stood and turned, and she saw Matías standing there, dark, handsome and certain.

So very like his brother, and yet not.

And she realized that none of it mattered. Because there was only one choice to make. There was only one direction she was going to walk.

Toward Matías. No matter what.

CHAPTER THIRTEEN

IT HAD BEEN shocking to see his brother and Liliana in the crowd at the wedding.

Matías had a feeling that *shock* had been Diego's intent.

Matías had made it his mission to keep his older brother away from Camilla through the entirety of the reception, and during the farewells that evening.

Though he had a feeling that if Diego had intended to approach her at any point, he would have done so. But he had not, which was actually no less unsettling.

Liliana, for her part, had looked beautiful, but pale. Drawn.

Her face adorned with no makeup, as she had often done, her long hair left loose, her curves highlighted by the flowing, lavender gown that she was wearing.

Diego never took his hands off her, his dark eyes sharp every time he looked at her.

It was a strange dynamic, and one that surprised Matías. Because he had imagined his brother would care nothing at all for his new wife. Had imagined that he had simply seduced her away from Matías in order to win at this ridiculous game they were playing to gain their grandfather's possessions. But there was something there. Something dark and tense. He commented as much when he and Camilla were finally alone. Headed back to his penthouse in Barcelona for their wedding night.

"She loves him," Camilla said softly.

"What the hell are you talking about?" Matías asked. "Don't you think that by now she has seen what manner of man he is?"

"Unfortunately, I think she knew from the beginning. I... I had a conversation with Diego before the wedding," she said, twisting her hands together.

"Were you going to tell me if I had not brought him up?"

"Possibly not. The whole thing made me nervous. He was clearly trying to intimidate me. Trying to scare me away. But he has never met me. So he did not know that was a losing proposition."

"I almost feel sorry for him," Matías said. "What did he say to you?"

"He confirmed that he *did* kidnap Liliana. Their marriage, however, is legal, so whatever happened after that, she consented to it. He talked her into it, he says. I imagine there was blackmail involved. But... I see the way she looks at him. I spent a good portion of the ceremony looking. I don't think she wants to be rescued," Camilla said softly. "Though I'm not entirely certain she's happy."

"How could she be happy with a sociopath? How could she love him?"

"Oftentimes these things don't make sense," Camilla said, her voice hard. "And why do you care? Just for her happiness? Or are you wishing that you had married her today?"

Frustration roared through him and he growled, pinning Camilla up against the wall in the penthouse. "I don't give a damn about Liliana. At least, not beyond her safety. Of course I don't want my brother holding her against her will, but as she traveled with him, and obviously married him, and has not fled him, I think it's safe to say that's not what's happening. I don't want her. I want you."

"Well, you seem awfully concerned about her."

"And you seem jealous," he said, taking a step back.

"I *am*," she confirmed.

He looked at his wife, standing there in the flowing white gown. His *wife*. She was his. Legally. A binding agreement. And suddenly, he wanted, more than anything, to hold her to that. To hold her to him. Wanted to do what Diego had done. To take her away, to hold her captive. To make her his, however that looked, whatever that might mean. Suddenly, being right, being good, didn't seem half so important as it had before.

Only having her.

And he could see just how thin that line that separated himself from Diego, Diego from his father, and his father from their grandfather, really was.

It was in his DNA, whether he wanted it to be or not.

"I married *you*," he said, his voice hard.

"Yes," she hissed. "And the inescapable truth is that if Liliana had been available you would have married her."

"Why do you want a fight?" he asked, moving nearer to her, closing the distance between them and wrapping his arm around her waist. "I can think of much better uses of our time."

He consumed her then, capturing her mouth with his own and pouring all of his frustrations, all of the intense, crushing feelings in his chest, out onto her. His pulse was pounding angrily, mirroring the heat and fire moving through his veins, the hardness, the desire coursing through his groin.

He wanted her, but that was not all.

No, it was not all. He was not a stranger to sexual desire, but this was entirely foreign to him. This was sexual desire mingled with something else. A need so fierce, so ferocious, that he thought it might destroy them both.

If he acted on it, certainly they would both go up completely in the conflagration. But if he did not act on it, he didn't think he would survive it.

He was all out of control. That control that he prided himself on, that he was so convinced made him a good man. A better man than his brother, better man than his father.

All of his certainty was gone. Every last bit. All that remained was need. Need for Camilla, for his wife. His bride. The woman he had spoken vows to, in front of his townspeople, in front of his grandfather.

They might have an understanding. They might have an agreement that was supposed to make things clear, that was supposed to make them easy, but right now it felt anything but.

Again, in this moment, they were nothing more than Camilla and Matías. The world outside them didn't exist.

Here, in his penthouse, this place that was his and his alone, she belonged to him only. Here, he had his bride on his wedding night. And whatever the future held for them, whatever the reasons for this marriage, he intended to claim this night for them. For himself.

Suddenly, he could wait no longer, his patience growing thin. He grabbed hold of the flimsy fabric of the bodice of her dress and tore it wide, letting the material fall loose around her waist.

She sucked in a shocked breath. "That was a beautiful dress," she said, faintly admonishing, but she did not pull away from him, neither did she look as scandalized as she was attempting to sound.

No, her eyes were dark, filled with desire. He could see that she was as tested for control as he was. That she was as hungry for this as he was.

That he was not alone in his desire.

And that only made the monster inside him growl even louder.

"Yes," he agreed. "It was a pretty dress. But your body, *mi tesoro*, is the most beautiful prize of all. Anything that gets in the way of that… I'm afraid I cannot allow it to be."

As if to prove his point he grabbed hold of the lacy bra that covered her breasts, concealed them from his view, and he tore it away from her body, as well, leaving those high, perfect breasts exposed to him.

He lowered his head, taking one perfect nipple between his lips and sucking hard. He was starving for her. And it did not matter that he had been with her every night that week. It did not matter that he had sated himself on her whenever he desired since that first night he'd had her. It was as if it had been years. As if he had been kept from her.

Perhaps it was simply that she was his wife now. No matter that neither of them intended for it to be permanent. Perhaps it had changed things somehow. Made him more possessive. Made all of this somehow more.

It seemed impossible, and yet, with all that heat and fire pounding through his body, he wondered. If somehow, she truly had become part of his flesh as they had spoken those words to one another at that altar. If somehow, there was a sacred bond here that could not be manipulated, that could not be fooled.

He dismissed those thoughts as he ripped the dress the rest of the way from her body, and took her panties with it, leaving her beautiful, golden form entirely exposed to him.

He examined those slim, perfect curves, her taut, toned belly, her womanly hips and shapely thighs. That glorious thatch of dark curls between them.

She was beautiful. A work of art. And she was his. All his.

He was still fully dressed, still wearing the suit he had worn to the wedding, and he quite liked that. This woman, completely naked before him while he remained fully clothed. It made him feel powerful. Gave him some semblance of control in the moment.

And it also made him hungry for more. To expose her to an even greater degree, to exert that power.

To do something to deal with that yawning, endless ache in his chest, and the rest of his body.

"You are mine," he said, words coming out on a growl. He picked her up, her lithe form soft and warm in his arms. "You are mine, and no other man's. Is that clear?"

"Yes," she said, the word hushed. For the moment at least, he seemed to have tamed her. He was not sure how to feel about that.

"And if my brother were to come in trying to carry you off, I would chase him to the ends of the earth before I let him keep you. I hope that is clear." He gripped her chin, holding her face steady, looking into her eyes. "I would chase that bastard to hell to bring you back to me. Do you understand? He would not be allowed to lay one finger on you, and if he did, it would be the last thing he did. He would lose that hand, and then he would lose everything else dear to him. Everything."

Honesty. Always with her it was that damned, unguarded honesty and he did not possess the strength to fight it on any level. Not now.

She shivered in his arms, and he wondered if perhaps he had gone too far, and then he decided he didn't care. Not at all. Not in the least.

If he was possessive, then so be it. If he was untamed, then so be it. If he was no better than any of the other men in his family, then he supposed he would have to accept that, not fight it. Not anymore. Not with her.

It simply was.

Suddenly, he understood the nature of that violence that coursed through Diego's veins. He understood that rage in his father. Because he felt it now all the same. It wasn't anger. It was something different. It was big. And it was hot, and it was something that owned him, body and soul. A possessiveness that he could not fight.

Possessiveness he *would* not fight, here and now.

He set her down on his couch, positioning her toward the back of it as he knelt on the cushions, spreading her thighs wide. And then he examined her femininity, all of that gleaming beauty, and the pearl that was the center of all her pleasure. "Beautiful," he growled, stroking his fingertips over her sensitive and responsive flesh. "And all for me."

"I am not the one who was supposed to marry someone else today," she panted. "I am not the one who deserves to be caught up in such a fit of possessiveness."

He tightened his hold on her thighs. "This is not about what either of us *deserves*," he said, his voice rough. "This is about what *is*. About what I'm going to take. I will have all of you, my bride. I hope you understand that."

"And you need to know, my husband," she returned, "that it is understood that if there is any doubt in your mind as to what you would do if Liliana came in here tonight and said that she wished to leave Diego, that you will keep your hands off me, that you will stand up and walk away from me now. Because you are not the only one who is possessive."

"If she came in here, what would you do?" he asked.

"I would fight her for you," she returned, that stubborn chin tilting upward. "Because I fight for what's mine. You know that I do. If I have to cut my hair off and change my identity, I will do it. But I fight for what's mine."

If she had been another woman it might have been tempting to be offended to be compared to her horses, to have that same sort of possessiveness given over to him. But it was not another woman. It was Camilla. And knowing the fierce possessiveness with which she regarded those animals, he did not think he deserved more. But rather, he suspected he deserved a lot less.

"And if she were to come in here," he said, "I would scarcely notice, because she is not the woman that I want. You are the woman that I want."

Understanding that when he said that, he knew there was a cost to it. Because if things had gone as planned, he would have full ownership over the Navarro family estate. If Diego had not taken Liliana, then all of it would be his. He would be in the clear.

But then he would not have Camilla.

Somewhere in the depths of his mind he was reminded of words that felt similar. A Bible story. A king offering his queen whatever she desired, even if it was half of his kingdom. And he realized then that if given the choice now, that was the trade he would make. It was the trade that had been made through no choice of his own, but it was what he would do if the need presented itself. If the choice were on offer again.

Half of his kingdom. With no hesitation.

"I have no desire for anyone but you," he reiterated, leaning forward, drawing his tongue across that sensitive bundle of nerves, wringing from her as much pleasure as possible with his lips, his tongue, his fingers. Working her body until she was boneless, breathless and spent, until the last vestiges of her release began to dissipate.

Then he picked up her boneless body and carried her into his bedroom.

"Mine," he growled, pressing a kiss to her lips. "My wife."

He pressed her down into the mattress, settling between her thighs. Typically, Camilla preferred to be the one doing the writhing. At least, that was how she preferred to begin their encounters. But not tonight. Tonight the possession was his. Tonight he was in control. Utterly and completely.

She also enjoyed pleasuring him, something that he was not averse to. Usually.

But again, tonight, he would not allow that. Tonight he would not surrender that to her. Tonight he would extract all of the control, all of the pleasure from her that he could.

He slid his hand beneath her hips, cupped her soft, perfect rear and lifted her up off the bed, angling her just so, so that he could thrust into the hilt.

He growled, realizing a moment later that he was bare, that he had not put a condom on. He was tempted, so tempted to press that. To keep doing this with nothing between their bodies. To spill himself inside her when he found his release, and damn the consequences.

It was that same, feral part of him that wanted to possess her completely.

But he would not. He would not do that to her. She wanted her freedom when all this was over. And it was that, that knowledge, that slowed his hand. That helped him hold on to his sanity. And only that.

"I must protect you," he said thickly, withdrawing from her body and making his way to the nightstand, grabbing a condom and sheathing himself quickly. "I'm sorry."

He thrust back into her, not bothering to clarify whether or not he was sorry he had entered her without protection in the first place, or whether he was just sorry that he had to get it.

He wasn't sure which thing made him sorrier, frankly.

Likely that he had to get a condom and he would rather feel her, all that silky heat, surrounding him.

He gritted his teeth, trying to maintain his control as he rocked his hips backward, then thrust home, pleasure almost blinding him as he did so.

He closed his eyes tight, sparks bursting behind them as he lost himself completely inside her.

There had never been anyone like this. There had never been anything like this.

She didn't just make him feel pleasure, she made him feel pain. Didn't simply satisfy him, she opened up on the heels of that satisfaction. Made him want in ways he hadn't expected to ever want before.

The build of his release was almost violent, was deadly, far too intense. And when it captured him, it didn't just send a burst of pleasure through him, it wrenched his chest open. He gritted his teeth, growling as his orgasm rocked him, pressing his forehead to hers and kissing her, deeply, fiercely, begging her, in Spanish and in English, to come along with him. It was the first time he had not ensured that she was satisfied more than once before he found his own release, but he had not had the control tonight. He had not possessed that kind of restraint.

He rolled his hips, grinding himself against her, and then finally, she gave him her pleasure. She pulsed around him, squeezing his arousal, pulling a few more spasms of pleasure from him as her own orgasm rocked her.

And when it was done, she clung to his shoulders, shaking, crying.

Her tears hit him with all the violence of a closed fist. Because his Camilla did not cry. She was strong, and she was lovely. That warrior goddess of his fantasies. She was weeping now, weeping like a child, because of something he had done.

"Camilla," he said, gripping her face, holding it steady, looking into those luminous dark eyes, gazing at her tearstained face. "Have I hurt you? What have I done?"

She shook her head. "Nothing," she said. "You haven't hurt me at all."

"Why are you crying?"

She sobbed, her entire body shaking. "Because," she said. "You didn't hurt me, you bastard. You made me fall in love with you."

"What?" he asked, drawing back.

"I'm in love with you, Matías. Oh, how I love you."

CHAPTER FOURTEEN

CAMILLA KNEW THAT she had made a grave mistake, and yet, she wouldn't go back and change it even if she could. She couldn't lie to Matías, not anymore. The relationship had started out a lie, and she would be damned if it continued one. He had asked her what she wanted. Not that long ago, he had demanded to know. Well, now he would know. She wanted him. She wanted this. Forever. No matter the cost.

"I love you," she repeated. "I didn't mean to. I wasn't supposed to. I was supposed to love the *rancho*, the horses and nothing more. I was supposed to want nothing beyond that. Nothing bigger than that life. Because that life was everything. At least, that life was everything to my father. And I love it, Matías, don't get me wrong. If I didn't, I never would have put myself at such a risk to come and work for you. But it's not everything. Not now. You are."

"This cannot be, Camilla," he said, his voice rough. "You cannot love me."

"I have never asked your permission to do anything, Matías. I'm hardly going to ask your permission for this. I don't need it. I don't want to. It just… It is." She had never been so certain of anything in her entire life.

Never been so certain of anything more than she was certain of this burning, deep conviction in her soul.

She would risk anything for this. For him. There was no pride in hiding away and denying feelings. She had too much experience watching someone else fall into that trap. Into that lie. That was her father's life. Shrinking everything down so that he could never be heard.

Wanting nothing beyond what he had in front of him. Nothing more than the *rancho*.

And she supposed her father had found a way to be happy in that. They'd had a good life. And he had never longed for the wife who wouldn't stay with him.

But Camilla did not want that life. She did not want a life reduced in order to avoid pain. She did not want a life where she could have Matías, where he was alive, where he was within reach, if she would only go after him.

She would exhaust every avenue before she accepted that.

She had always seen her mother as flighty. As unfeeling. Running continually, unavailable to her father.

But now she wondered. She wondered if Cesar Alvarez had ever gone after his wife, or if he had simply let her leave.

If he had simply assumed that love was beyond their reach.

Camilla was not going to do that. Not with Matías. It was too important. He was too important.

"I love you," she repeated. "I didn't know that I wanted this. I didn't know that I wanted more than a life on the *rancho*. But I do. You asked me once, Matías, what I needed to be happy. And I have decided that I need you."

"You little fool," he said, the words almost despairing, as much as they were enraged. "You could have had a life that made you happy, if you had not decided that you wanted me in it."

"Why can't we be together? You were going to have a wife. You were going to have Liliana. You had committed to that. So why can't you have me?"

"Because I have seen where it ends," he said, exploding now. "It ends in brokenness. It ends in despair. For everyone involved. And I will not be part of that."

"Why wouldn't it have ended in despair with Liliana?"

"Because I—" He cut those words off.

"Because you felt nothing for her. But you feel *something* for me. Admit it. You care for me, Matías, and if it isn't love, it could be someday."

"I will admit no such thing," he said. "This is not love. This is an abomination. It is a lack of control, a lack of control that I swore to myself I would never experience. And here I am, at the very end of everything, because of you. Liliana would have been safe because she didn't challenge me. Because she didn't make me feel so much like I might understand the man that my father was."

"Do you honestly think you would hurt me? You have never once threatened me. Ever. You have never demonstrated any such tendencies, and I'm not going to believe now that that's the reason that you can't be with me."

"There is a thin line between love and hate. Between passion and destruction. And I never appreciated that fully until tonight. Until I could not control myself with you. Until I had to fight every last one of my impulses to keep from going and killing Diego, not because he was standing there with Liliana, but because he was within reach of you. Knowing that he went and spoke to you tonight…that he was alone with you… I don't know myself when I'm with you, Camilla, and if I can't control myself… I fear that is a man neither of us wants to know."

"You think you're going to break me?"

"I know it's possible."

"It's not. It isn't."

He advanced on her, then reached out, pressing his palm against her throat, beneath her chin. She lifted her fingers to his, curving her fingers around his knuckles, forcing his hold tight.

"You think that I should be afraid of you?" she asked. "You think that you might harm me? Do you see how I trust you?"

He growled, tightening his hold on her and pushing her back against the wall, something in his gaze sharp, desperate. "You test me, because you don't know better."

He released his hold and turned away from her, walking away. "There are ways to break people that have nothing to do with the physical body. You can break them in a thousand different ways, and believe me, Camilla, I have seen it. My father killed my mother that day, but he broke her long before. He broke her by denying her the one thing that she wanted. His love. It's the way that he tried to break all of us." He let out a long breath. "In a home like that, you have two options in the end. You either decide that you don't need love, or you die from the lack of it. I learned to live without, and I can't ask you to do the same."

"You think it would kill me?"

"Not physically."

"You think you would make me that miserable?" she implored.

"I know it," he bit out.

"We have months to work this out," she said. "This doesn't have to be the end. We can figure out what will work between us. I know that we can."

"No," he said, his tone bleak.

"Yes," she insisted. "I love you, but I'm not asking you for anything in return. I'm asking that you try. Let's try. The two of us. We can make something better, you and I. Better than what we had. Than what we saw. I'm not my mother. But I'm not my father, either. I'm not going to allow the one that I've said was you, the one that I have decided that I love, to walk away from me without a fight. I will be damned if I do, Matías. You're mine, and I'm not going down without a fight. You're right. I'm not Liliana. I will fight for you. Perhaps that's why I scare you. Because you know that she would've let you hide away. That she would never have demanded your love. But I am. I'll work for it. You don't have to give it now. But I will win it someday."

"No," he said again. "This is the end."

"It can't be. Matías, you know that it can't be, because if it is then Diego will get that stake in your company. And you won't get the *rancho* at all."

"It is the end." He picked up his phone, and she just watched, in shock as he dialed. "Grandfather," he said, his tone almost casual, as if he wasn't calling the old man past midnight. "I regret to inform you that my marriage is not going to work out. Camilla and I are going to seek an annulment. On the basis of fraud. I lied to her, you see. I led her to believe that our relationship was real, when it was not. It never was." His horrible, blank gaze was rested on her as he spoke those words. And somewhere, down deep, she knew that he was only doing this to harm her. To make her leave him be. To make her walk away. But knowing that didn't make it less painful. "Yes, I am aware of what that means," he said. "I'm aware that it means I'm forfeiting all that could be mine to Diego. I'm aware that it means I'm walking away from the inheritance. I only ask for one thing. I want the horses that were purchased from Cesar Alvarez. They are assets of the *rancho*, but I wish to return them to Camilla for her trouble. Otherwise, I will return to running my business, and Diego will have control of the Navarro assets. Whatever that might entail."

There was a pause. And then Matías nodded once definitively. "Then we have a deal."

He hung up. "The horses are yours," he said, his tone completely void of emotion. "The *rancho* will be Diego's."

"No," she said, crumbling inside. He was giving all of this up rather than being with her. All of it. He was committing an extreme act to get away from her, and if anything could possibly speak more to the fact that he didn't love her, that he wanted to escape her, she didn't know what it could be.

She had not expected this. Of all the things she had expected, it had not been this.

"It was never my intention to hurt you," he said. "I thought that I made it very clear what was to happen between the two of us. But obviously, I did not make it clear enough. We will not work. This will not work. I will return you to your family *rancho*. All of your assets should be returned to you. And then we can go on as though this never happened. As though we never met."

He began to get dressed, walking away from her, moving to the front of the apartment. She stood, frozen, numb, watching him prepare to go. "That's it? You're leaving tonight?"

"Yes," he said. "I'm going to go deal with a few business matters, the first of which being the restoration of your *rancho* to your ownership. You will not have to see me again."

"But what if I want to?" The question was small, and there truly was no pride at all left in it. There was none left in her entire being.

"It does not matter what you want," he said. "This is what must be."

And then Matías Navarro walked out of the penthouse, and out of her life.

Camilla Alvarez was certain she had experienced the lowest moment anyone possibly could. The death of her father, followed by the loss of the ranch, the loss of the horses.

But she had been wrong.

The most painful loss of all was the loss of her heart.

Her heart that had just told her she would never see him again.

And sadly, she believed it.

Matías had gotten on a plane to London directly after leaving Camilla in the penthouse. He had worked at a punishing pace for days, completely unnecessarily from his office there. He had not needed to go there. He had not needed to leave the country at all, not to deal with transferring ownership of a ranch back in Spain. But this was not about business. It was about needing to get distance between himself and the woman who had bewitched him in great and terrible ways.

He had never been for her. Ever. He had never meant to mean something to her. In fact, he had imagined she would be the last woman on earth who would fall in love with him.

Those words echoed in his mind. She had fallen in love with him.

How many times had he told her that he did not hire women because they only fell in love with him?

How many women had said they loved him in the past? Countless. But it had been nothing like this.

When he'd sent them away they had pouted. They had cajoled. They had been annoyed. But they had not been wounded.

Camilla had been *wounded*.

She loved him. She truly did. She might have been the only person in all the world who ever had. He had sent her away.

There'd been no other choice. Not really.

If he had kept her, he would only break her. It had hit him when he'd realized that he...that he understood his father. His brother. That the unhinged, uncontrollable things in them he'd always despised lived inside him, too.

Control was everything. A lack of it was destructive. And love was...it was a force that couldn't be tamed. It was a hurricane.

That was what love was. Being broken apart.

He swallowed hard. Then he stood from his desk and made his way over to the sideboard, grabbing a bottle of whiskey and pouring himself a generous tumbler full before knocking it back.

Love was pain. And nothing more.

He had never intended to revisit this kind of pain on himself. Not again.

He shook his head and looked around the pristine office space. This was his. And perhaps, Diego would end up with a small amount of shares in the company. That would irritate him, but it would hardly give his brother any control. Of course, anything Diego touched had a tendency to get turned into fire and brimstone.

But then, so be it.

He had that thought before he had entered her body for the last time, that he would give her anything, even half of his kingdom.

Apparently, he was not averse to giving away the entire thing.

He still couldn't believe he had done it. That he had cut ties with her quite so definitively. That he had made such a bold statement to his grandfather.

That he had given it all away.

It was late, and he did not expect it when his secretary called into his office phone line.

"Someone is here to see you, Mr. Navarro," she said in her cut-glass English accent.

Penelope was at home, not in the office, but if somebody wanted to be let in, the call still went to her even after hours, and she could control entry into the office building from her computer.

"Who is it?" he asked.

"He says he's your brother."

Matías swore. Of course. He should have known that he couldn't avoid that snake for long. He would know by now that he had won. And he would want to gloat.

"Let him in."

Matías stood from his desk again and poured another measure of alcohol. By the time Diego walked in he was standing there with two glasses in his hand and a smile on his lips.

"You would only smile when offering me a drink if it was poisoned," Diego said, producing a flask from inside his jacket. "I'm good."

His brother was smiling, but Matías could see that

something had begun to fray around the edges of his personal brand of dark charm.

"To what do I owe the displeasure?"

"I heard that you had forfeited our little game," Diego said.

"Because it quit being a game to me."

"Oh, I see. So it was still a game when I stole Liliana right out of her bedroom, but it's not a game now. Fascinating."

"Liliana said that she wanted to be with you," Matías pointed out. "I was hardly going to rescue a woman who didn't wish to be rescued."

"Yes," Diego said. "She did tell you that. Because I'm blackmailing her. Her father is not the upstanding citizen that he appears to be, and Liliana was quite shocked to find out the Hart family name was not built on the pristine foundation she had once thought. A tragedy all around."

"Not for you, though."

"Indeed," Diego said. "I have met very few tragedies that I didn't want to exploit. And this was no different. However," he said. "I think it is time we finish this."

"I agree," Matías said. "And you've won."

"No," Diego said. "*Abuelo* has won. At least, if we allow him to." His brother rubbed his chin thoughtfully then took a drink from his flask. "So, you wish to discontinue this, to call your marriage a sham and be done with it. I wish to do the same."

Matías could only stare at his brother. Shocked at the words he'd just spoken. "Why?"

"I suspect for the same reasons you do," Diego said, taking a drink from his flask. "The game got away from you, didn't it?"

"Has it gotten away from you?"

"Liliana Hart," Diego said, "was supposed to be the simplest and softest of targets. I have watched her for years while doing business with her father. Sheltered. Meek, or so I thought. She is such an innocent, Matías. You have no idea. At least, she was."

Matías could scarcely believe what he was hearing. Because by all accounts it appeared that perhaps his brother—his brother he would have said had no heart at all—had fallen in love.

And if he knew Diego at all, he also knew that his brother would not be able to accept it.

It was a strange thing, imagining that such a soft, pale creature would appeal to Diego. But then he supposed that stood to reason as much as anything else in this messed up world.

As much as the ways in which Camilla had destroyed him from the inside out.

"So, neither of us play?" Matías asked. "That's what you're proposing?"

"Yes," Diego responded. "I already called Grandfather and told him that Liliana was divorcing me."

"Is she?"

"I have already put her on a plane back to America. Along with all of the evidence of her father's misdeeds so that she has no fear I will use it against her."

"We are in a similar place, then. As I have sent Camilla away. Back to her family *rancho* and have just finished procuring documents for her to sign that will restore her ownership."

Diego laughed darkly, then he reached out and grabbed hold of the whiskey tumbler in Matías's hand. He took a drink, quick and decisive.

"I thought you were afraid that was poisoned," he pointed out.

"At this point, I feel it would be all the same either way."

Matías shrugged and took a sip of his own whiskey. "You may not be wrong."

"I have always found it astoundingly simple to take what I want," Diego said, looking merely confused. "Why was it not with her?"

"You're not going to like my conclusion."

"Oh, probably not."

"Love." The moment he said it he knew it was true. But not about Diego. About himself.

Matías loved Camilla. And the real issue wasn't so much that he was afraid he might break her, but that she might break him. That she might destroy him, utterly and completely.

"I've already tried love," Diego said. "Against my better judgment."

He was speaking of his first wife, Matías knew. "It ended badly."

"Yes," Diego said slowly, "though not in the way that people think."

"I knew that already."

The two brothers stared at each other for a moment. They had never been close. The way they had grown up had simply made it impossible. A wedge had always been driven between them, first by their father, and then later in life by their grandfather.

Suddenly, Matías wanted to fix it. If he could fix nothing else, he wanted to fix this.

It had occurred to him last night that he was much more like Diego than he had ever allowed himself to believe, but now he felt that might mean something different than he had originally thought.

"I know that our father killed our mother," Diego said, his tone grave.

"Dios." Matías breathed it, as a curse or a prayer, he didn't know. "Why did you never say?"

"I don't know how to talk about such things," Diego said. "And he…threatened me. And as a boy I was too frightened to stand against him. I am a coward, Matías, and I have to live with that."

"You were a child, not a coward."

Diego went on as though Matías hadn't spoken. "And I know that…that I am broken. Just as he was."

"No," Matías said, suddenly finding it much easier to deny it when the words were coming from his brother's mouth rather than from somewhere deep inside himself. "You're not. He was. *Abuelo* is. We can be something else."

"Can we?"

"Does Liliana love you?"

Diego shook his head. "I don't think so."

His brother was lying. Matías could see that. Though whether to himself or to Matías, he didn't know.

"Camilla says she loves me. And I feel that… I feel that if she can love me then perhaps I'm not broken."

"The concern," Diego said, his voice rough, "becomes breaking them."

"Yes," Matías agreed. "But I wonder…if love is the difference."

Diego chuckled. "That is the one thing I can confidently say our father and grandfather do not possess at all. Though that highlights other failures of mine, sadly."

"No one ever taught us how to love, Diego," Matías said. "They taught us to be ruthless. They taught us to play these games. To be cold, unyielding men who cared for nothing beyond our own selfish desires."

"I would say they taught us everything we should have tried not to be. And you," Diego said, "have certainly come the closest."

"I still didn't have love. So I'm not sure if it made any difference in the end."

"Is it too late now? Do you think it's too late to have it now?"

He remembered what Camilla had said. About how she would not be like her father. How she wouldn't let go of what they had until there was no other path. Until she was certain there was no more hope.

"It's never too late," he said. "I have to believe that. And then, even when it is too late, I feel that you have to keep trying. Beyond hope. Beyond pride or reason. Because love has no place in any of those things. Love is something entirely different."

"When did you become such an expert?" Diego asked.

"I'm not," Matías said. "But I know about pride. I know about failing. I know about loss. I know about selfishness. I know about anger. And nowhere, in any of that, did I find peace. Nowhere was there love. I can only assume it's this thing," he said, grabbing hold of his chest. "This thing that feels foreign. This thing that I don't know at all. This thing that has taken me over, body and soul. And… I wanted. I would've given it all up for her. We were both acting fools for this, and we were willing to give it up for them. Would our father have ever done that?"

"No," Diego said without hesitation.

"No," Matías agreed.

"Well, then," Diego said. "Perhaps we are not broken after all."

Matías agreed. Perhaps they weren't broken. And perhaps, he would not break Camilla.

Losing her would break him, though. As the loss of his mother had done. But it was a risk he had to take. Because the alternative was life without her.

And that was no life at all.

CHAPTER FIFTEEN

CAMILLA STEPPED THROUGH the front door of the ranch house, feeling the uneven tiles beneath her bare feet. Finally. It was what she had longed to do ever since she had lost this place all those months ago. It was all she had dreamed of. And yet, for some reason, the stones did not feel as warm or welcoming as she had imagined they might. For some reason, it did not feel like home.

"Because home is where the heart is," she said, the words falling flat in the empty room.

And sadly, Matías Navarro was her heart. Her soul. Her everything.

She had been out riding, and while she had most definitely found some pleasure in it, it had not been the deep, unmitigated joy she had once known when she was on the back of a horse. It was different now. She was different.

She was something more than she had been. And it galled her, because of course these simple things no longer provided her with the expansive feelings of happiness that they once did.

Her life had taken on a deeper, richer dimension. And with that had come deeper, richer pain. And it tinged everything. Even this victory. Even having Fuego back out in the fields.

She had not expected Matías to do that. She was *angry* at him for it. He should have kept the horse. Because…at least then it would have been easier to pretend that he really did feel nothing for her. Nothing beyond a sense of honor. A sense of duty and a need to do the right thing.

Giving back all the horses, most especially Fuego, felt like the actions of a man who cared. And she would rather not have to feel that he might. It was too hard. It hurt too bad. She just wanted to believe that initial feeling she'd had when he had sacrificed everything to get rid of her.

Now, as the weeks had passed, she was beginning to see it differently. She was beginning to wonder if it wasn't as she had first thought.

If he wasn't so desperate to get away from her, but if he was that afraid. So afraid of what might happen if he gave them a chance, that he had been willing to give up everything to protect her.

The idea that he was protecting her from himself made her ache. Because of course, she feared nothing when it came to Matías. Nothing but never being with him again. That was the real fear.

Her real, true fear.

She walked into the kitchen and grabbed an apple, then made her way back outside. She was too restless to spend the afternoon in the house and there was nothing to do in there anyway.

Work was the only answer.

She left her shoes on the front porch and walked down the dusty drive out into the sun. She closed her eyes, trying to recapture her joy in these simple pleasures. In the feel of the dirt beneath her bare feet, in the taste of the apple—sharp and crisp. But there was just nothing. It was all hollow. All desperately sad.

She was sad. All the way down.

She remembered that last time she and Matías had been together. When he had entered her first without a condom, and then thought better of it.

How terribly small and selfish it was of her that she wished a baby had resulted from that. So that she had something to tie her to him. Someone to keep her company.

But it had not. And anyway, she should be relieved by that.

She wasn't. The paperwork had been sent back to her, and the *rancho* was hers. She had signed all the appropriate documents. And still, she felt unsettled. Unfulfilled.

But she knew that there was more to life now. More to life than horses and ranches. More to life than simply protecting yourself from loss.

There was love. Oh, there was love. Deep, all-consuming love that hurt as much as it did anything else.

She sighed heavily and walked out toward the stables. And then her heart jolted when she saw a man standing there. Tall and broad. He was wearing the kind of hat *caballeros* liked to wear, and he had on jeans. A work shirt.

Still, there was no mistaking the man himself. He didn't need a suit to be him. Perfectly, undeniably him.

Matías.

It didn't seem possible. But there he was. Standing right out there in the hot sun, dressed like a ranch hand.

"What are you doing here?" she asked.

"I came to see about a job," he responded.

"I'm sorry," she said. "I don't hire international bil-lionaire businessmen."

"Why is that?"

Her throat tightened, her heart squeezing. "Because I always seem to fall in love with them."

She turned away from him, horrified when tears began to well up in her eyes. She didn't want to give him any more of her weakness. She'd been willing to fight to the end, but the end was long past, and now it was simply pathetic.

"That's strange," he said, his voice dark. "That isn't the reason I thought you might give."

Her body stiffened. "What reason did you imagine?"

"I thought it was perhaps because they were unable to prevent themselves from falling in love with you."

She put her hand over her mouth, trying to regain her composure. Trying to get a foothold. "I don't think that's the case," she said, shaking her head and straight-ening her shoulders, walking away from him resolutely. She was not going to allow him to play games with her. Not anymore.

"It is," he said. "Camilla, it is true. But I was too much of a coward to admit it. I have been... I have been trying to sort through all of that. Over the past weeks. And I've come to the conclusion that... I am nothing more than a little boy, hiding in a tree and hoping that the dark things don't find me."

That made her heart crumple. She couldn't resist him then. Not with that.

She turned to him. "You're not a little boy."

"Listen to me," he said, the words tinged with des-peration. "My world as I knew it ended forever the day that my father killed my mother. I think it killed some-thing in me, as well. Or at least wounded it desperately.

I couldn't get the image out of my head. Of what he had done to her. Watching Diego's disastrous attempt at a first marriage only convinced me even more that I could never have such a relationship myself. That I could never let go of my control. But then there was you. And you're so strong. You don't fit any mold of anything that I thought I might find. Of anything I thought I might need. You are strong in ways that I could never hope to be."

"That's not true," she said.

"Yes," he said, "it is. You have never faltered. You told me that you loved me, in spite of the fact that I gave you no indication I love you back. In spite of all that I told you about me and my life. In spite of everything you had seen of a marriage growing up. In spite of the betrayal of your mother. You told me that you loved me. You set your pride aside, and any fear, and you laid it out there. You were the one. You have always been. Brash. Fearless."

She shook her head. "I'm not fearless, Matías. I was overwhelmed by fear, overcome by it that night, but I couldn't hold it back. I couldn't. Because I've seen what happens when you do. When you let love walk away so that it doesn't make a fool of you. I would rather be a fool. Ten times over. And I… I have been. I've felt like nothing but a fool these past weeks. A brokenhearted one at that."

"That's not fair," he said. "What I did to you. You did not deserve it."

"Were you so afraid? For me? *Of* me?"

"Yes," he admitted. "Both. I was afraid of what I might do to you. But more than that, I was afraid of what letting myself love you might do to me if I wanted you, but then could not keep you. If I somehow turned into my father the minute that I released my hold on that control. The minute I admitted that you were more important than air… Well, what would happen if I felt threatened?"

"You would let me go," she said. "And shower me with gifts. You proved that."

"I did," he said, his words torn from him. "But I didn't realize then, I wouldn't let myself admit that, that I loved you already. That love was already there, and it made all of the difference."

"What do you mean?"

"Remember we talked about how your mother loved herself more than she loved your father. More than she loved any of the men she has taken up relationships with."

"Yes," she said.

"My father loved himself more than he loved anyone in his own life. My grandfather is the same. He doesn't love Diego and me the way a grandfather should love his grandsons. He didn't love his own son the way that he should have. And my father certainly didn't love our mother or love us. It is not a decision in your head that keeps you from harming those around you. It's self-lessness. And that only comes from one place. It comes from love. It comes from loving someone more than you love yourself. From the desire to see them happy even if you're miserable. And I… I felt that for you. Even as it tore me apart to send you away. That is not a testament to my own strength, or to my own goodness, but to you. To the fact that you reached inside me and found something there I didn't think existed. That you make me want something I didn't think I could want."

"Matías," she said, closing the distance between them and kissing him, fiercely, ferociously. "I love you.

And I think… I think you are a good man. I think that you are better than your name. Than the legacy of your father and your grandfather."

"I should hope so. Because I actually do need the job on your ranch."

"Do you?"

"Well, we shall see how it goes, but Diego and I have both forfeited the game."

"What do you mean?"

"He has told our grandfather his marriage has ended, and I already announced to my grandfather I was divorcing you. And so, neither of us is married. Neither of us has fulfilled the terms of my grandfather's will. We refuse to play."

"Why did Diego do that?"

Matías sighed heavily. "For the same reason I did. For love. Because in the end we would rather do the right thing for the women we love than the right thing for ourselves, and I believe that's the first time either of us have ever felt that way."

"Has he told Liliana?"

Matías shook his head. "Not when last we spoke. But it was my conversation with him that made me realize I had to come to you. That I had to try."

"I love you," she said again. "I love you. More than myself."

"And I love you more than myself. And I will do so for the rest of my life, as long as there is breath in my body."

"I trust you."

He smiled, those simple words obviously touching something deep inside him.

"You are everything I need," he said, dropping a kiss on her lips. "You are strong, but you are fragile. Beautiful. My wife, and my stable girl."

She laughed. "I believe, my dear, that you might end up being my stable boy. After all, I am the owner of this *rancho*."

"So you are. I shall have to comfort myself with my billion-dollar industry."

"Well, if it won't keep you warm at night, I promise that I will."

He picked her up, holding her tightly in his arms. "Well, that, my lovely wife, I do believe."

And this time, when she passed over the threshold of her house, she truly felt like she was home. Because her heart was with her. And she was in his arms.

EPILOGUE

MATÍAS STEPPED OUT onto the balcony at the Navarro *rancho*, overlooking the fields before him. And he smiled when he saw his wife, riding up the path on the back of Fuego, who she had brought out to stay with them for the weekend.

She was still wild, that woman, even after several years of marriage. And he would have her no other way. He lived to watch her ride. To watch her race.

It had taken some convincing but he had finally talked her into acting as the jockey for Fuego and the two of them had had a few very successful years. Until she'd had to take time off for her pregnancy. And then for the next one.

"Papá."

He looked down at his son, who was standing there staring up at him with wide, dark eyes. His mother's eyes.

"Yes, Cesar?" he asked, bending down and picking the little boy up, holding him in his arms.

"Is *Mamá* coming back soon?"

"Yes," Matías said. "She's on her way for supper. You know how she likes to ride in the afternoon."

"Me, too," said his son.

Matías knew that was true. Because it was in his blood. Just as it was in Camilla's.

During dinner they ate on the terrace and Matías held baby Amelia on his lap while Cesar peppered Camilla with questions about each and every horse. A routine evening. One he loved more and more with each passing day.

But not half as much as he enjoyed what transpired after dinner. After the children were in bed. Tonight he and his wife sat outside in the warm air, a fire lit in the ring in front of them the only light besides the stars.

She kissed him passionately, switching positions so she was straddling his thighs. "I think tonight," she said, "I would like to have you out here."

"Something you won't be able to do when Diego and his family arrive," he pointed out.

His reconciliation with his brother had occurred after they'd both decided to quit playing their grandfather's game. And it turned out the old man had been so entertained by being outmaneuvered by his grandsons that he'd ended up gifting the estate in equal parts. And then had kept on living. Much to everyone's surprise.

"Which is why I must make the most of it now," she whispered against his lips.

When they were sated he carried her up to bed, and held her in his arms.

And when he dreamed it was only of her.

* * * * *

MILLS & BOON

Coming next month

THE SICILIAN'S BOUGHT CINDERELLA
Michelle Smart

'But...' Aislin couldn't form anything more than that one syllable. Dante's offer had thrown her completely.

His smile was rueful. 'My offer is simple, dolcezza. You come to the wedding with me and I give you a million euros.'

He pronounced it 'seemple', a quirk she would have found endearing if her brain hadn't frozen into a stunned snowball.

'You want to pay me to come to a wedding with you?'

'Si.' He unfolded his arms and spread his hands. 'The money will be yours. You can give as much or as little of it to your sister.'

It took a huge amount of effort to keep her voice steady. 'But you must have a heap of women you could take and not have to pay them for it.'

'None of them are suitable.'

'What does that mean?'

'I need to make an impression on someone and having you on my arm will assist in that.'

'A million dollars for one afternoon...?'

'I never said it would be for an afternoon. The celebrations will take place over the coming weekend.'

She tugged at her ponytail. 'Weekend?'

'Aislin, the groom is one of Sicily's richest men. It is a necessity that his wedding be the biggest and flashiest it can be.'

She almost laughed at the deadpan way he explained it.

She didn't need to ask who the richest man in Sicily was.

'If I'm going to accept your offer, what else do I need to know?'

'Nothing… Apart from that I will be introducing you as my fiancée.'

'What?' Aislin winced at the squeakiness of her tone.

'I require you to play the role of my fiancée.' His grin was wide with just a touch of ruefulness. The deadened, shocked look that had rung from his eyes only a few minutes before had gone. Now they sparkled with life and the effect was almost hypnotising.

She blinked the effect away.

'Why do you need a fiancée?'

'Because the father of the bride thinks going into business with me will damage his reputation.'

'How?'

'I will go through the reasons once I have your agreement on the matter. I appreciate it is a lot to take in so I'm going to leave you to sleep on it. You can give me your answer in the morning. If you're in agreement then I shall take you home with me and give you more details. We will have a few days to get to know each other and work on putting on a convincing act.'

'And if I say no?'

He shrugged. 'If you say no, then no million euros.'

Continue reading
THE SICILIAN'S BOUGHT CINDERELLA
Michelle Smart

Available next month
www.millsandboon.co.uk

COMING SOON!

We really hope you enjoyed reading this book. If you're looking for more romance, be sure to head to the shops when new books are available on

Thursday 10th January

To see which titles are coming soon, please visit

millsandboon.co.uk/nextmonth

LET'S TALK

Romance

For exclusive extracts, competitions
and special offers, find us online:

f facebook.com/millsandboon

🐦 @MillsandBoon

📷 @MillsandBoonUK

Get in touch on 01413 063232

For all the latest titles coming soon, visit
millsandboon.co.uk/nextmonth

AGE: 400 maybe

MOBILE: 07713 122

SCHOOL: I used to go to St Beckham's, a long time ago

THINGS I LIKE: Gorillas, swinging through trees; my hammock aboard the 'Betty Mae'; practising cutlass fighting; Braemar; Jenny and Granny Green

THINGS I HATE: Joseph Craik (a bully); Captain Cut-throat (a bully);

The P... ...wabbing; being

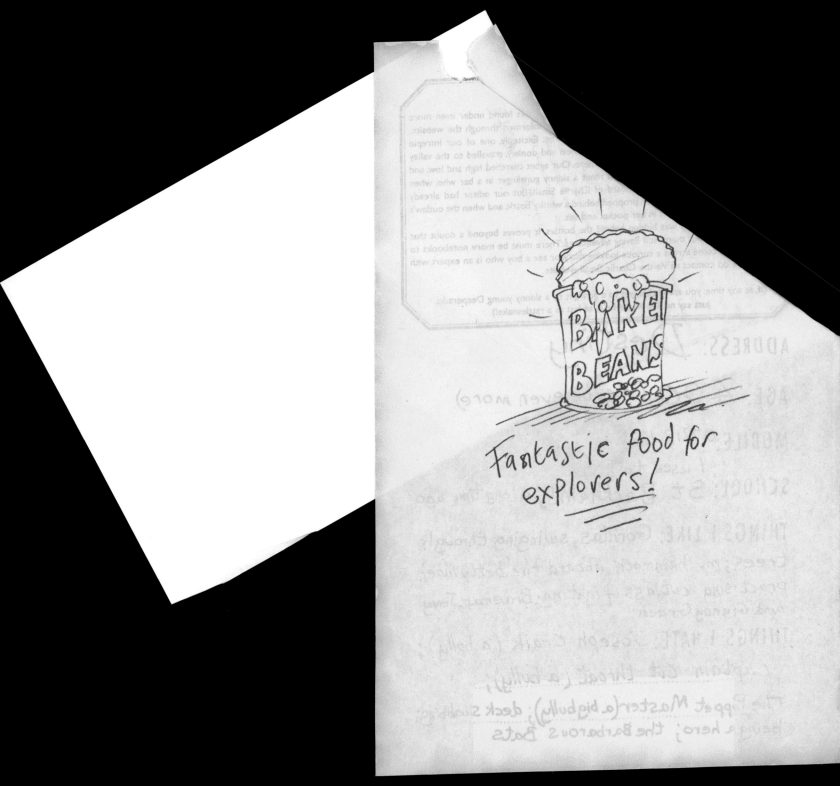

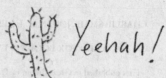
Yeehah!

THE AMAZING ADVENTURES OF CHARLIE SMALL (400)

MARSHAL

Notebook 4

DESTINY MOUNTAIN

RED FOX

CHARLIE SMALL JOURNAL 4: DESTINY MOUNTAIN

A RED FOX BOOK 978 1 782 95320 3

First published in Great Britain by David Fickling Books,
(when an imprint of Random House Children's Publishers UK
A Random House Group Company)

First published as *The Daredevil Desperados of Destiny*

This Red Fox edition published 2014

1 3 5 7 9 10 8 6 4 2

The Random House Group Limited supports the Forest Stewardship Council® (FSC®), the
leading international forest-certification organisation. Our books carrying the FSC label are
printed on FSC®-certified paper. FSC is the only forest-certification scheme supported by the
leading environmental organisations, including Greenpeace. Our paper procurement
policy can be found at www.randomhouse.co.uk/environment.

MIX
Paper from
responsible sources
FSC® C016897

Set in 15/17pt Garamond MT

Red Fox ... UK,

Addresses for ... and at: www.

A CIP catalogue record for this book is available from the British Library.

If you find this book, PLEASE look after it. This is the only true account of my remarkable adventures.

My name is Charlie Small and I am four hundred years old, maybe even more. But in all those long years I have never grown up. Something happened when I was eight years old, something I can't begin to understand. I went on a journey... and I'm still trying to find my way home. Now, although I have destroyed a terrible two-headed vulture, robbed a bank and been caught in the middle of a bison stampede, I still look like any eight-year-old you might pass in the street.

I've travelled to the ends of the earth and to the centre of the earth. I've been chased by a merciless posse, I've really rattled a rattlesnake and caught a cougar by the tail! You may think this sounds fantastic; you could think it's a lie. But you would be wrong, because EVERYTHING IN THIS BOOK IS TRUE. Believe this single fact and you can share the most incredible journey ever experienced!

Charlie Small

Wild
Bob
Ffrance

Looking Down The Barrel Of A Colt 45

BUMP!

'Ouch!' I cried as I rolled to a stop. Looking back I could see that I had tumbled down a huge gorge between two cliff walls. The ground beneath me was dusty and scrubby, and I was just about to get up and dust myself down, when I heard a familiar click behind my left ear.

'Where d'ya think you're goin', boy?' asked a soft voice. I turned around carefully, with my arms raised, and found myself staring down the barrel of a Colt 45.

'Oh, shucks! It's a bad day for you, boy,' said the young man looking at me. Piercing blue eyes shone from a dirty, grimy face; his long, greasy hair hung down to his shoulders, and he had the meanest grin I've ever seen.

'I'm Wild Bob Ffrance, the most wanted outlaw in the whole of the wild and wicked west – and you've just barged into my camp.'

Oh no! Help!

Things Go From Bad To Worse

With a twitch of his pistol, he signalled me towards a campfire that glowed behind some scrubby bushes, and from where the smell of cooking drifted.

'Hands behind your head, boy, and no funny business or I'll splatter your brains on the ground like a mess of baked beans.'

I did as I was told! I put up my hands and walked towards the fire, expecting to hear the bang of his gun and feel the sting of a bullet between my shoulder blades at any second.

This is just typical, I said to myself. There you were, safe and sound and living the life of a hero with old Granny Green, when you decide you want to go exploring again; then you want to find your way back home. And before the end of the very same day, here you are being marched at gunpoint by a crazy, trigger-happy cowboy. Brilliant!

'Turn around. Now, sit down on that rock and keep quiet,' said Wild Bob Ffrance, and again I did exactly as I was told. Well, almost!

'Look, I'm no threat to you,' I began to say.

'I just stumbled down . . .'

P'TANG! Wild Bob's gun spat a tongue of orange flame and a bullet ricocheted off the rock where I sat. *P'tang . . . p'tang . . . p'tang!* The sound echoed across the evening sky.

'What part of "sit down and keep quiet" do you not understand?' said the man, spitting into the dirt at his feet.

'Well, I . . .'

P'TANG! Another bullet chipped the rock, just by my left hand, stinging my fingers. OK, I got the message!

'Now, let's see what you've got in there,' he said, pointing to my rucksack. 'Hand it over, nice and easy.'

Accused

PTANG!

The outlaw took my rucksack, his gun still trained on me, and tipped it up. My telescope and magnifying glass, the maps, my journal and all the other paraphernalia, fell to the ground.

'It's my explorer's kit,' I said helpfully.

'It looks like a spy's kit to me,' said the gunman through gritted teeth. 'You were sent by Horatio Ham to spy on me, weren't you, you low-down dog.'

'Ham! Who's Horatio Ham? I'm just trying to . . .'

'Shut your jabbering, boy,' the cowboy replied. 'I know a sneaking, slinking spy when I see one. Well, you've been spying on the wrong man this time.' He flicked open the chamber on his pistol and started reloading it with bullets from his gun belt.

Charlie
↖ *A bullet with my name on it!*

Yikes! Was this going to be the end of all my adventures?

Challenged

'Hold on a minute,' I said. My heart was thumping so hard I thought it might burst out of my chest. 'What are you doing?'

'Don't worry, Mister Spy,' said the outlaw, clicking his gun shut. 'I'm not a murderer. It's going to be a fair fight; don't let anybody say that Wild Bob isn't fair. I'm challenging you to a fastest-to-the-draw gunfight!'

Fair! Who was he trying to kid?

'I can't use a gun,' I cried, very scared indeed. 'I've never even held one before.'

'Don't give me that. Everybody knows how to use a gun. Why, I was given one as a christening present!'

'Well, I was given a silver napkin ring for mine,' I said. 'I really don't know how to use a gun. So, sorry, but I'm afraid I can't fight you!'

Wild Bob Ffrance stared at me for a moment, then smiled and put his gun down on a rock. Phew! I thought. I've got out of that one!

'OK. Maybe you can't fight with a gun,' said Ffrance. 'So, I'll make it easy for you; follow me.' And he led me into a clearing by the cliff where I had fallen. It was scarred with cracks and caves of all shapes and sizes.

The outlaw turned his back to the cliff and faced me. 'If you can't use a gun, you'll have to use something else,' he said. 'So, choose your weapon, boy; any weapon you like.'

With that, he took a huge Bowie knife from his boot and sent it juddering into a nearby tree. Before it had even finished vibrating, he pulled a slingshot from his pocket and launched a stone through the air, knocking a crow from the branch of a cactus plant; finally, he unfurled a long leather whip from his belt and flicking it with a loud crack, plucked the knife back out of the tree; the knife span up into the air, and he casually caught it in his free hand. 'What's it to be, boy?' he asked.

Boing!

I was done for. This outlaw was a phenomenon! He was an expert with a gun, a knife, a slingshot, a whip and who knows what else? I wasn't an expert at anything. (Well that's not entirely true; the Perfumed Pirates of Perfidy had taught me to be an expert sword fighter.)

'Do you have any cutlasses?' I asked, praying that he would say no so I didn't have to fight.

'Not much call for cutlasses in the Wild West,' replied Ffrance, and spat on the ground. 'You'll have to choose something else.'

It was obvious that he wasn't going to let me off and I was going to have to fight. But what else was I good at? It was then I noticed the lasso, curled around the pommel of a black leather saddle that had been placed in the shade of the cliff face.

Well, I was good at swinging through trees and climbing the rigging of a pirate ship. I was an expert at dangling from the end of puppet strings; I had become very good with all sorts of rope on my various adventures. Maybe I would be good with a lasso as well! There was only one way to find out. I pointed at the rope.

'The lasso?' asked the outlaw. I nodded. 'So, you're a rope merchant, are you?' And he tossed the coil of rope to me.

The Fight

'Oooof!' The weight of the lasso knocked me to the ground, and Wild Bob Ffrance smiled as I struggled back to my feet. This was ridiculous. How on earth was I supposed to throw the lasso when I could hardly lift it up?

'It looks like you're having a bit of trouble, boy,' chuckled Wild Bob. 'So, just to make things a bit fairer, I'm gonna fight you barehanded . . . with one arm behind my back . . . standing on one leg . . . and with one eye closed!'

I think he was starting to find me a bit of a joke!

'Ready?' he asked. I unfurled the coil of rope until I found the loop of the lasso, and started to swing it over my head like I'd seen the cowboys do on telly.

'Ready!' I cried, but the rope got tangled around my arms, slipped down over my head and ended up curling around my ankles. I toppled over once again.

Wild Bob smiled as I scrambled to my feet once more. 'Are you ready now?' he asked again. 'Now, FIGHT!'

And he hopped towards me on one leg, while looking through one eye. He should have looked ridiculous, but he looked as mean as a wild cat.

Clumsily, I swung the rope and threw it, hoping that somehow the loop would fall around the outlaw and I could bring him down . . . but it went sailing off in completely the wrong direction!

What happened next happened very, very fast!

As I threw the lasso, I saw to my horror that

the mouth of the cave right behind Wild Bob Ffrance was suddenly filled by the biggest, sleepiest and grumpiest grizzly bear I've ever seen. As my lasso sailed away in the wrong direction, the grizzly bear raised his huge paws above Wild Bob's head and gave an ear-shattering roar. Instantly, the outlaw dropped to one knee, turning to face the grizzly and going for his gun at the same time. But his gun wasn't there; it still sat on the rock where he had left it with his other weapons.

The ghastly Grizzly bear.

The bear began to lumber towards the defenceless outlaw. At the same instant my wayward lasso fell onto Ffrance's revolver, sending it clattering from the rock. The gun hit the ground and went off. P'TANG! The bullet hit the rocks above the mouth of the cave, and a lump of granite the size of a pineapple fell straight onto the grizzly's head with a sickening *crack!*

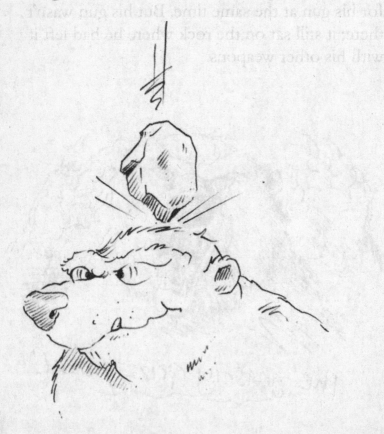

The bear stopped in his tracks. He blinked once; he blinked twice, and slowly went cross-eyed. With a huge sigh, like a deflating bouncy castle, he dropped down onto all fours. Wild Bob rushed to get his gun, but the grizzly bear had ambled away in a complete daze. He didn't know what day it was any more!

'WOW! That was some mighty fancy rope work, boy,' said Wild Bob. 'You saved my skin and no mistake, even if you are a spy for Horatio Ham.'

'Oh, it's OK,' I said nonchalantly. 'But I am not a spy for Horatio Ham, honest I'm not. My name is Charlie Small, and I'm just a boy who's trying to get home.'

'I think I believe you; but don't you know it's not safe to be wandering through this territory while Ham is about?' said Bob. 'I think you'd better stick with me for the time being.' And the young man came striding over to me and shook my hand. 'You've just made a friend for life, Charlie Small; and after the way you lassoed my pistol, I'm going to call you the Lariat Kid from now on.'

'What's a lariat?' I asked.

'A lariat is another word for a lasso,' said Wild

Bob. 'I thought you would have known that, being an expert and all.'

'Oh yes, lariat. I remember now,' I said, quickly.

Wild Bob chuckled. 'Whatever,' he said. 'Now, let's go and see if my supper is ready.'

Wild Bob's Fireside Story

Now I'm ready for bed, camping out under a large, pale moon that floats in an indigo sky. My head is spinning from Wild Bob's tales, and I'm writing up my journal before I go to sleep.

Earlier today, back in Wild Bob's camp, I collected up the bits and pieces of my explorer's kit, checking they were all there as I put them back into my rucksack.

1) My multi-tooled penknife
2) A ball of string
3) A water bottle
   (full to the brim once more)
4) A telescope
5) A scarf

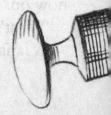

COMPLIMENTARY

TICKET TO ANYWHERE
ONE WAY OR ANOTHER

DATE:
ANYTIME

16 2973

6) An old railway ticket

7) This journal

8) A pack of wild animal collector's cards

9) A glue pen (to stick any interesting finds in my book)

10) A glass eye from the steam-powered rhinoceros

11) The hunting knife, the compass and torch I found on the sun-bleached skeleton of a lost explorer

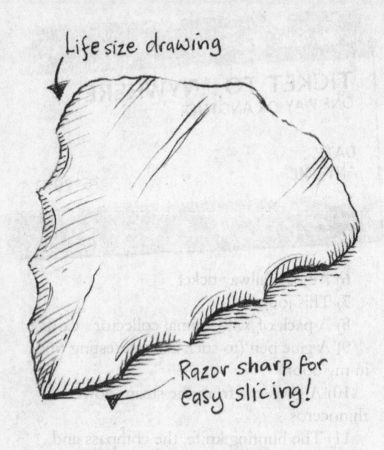

Life size drawing

Razor sharp for easy slicing!

12) The tooth of a monstrous river crocodile
13) A magnifying glass
14) A radio
15) My mobile phone with wind-up charger
16) The skull of a Barbarous Bat
17) A bundle of maps, collected during my travels
18) A few doubloons from the *Betty Mae*

I have lost some things on my journey (my pyjamas had been shredded by the giant snow worms; Jenny and I scoffed the Paterchak mint humbugs and Kendal mint cake as soon as we had freed ourselves from our puppet prison; the large slab of whale meat was devoured by Braemar, the white wolf) but I replaced them with equally useful stuff from the store in the village where Jenny and her grandmother live.

19) A bag of marbles
20) An automatic travel umbrella
21) A large slab of Granny Green's toffee
22) A plastic lemon full of lemon juice.
(A squirt of lemon juice can make the most
  disgusting ingredients just about edible!)

A useful collection of things, I think you'll agree.

A plastic
squirty lemon.

Then, as coyotes howled in the distance and the tumbleweed rustled in the breeze, Wild Bob handed me a delicious plate of beans and bacon. As we ate, he told me the story of how he had become an outlaw. I soon realized he was as innocent of being a bandit as I was of being a piratical terror on the high seas.

(See my Journal Pirate Galleon)

It all began a long time ago when Bob was about eight years old. His mum and dad had a small farm called Two-Eyes. They had a very happy life until, one day, a man called Horatio Ham bought the rest of the land in the valley and started up as a cattle rancher.

Now Ham was a bully, pure and simple, and he wanted to own the whole valley, especially the river that tumbled out of the surrounding hills and flowed straight through the Ffrance farm. If he owned the river he could control the supply of water to the nearby town of Trouble, and therefore the town itself.

First he tried to buy the farm, but Bob's parents weren't interested. So he had his men sneak onto the land at night and smash the farm machinery; when he drove a herd of cattle through the farm and ruined all the crops, he won. Bob's parents couldn't take any more and they packed up and moved into Trouble.

Bob's mum and dad never recovered. They became ill and went to an early grave, but as their coffins were lowered into the ground, Bob swore that he wouldn't rest until he had got even with Horatio Ham.

Bob Ffrance Becomes An Outlaw

Young Bob wanted to stay with his friends in Trouble Town, but by now Ham had moved onto the Ffrance land, and had control of the river. He threatened to cut off the water supply if anyone in Trouble Town helped the young Ffrance boy.

Some of the townsfolk tried to

NOTICE
Anyone caught
Helping Young
BOB Ffrance
will bE Shot!
By order of
Marshal McKay

hide Bob, but when Ham made his vicious cousin, Mad Mickey McKay, the marshal of Trouble County, Bob knew he couldn't put his friends' lives at risk any more. One night he slipped out of his hiding place, and in an act of bravado, stole the marshal's horse and rode silently out of town.

'From then on,' said Bob, rolling out a blanket and throwing another over to me, 'I was an outlaw, wanted as a horse thief; anything I needed, I had to beg or borrow from the kind folk of Trouble, or steal from Horatio Ham and his cohorts.'

'But how did you survive, where did you grow up?' I asked.

'Oh, that's a long story, boy,' smiled Bob. 'Sometimes I lived on my own, sometimes with the Rapakwar Indians. They're good people and have as much cause to hate Horatio Ham as I have. He had a gang of hired gunfighters run them off their hunting grounds. Now they live way beyond the valley, waiting for the time when they can return home. Same as me. They taught me how to track and hunt and survive out in the open, as well as when to fight and when to run.'

This Horatio Ham sounds like a real twit!

'And where do you live now?'

'I live with a few others who have also been made outlaws by Horatio Ham, in a very secret hideout, and tomorrow I'll take you there. First we will have to get you a good, strong steed and that means going to Trouble; but all that can wait until morning.' With that, Wild Bob Ffrance pulled the blanket up under his chin and within a few seconds was snoring gently in sleep.

I Phone Home

I wish I could get to sleep as easily, but my head is full of cowboys and bandits, Indian braves and no-good varmints, so I've taken out my journal again. Will I find trouble in Trouble? Will I meet the horrible Horatio Ham and his cousin, Marshal Mad Mickey McKay and, if we get there, will Wild Bob Ffrance's gang of Desperados welcome me into their camp?

All of a sudden I felt further from home than ever, lying out under the vast night sky with just a snoring stranger for company, so I decided to give my mum a ring. I knew exactly what she would say; it was ages ago that a great bolt of lightning had hit my little raft and I had been swept down a mysterious tunnel into a vast jungle, but somehow for Mum it remains the very same day I started my adventures. Although she says the same thing every time I call her, the sound of her voice always makes me feel better. I picked up my mobile and called the number.

'Charlie? Is that you?' said Mum. 'Is everything all right?'

'Yes, Mum. I'm camping out with a notorious outlaw in the middle of the Wild West!'

'Sounds wonderful, dear,' she replied. 'Oh, wait a minute, Charlie. Here's your dad just come in. Now remember, don't be late for tea, and if you're passing the shops on the way back, please pick up a pint of milk. Bye.'

'Mum?' I called. But she had already hung up. Oh well, at least I know she's not worrying about me, even if I have been gone for years and years!

Now I've brought my journal up to date, I must get some sleep. Who knows what tomorrow may bring? I'll write more just as soon as I can. Goodnight, partners! Zzzzzzzzzz!

Riding Into Trouble

We woke up early the following morning and after a quick cup of hot, bitter coffee, were ready to go. Wild Bob Ffrance led his horse into the clearing from where it had been tethered to a tree for the night. Although Bob was dusty and greasy, and his clothes were all tattered and torn, Fortune, his magnificent black stallion, gleamed like a piece of jet. Bob put a dirty boot into a shining stirrup, swung a leg over the stallion's back and then leaned over and lifted me up onto the saddle behind him.

'Let's go and get you a horse,' he said, and nudged Fortune into an easy trot.

We rode across the wide expanse of a dry and dusty valley. This valley, according to Wild Bob, had once been a fertile place full of trees and long grasses. Then Horatio Ham had dammed the river that fed it and now the whole area had become a dust bowl. The watering holes had long dried up; great cracks ran across the

parched ground and
bare tree stumps stood
where lush and leafy
glades had once grown.
Again, another
poor farmer had
been forced off
his land.

'It's like that all over the state,' said Wild Bob.
'Everywhere you go, Horatio Ham is taking
over. But he'll get what's comin' to him. It ain't
for nothin' that we've become known as the
Daredevil Desperados of Destiny.' And Bob
patted one of the six-guns that hung from his
belt.

Eventually we came to a high escarpment and
looked down on a bustling town of clapboard
houses, shops and inns.

'That's Trouble for you,' said Bob. 'I think
we'll go in the back way. Most of the townsfolk
are friendly – they hate Ham as much as I do –
but he's got spies everywhere. We don't want to
bump into one of them before we have to.' And
he urged his horse forward, taking a rough track
that led behind the buildings that lined Trouble's
Main Street.

We stopped at a large pen fenced with rough poles. It was called a corral and held about twenty beautiful horses. On one side of the pen was a large wooden stable. Wild Bob dismounted and tethered his horse.

'Come on, Kid,' he said and I jumped down and followed him as he quietly entered the stableblock through a back door. Bob crept noiselessly towards the front of the stables where large, double doors were open on to the main street. Here a small, stocky man was grooming a very small and stocky pony, whistling to himself.

There was a slight click as Bob cocked his gun.

'Don't you know any other tunes, you no-good varmint?' he asked from the shadows, and the groom froze with one hand on the pony's back. He slowly turned to face us and I don't know how he did it, but a gun had appeared in his hand, its dull sheen glinting in the subdued light.

'Come out of the shadows,' he ordered. 'Come out real slow, or I'll blow you to kingdom come.'

No, I thought. This can't be happening. I had

only been in town a couple of minutes and I was already involved in a gunfight!

'Don't,' I started to say, but Bob stepped out of the shadows, his gun still raised, and said, 'Not bad for an old-timer!'

The man stared into the gloom. 'Well, well, well,' he said, with a sly smile. 'If it ain't Wild Bob Ffrance, Daredevil Desperado and arch enemy of Trouble's noble benefactor, the honourable Horatio Ham.' And with that he spun his gun back into his holster and smiled. 'Where've you been the last few months, Bob?' And the two men stepped forward and embraced each other in a big bear-like hug. 'We thought maybe you'd been taken!'

Freecloud

'Wild Bob, taken by that lump of lard, Ham? That'll be the day!' said Bob with a wide grin on his face. 'It's good to see you, Cody,' he continued. 'I need a mount for my young partner here, the Lariat Kid.'

Cody

I blushed at my new nickname, feeling slightly foolish, but I have to admit it made me feel pretty good too!

'No problem, you know that, Bob,' replied Cody. He was a bony, white-haired old man, with a chin full of wiry whiskers and a mouth that contained just three teeth. 'Everyone in this god-forsaken town is behind you. Just take your pick; we've got some real good stock out back.'

'Yeah, I saw them,' said Bob. 'But what about the one you're sprucing up right now, Cody? He looks about the right size.'

Cody's whiskery jaw dropped. 'Oh boy, that would be beautiful,' he chuckled. 'This here pony is a birthday present from Ham to his son, and they're due in town any minute to pick it up!'

'Couldn't be sweeter,' said Bob, laughing.

'You'll have to tie me up, though, Bob. Make it look like a robbery, or Ham will have my guts for braces.'

'No problem,' Bob agreed, then turning to me he said, 'Say hello to your new best friend, Kid. What's her name, Cody?'

'Freecloud,' he answered. 'She's called Freecloud.'

She was certainly a beautiful pony, quiet and strong and a wonderful caramel colour, but she was also very small. She wasn't much bigger than a Shetland pony!

Freecloud

'She's a bit small, isn't she?' I said. 'I don't want to look daft!' And Freecloud snorted and looked at me as if to say, *daft am I? We'll soon see about that!*

'She's small but she's mighty fast,' said Cody.

'Take it from a man who knows horses,' Wild

Bob said. 'If she wasn't a bit special, there's no way that Ham would buy her for his son.'

But there were other things bothering me about my new 'gift'.

1) I didn't know how to ride a horse. Mechanical rhinos yes, horses no!

You can read about that in my journal Gorilla City.

2) Freecloud wasn't Cody's horse to give away. Did I really want to annoy Horatio Ham, nasty land-grabbing tyrant or not, before I'd even met him?

Wild Bob must have guessed what I was thinking. 'Don't worry what Ham will think, Kid,' he said. 'You're in trouble just knowing me, and it's the duty of every Desperado to annoy, incense, railroad and disrupt Horatio Ham's existence in any and every way possible. You are on our side, aren't you, Kid?'

I didn't really have any choice, did I?

'Yeah, sure.' I sighed. 'Freecloud it is!'

How Not To Get On A Horse

After Cody had saddled Freecloud, Wild Bob tied and gagged the old-timer to make it look as if there had been a robbery. Then he brought Fortune through to the front of the store and mounted him. I watched very closely, but it looked simple enough. So, copying Wild Bob, I put my foot in a stirrup, pulled myself up with the saddle and swung my free leg over Freecloud's back.

Yikes, I thought, Freecloud's head has come off! But as I leaned forwards and cautiously looked down, I saw her tail, swishing patiently from side to side. How embarrassing, I had mounted my horse the wrong way round and ended up facing her bottom!

'*Wumpf mff!*' I could hear Cody sniggering from behind his gag, and I felt my face blush.

'C'mon, Kid,' said Bob sternly. 'This is no time to mess around.'

'Sorry,' I said, and I slipped down from Freecloud and remounted – again facing her bottom. How was that? I'm sure I did everything right.

'Wumpf mff munm!'

'All right, so I don't know how to ride a horse,' I cried. 'It's not that funny. We don't ride horses where I come from!'

'Did you hear that, Cody?' gasped Bob in astonishment. Cody's bony shoulders were shaking with laughter and tears were running down his face, and that got Wild Bob laughing too. 'What *do* you ride where you come from, then?' he sniggered.

'Rhinos mainly,' I said nonchalantly, remembering my long trek across the jungle plain on the back of Jakeman's marvellous mechanical rhino. 'I know how to ride rhinos!'

'What's a rhino when it's at home? Some special sort of horse that walks backwards?' said Bob. 'Oh, never mind. Let's get going; you'll just have to pick it up as you go along. So long, Cody, and thanks for all your help.' And he gave Fortune a nudge with his heels and moved off down the street.

A Quick And Painful Riding Lesson

Still blushing, I tried to swivel around in my saddle, but before I could, Freecloud had jogged out of the barn after Fortune. I leaned forward, flattening myself against Freecloud's back and stretched my arms as far around her fat tummy as they would go.

'Stop, Freecloud. STOP!' I begged, holding on for dear life.

All of a sudden, and I'm sure out of sheer vindictiveness, Freecloud broke into a fast trot.

'Help!' I yelled as I passed Wild Bob, still facing the wrong way. 'I don't know how to stop. *Ooof, ooof, ooof, ooof!*' I bounced wildly up and down on Freecloud's back, as if I was riding a bike down a steep flight of steps.

Now the townsfolk had started gathering around to join in the fun, pointing and laughing.

'Look,' someone cried. 'The circus has come to town!' This was so embarrassing; to think that I had once wrestled a giant river crocodile and now I was being made a fool of by a preposterous mini-pony with attitude! Oh, if only I had one of Jakeman's marvellous inventions to ride instead.

During my many adventures, one of Jakeman's inventions has always turned up, just in the nick of time. I don't know why and I don't even know who Jakeman is, but his magnificent mechanical rhino, his jet-powered swordfish and his super submawhale had helped me out of some very sticky situations. Why couldn't I have found a Jakeman's automated horse to ride – something that would do as it was told!

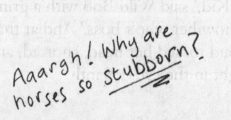

Aaargh! Why are horses so stubborn?

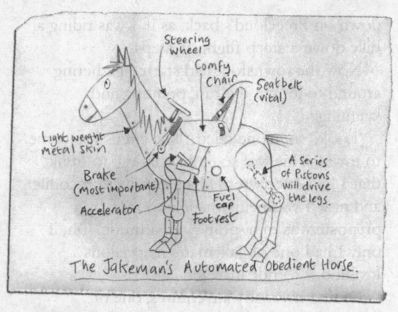

Steering wheel

Comfy Chair

Seatbelt (vital)

Light weight metal skin

A series of Pistons will drive the legs.

Brake (most important)

Accelerator

Fuel cap

Footrest

The Jakeman's Automated Obedient Horse.

(Here is my idea of what a Jakeman's Horse might look like!)

All of a sudden, Wild Bob was beside me. He grabbed Freecloud's reins and pulled us to a stop. Immediately, Freecloud kicked up her hind legs and I went sailing over her head, landing with a thump on the ground. The crowd roared with delight.

'Don't worry, Kid,' said Wild Bob with a grin. 'You've got to show her who's boss.' And at that moment Freecloud tossed her head, snorted, and looked me straight in the eye defiantly.

'Now try mounting her using your other foot,'
Bob suggested. And do you know what — it
worked! I found myself perched on Freecloud's
back and pointing in the right direction.

'Brilliant!' I cried. 'Now, how do you steer and
how do you stop?'

'Just pull on the reins,' said Bob. 'Left to go
left; right to go right, and both together to stop.
It's easy.' But as Freecloud tossed her head and
stamped her hooves, I wasn't so sure that was
true!

'Hadn't we better get going, before Horatio
Ham finds out what we've done?' I asked. I
really didn't want to bump into him while sitting
on his son's new pony.

'All in good time, Kid. I need to get some
supplies first,' said Bob with a grin. 'Anyway,
Ham will already know all about us. He's got
spies everywhere. So we may as well stick
around and have some fun!'

Fun? What sort of fun? I didn't like the
sound of this. I just wanted to get out of
Trouble and ride far away — but it seemed Bob
was determined to hang around until Ham
showed up.

What on earth was going to happen then?

Horatio Ham

We carried on down Main Street, my eyes nervously scanning the crowds for someone who might possibly be Horatio Ham. But everyone appeared to know Wild Bob and was very friendly.

At the general store, Bob stopped and dismounted. 'We need some supplies,' he said. 'Come and lend a hand.' I pulled on the reins to stop Freecloud, but she tossed her head and took no notice. Much to everyone's amusement, I continued on down the road. Not again!

I pulled and pulled, but still nothing happened. Where's a brake handle when you need one? I heard Bob tut as he loped down the street after me and took the reins.

'You're really showing her who's boss,' he said with his silly grin as he led me back to the storefront.

As we entered the shop door, I caught a glimpse of a suspicious and scruffy-looking cowboy from the corner of my eye. He was sneaking hurriedly off towards the large saloon that stood on the far side of a square at the end of the street.

'Bob . . .' I started to say, but without even looking around, Bob smiled and said, 'I know.'

Inside the dark shop, the owner greeted Wild Bob as a friend. Bob picked up a large sack of flour and a brand-new lasso, which he handed to me. 'A brand-new lariat for the Lariat Kid,' he smiled and went to the counter to pay; but the shopkeeper refused to take his money.

'No way, Bob,' he said. 'You're a true friend to this town and we admire what you're doing against Ham. You've heard the latest, have you?'

'What might that be?' asked Bob, putting the fold of notes back in his pocket.

The Scorekeeper

'Horatio Ham has made himself President of Trouble Bank,' said the shopkeeper. 'Now he won't let us have our savings. He's got big plans for the town, says he. He needs the money more than we do, says he. It ain't fair! He's already built himself a brand-new ranch house. It's like a palace – indoor thunderbox and everything!'

'Is that so?' said Bob, going very quiet. 'Well, we'll have to see what we can do about that, won't we?'

'Good old Bob,' said the man, smiling widely behind his huge moustache. 'I knew we could depend on you.'

'So you can, friend,' said Bob. 'But first I have to get this stuff back to camp.' With that, Bob swung the bag of goods onto his shoulder and we walked out into the sunshine . . . and straight into a welcoming party of men, bristling with rifles.

'Good morning, Wild Bob Ffrance,' said a deep, gravelly voice from the centre of the group, and I knew who it was straight away: Horatio Ham. He was very tall and rather fat, with a fancy waistcoat stretched across his big, barrel-shaped belly. His eyes were tiny black slits that peered from the deep folds of his chubby cheeks, and he was staring at us with an arrogant sneer. He looked a thoroughly nasty piece of work.

'Aren't you going to introduce me to your new friend?' Ham asked, and with every

Horatio

Ham

movement he made, little waves of flesh
rippled across the greasy expanse of his face.
'I do so hate to arrest someone I haven't been
introduced to!'

Gunfight At Trouble Town

'Well, if it isn't the honourable Horatio Ham,' Bob replied, ignoring his question. 'I thought I might bump into you. Out for a walk with your bunch of bully boys?'

'I came to pick up a birthday present for my boy, Silas,' said Ham, and I noticed a large and bulky boy of about my own age, sticking his tongue out at me from behind his father's coat tails. 'I chose a nice little pony for him, but when I got to the stables I was told that someone had already taken it. You wouldn't happen to know anything about that, would you, Ffrance?'

Silas Ham.

'Sure,' said Wild Bob pushing his hat to the back of his head. 'We saw the horse, and the Kid here thought it was just the ride for him. The stable boss said it was for you, but as we're such old friends I didn't think you'd mind if I took it instead. You don't mind, do you, Ham?'

Horatio Ham's face darkened and his cheeks quivered with anger. Hold on! I thought. Don't get me involved – I didn't want to take the

40

horse. But I knew I was already involved; I was standing next to Wild Bob Ffrance and that was enough to condemn me.

'Did you pay for the horse?' asked Ham through gritted teeth. Wild Bob didn't answer. 'Did you pay for those goods you're carrying now?' Again Wild Bob said nothing, while readjusting the heavy sack on his shoulder.

'Get ready to run, Kid,' he whispered from the side of his mouth. 'Run straight for your horse and ride like the wind.' *I can't ride a blooming horse*, I wanted to remind him, but I knew it wasn't the time or the place. Things were very serious indeed and I couldn't see a way out.

'So, you *haven't* paid. I thought as much,' said Ham with a smirk. 'Now you are a horse-thief twice over. It will be my pleasure to add the crime of shoplifting to your long list of misdemeanors. I'll take you over to the jail myself, right now.' As Horatio Ham started to take his gun from its holster, the group of men cocked their rifles and my knees started to knock. Wild Bob let the heavy sack fall from his shoulder and in one movement swung it up into the air. Everyone's eyes followed it as it sailed high over Ham's head.

As if by magic a gun appeared in Wild Bob's hand and he fired. *Bang! Bang! Bang!* The bullets ripped into the sack which exploded in a thick cloud of flour, filling the air around the gunmen's heads, clogging their eyes and ears and noses, and they doubled over in fits of coughing and swearing and sneezes.

'Time to go!' said Bob, and we raced down the sidewalk towards our horses. With the gorilla skills I'd learned in the jungle, it was no problem to leapfrog over the rail and land on Freecloud's back. For once she behaved herself, and with a kick I galloped down Main Street after Bob's stallion, with my eyes half-closed and holding onto Freecloud for dear life.

By the time Ham and his men had cleared

their eyes and lifted their rifles to their shoulders, we had rounded the corner and were racing out of town.

'Keep going, Kid,' yelled Bob. 'It won't be long before they're after us. Yee-hah!'

Sure enough, it was only a matter of a minute or two before I could hear the thundering of hooves behind us.

Help, how did I get into this mess!

The Lariat Kid

A deadly wasp!

Freecloud was small and fast and strong, but the horses after us were bigger and faster and stronger, and it wasn't long before red-hot bullets were whizzing round my ears like swarms of deadly wasps. Ham and his men were gaining on me every second.

I galloped along in a thick cloud of dust thrown up by Wild Bob's stallion. It made me cough and splutter and spit, but it was only this dust cloud that saved me from the chasing posse, making us all but invisible as they fired blindly into the fog of dirt. I could hear them getting nearer and nearer.

Then through the dirt cloud I saw Wild Bob gesturing towards a small track leading off to the right. As we reached it, Bob turned his horse without breaking stride, and – help! – how do you steer a horse again? I pulled on the reins, this way and that way, but it was too late. I went thundering straight past the turn, bouncing about in the saddle like a sack of potatoes.

Yikes! What was I going to do now? I yanked on the reins, Freecloud screeched to a halt and once again I went sailing over her head and crashed to the ground, my new lariat landing on top of me. With a whinny, Freecloud galloped away down the track after Fortune and Wild Bob.

'Freecloud, come back you stubborn old nag,' I cried chasing her down the track a little way.

I could hear Ham's posse getting closer every second; soon they would be on top of me. What could I do? I had to think fast. What would the Lariat Kid do? I sat up and as the rope slipped to the ground, an idea popped into my mind. I leaped to my feet and, finding the loop of the lasso, threw it over the stump of a nearby tree. Quickly I ran across the track, unravelling the lasso all the way. Finding a tall standing stone on the other side of the track, I looped the rope around it and dived to the ground just as the posse came charging into sight.

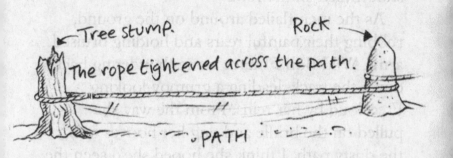

Tree stump.

Rock

The rope tightened across the path.

PATH

'Off to the right,' Horatio Ham was yelling. 'They turned up that track; can't you see the dust trail?' The posse turned onto the track and as they rode level with me, I pulled on the rope. It leaped from the dust, tightening across the path a few feet from the ground. Ham saw it too late and his horse galloped straight into the trap, tripping and stumbling and throwing Ham from its back. The rest of the riders ploughed into the back of his horse, and as their mounts reared and kicked and whinnied, they fell to the ground, dropping their rifles in the pandemonium. Ham landed with a sickening thump on the ground, the pistol in his holster went off with a crack and he yelled to one of his men.

'Yow! Take me home, Virgil, I think I've just shot myself in the foot!'

As the men flailed around on the ground, rubbing their painful rears and holding bruised arms, Wild Bob Ffrance came thundering back down the track, leading a grumpy-looking Freecloud by her reins. From the way she pulled on the bridle and dug her hooves into the dusty path, I think she hoped she'd seen the last of me.

'That's some mighty fine lasso work, Kid,' Bob smiled, hauling me onto the pony by the scruff of my neck. 'That should teach you,' he added to Ham. 'Don't ever mess with the Lariat Kid!' And with a slap to the rear of my irritated pony and a 'Yee-hah!' we galloped away down the track again, followed by a couple of half-hearted shots from Ham's posse.

~~Destiny~~ Destination Destiny

We rode at full gallop for another half-hour, along dry riverbeds, through isolated groves of cactus trees and across a wide and empty plain towards a range of low mountains. All of a sudden a huge shadow passed over the ground in front of us, and for a moment the air turned chilly. I shivered and looked up into the sky, and caught a glimpse of a large black shape disappearing into a bank of clouds.

'What was that?' I asked.

'Mapwai,' muttered Wild Bob with a shudder, staring up into the now empty sky with wide, fearful eyes. This was the first time I had seen the outlaw look scared.

'What's Mapwai?' I asked.

'With any luck, Kid, you'll never have to find out,' said Bob seriously. 'C'mon, we've still got a little way to go.'

As we grew nearer, I could see that one of the mountains was perfectly conical in shape, its summit chopped flat and emitting large puffs of smoke. It's a volcano, I thought. A volcano that looked as if it might erupt at any minute; what on earth were we heading towards that for?

'There she is,' said Wild Bob, pointing at the funnel-shaped flame-thrower of a mountain. 'That's home. That's Destiny Mountain!'

DESTINY!

Oh, brilliant, I thought. Things just keep on getting better and better!

We rode straight towards the volcano. When we reached the base I thought Bob was going to try and ride straight up the sheer sides, but at the last minute he turned his horse and we trotted through the scrub that grew around the base of the mountain. Gradually the bushes started to get thicker and thicker, and Bob turned this way and that, following an invisible path through them.

Then, once again, the side of the mountain rose before us like a huge wall. It seemed we could go no further, but Bob turned back on himself and followed the side of the mountain for a bit, before disappearing into thin air!

Entering Destiny

One minute he was there and the next he was gone. I was alone in the bush, staring at the empty space he had just occupied. My jaw dropped open in amazement, and for a minute I sat there on Freecloud's back like a complete lemon, looking this way and that. Midges buzzed in the warm air and somewhere I could hear the sound of a waterfall, but everything else was quiet. I couldn't hear the clop of Bob's horse, or the thin whistling that he constantly made between his teeth as he rode. I was alone. I was lost. I was . . .

'Are you coming, or are you just going to sit there for the rest of the day?' asked Bob, and once again I stared in wonder, for all I could see was his head. It seemed to float in mid-air about four metres up the side of the mountain. Then his stallion's head appeared, followed by its neck, and I began to understand exactly what I was seeing.

There was a separate wall of rock that followed the curve of the mountainside about a metre and a half in front of the mountain itself, and it so completely matched the colour and texture of the volcano as to be almost invisible. As I nudged Freecloud forwards, I came to the spot where Bob had disappeared and saw a narrow entrance to a path that led up the side of the volcano, completely shielded from view by the solid wall of rock on the other side.

'Pretty sweet, eh?' said Bob, smiling widely.

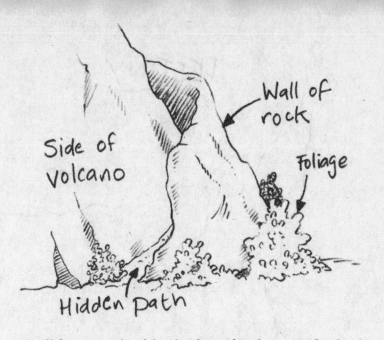

Side of volcano

Wall of rock

Foliage

Hidden path

'It'll be pure bad luck if anybody ever finds the entrance to Destiny.' He kicked his horse and I followed him up the rocky pathway. Every now and then, there was a small gap in the outside wall and, looking out, I could see we had risen hundreds of metres above the surrounding plain. It was a wonderful view and a fantastic lookout post. You would be able to see any enemies for miles. So it seemed strange that there wasn't a lookout. If anyone did find the hidden path, it seemed that they could walk straight into the Desperados' camp.

Then I heard a whistle, surprisingly close by, and it was answered by the hoot of an owl and

DESTINY

I realized we had been watched all the way. The path entered the large archway of a tunnel in the mountainside, and looking up, I saw holes in the tunnel roof, like the murder holes in a castle gateway. If we had been enemies I am sure that we would have been showered with all manner of rocks and boulders.

Suddenly we were through the tunnel, emerging into the bright sunlight on a platform of rock that looked down into the interior of the volcano. What a wonderful sight it was!

The sides of the volcano were sheer and high and completely hollow. Large hawks soared over the circle of sky above our heads; on all sides water cascaded down, forming deep green pools amongst the rocks at the base of the cliff face. The floor of the volcano was covered in lush grass on which the horses could feed, and near the centre were a group of rickety wooden huts, from where a group of men looked up at our approach. I began to feel very nervous as we trotted down into the interior of the volcano to meet them.

The Desperados

Almost immediately we were surrounded by a gang of the most disreputable looking characters I'd seen since escaping from the grisly lady pirates. They were dirty, smelly and armed to the teeth with an amazing assortment of guns and rifles and daggers. One of them even had his pockets stuffed full with sticks of dynamite. If he tripped over we would have all been blown to kingdom come. So, these were the famous Daredevil Desperados! They looked fierce and unfriendly, and they all started talking at once.

'Everything go OK, Bob?'

'Who's your prisoner, Bob?'

'Are we going to torture him straight away, or wait until after dinner?'

'Whoa! Hold your horses, boys. This here is the Lariat Kid, and he's not a prisoner, he's a friend, a good friend. We really had some fun hounding Horatio Ham. Cornelius, if dinner is ready, serve it up and I'll tell you all about it.'

As we sat around the campfire, eating generous portions of bacon and beans (don't cowboys eat anything else?) and drinking glasses of something called Red-eye, Wild Bob told them all about how I had rolled into his camp, and how I had swiped Ham Junior's horse, and how I brought down the whole of Ham's posse with one flick of my lasso! The Desperados were delighted.

'Oh, real sweet, I wish I'd seen that,' said one of the gang, snorting down his nose. His shoulders were shaking with mirth, but his face stayed as long as a wet Sunday. 'My name's Sneaky Pete. Glad to make your acquaintance, Kid.' And with that, all the Desperados started to introduce themselves, welcoming me as one of their own. All except one man who sat slightly apart from the group and just sat watching me, making me feel very uneasy.

'That's Gentleman Jim, a real pistolero,' said Sneaky, pointing over at him. 'He's Wild Bob's number two. He don't say much, but he's OK . . . as long as you don't cross him.'

We had a fine old feast; the beans and the Red-eye flowed

The Desperados loved this drink.

RED-EYE
OLD
GUTROT

freely and the Desperados danced and sang, stamping their boots in the dust as Sneaky Pete played a battered old banjo. *Yee-hah!* This is the song that they sang:

When Ham rode into town, the wind howled just like a hound,
Lightning split the heavens and thunder shook the ground,
Daytime turned as black as night and clocks stopped on the shelf,
When Ham rode into Trouble, we thought it was the hound of hell himself.

Horatio Ham is a devil of a man, he'll take just what he wants then say goodbye,
Horatio Ham is the devil's own man, he'll stake you out in the noonday sun and leave you there to fry.

When Ham takes a walk down Main Street, flowers shrivel up and die,
The ground begins to tremble and children start to cry,
But when Wild Bob catches up with him, he'll know he's met his match,
Because Ham will need the doctor, but Bob won't bear a scratch.

Horatio Ham is the devil of a man, he'll take just
what he wants then say goodbye,
Horatio Ham is the devil's own man, he's sold his very
soul and now he is bound to die.

My New Pals

Keeping to my promise to record all the strange
and wonderful people and creatures I meet, here
are a few sketches of my new friends. And what a
lovely bunch of vagabonds they are!

Wild Bob Ffrance
Wild Bob is leader of the
Daredevil Desperados.
You've already met him
and know him for
the amiable, brave
and reckless hero
of the people
that he is.

Sneaky Pete was always jolly!

Sneaky Pete

Poor old Sneaky is blessed with the most miserable face I've ever seen. It's a real shame because he is really very cheerful and always ready with a joke. No one has ever seen Sneaky Pete smile; if something amuses him he just gives a loud snort through his nose. He is the gang's intelligence gatherer.

Gentleman
Jim Silver
Gunfighter

Gentleman Jim Silver

Gentleman Jim is a real dandy and dresses in black from head to toe. He has pure white hair and wears a hat pulled down low to protect his pale pink eyes. His boots sport sparkling rhinestones and silver spurs and he wears two silver revolvers with pearl handles. He is a quiet thinker, a slow talker, and a very dangerous gunslinger. Of all the Desperados, I find Gentleman Jim by far the scariest.

Mick the Miner

A giant of a man and the hairiest thing on two legs I've seen since meeting Thrak, King of the Gorillas. He is an expert at digging tunnels, and is able to take a full-grown man in each hand and lift them clean off the ground. Whatever you do, don't get into a wrestling match with Mick the Miner; he will make mincemeat of you!

Mick the Miner is so hairy, he looks just like a scribble!

Jake 'Pint-pot' Penley

A fierce and tiny powerhouse of a Desperado, with just one eye and one leg. Rumour has it that his wooden leg has been specially adapted to help him fight, and he has to be seen to be believed! I don't know if this is true.

Now it's late in the evening and everything is quiet except for the call of the coyotes in the distance. I'm plum-tuckered out after my day's amazing adventures. Not surprising, really; I've made friends with a bunch of outlaws, outwitted the most powerful man in the territory and stolen his son's horse. (Though if I'd known then what I know now about Freecloud, Silas Ham could have kept the bad-tempered, disobedient, grumpy, good-for-nothing brute!)

I have been given a berth in a small bunkhouse, which consists of four bunks, a locker for each man, a stove and a small table and some chairs. It's nice and snug, and now I've finished bringing my journal up to date, I must get some sleep. Goodnight, partners!

Three Hours Later

Boy, do these Desperados snore. What's more, with the after-effects of so many baked beans, that's not all they do; I've been woken up three times already, thinking that the volcano was erupting!

phwar!

Pooee!

Joining The Desperados!

The next morning after a long breakfast (bacon and beans!) and a very, very quick wash under a freezing cold waterfall, Wild Bob made an announcement.

'Now listen, partners,' he said. 'The Lariat Kid has saved my life once and upset Horatio

Ham twice. So, I propose we make him a full member of the Daredevil Desperados. What do you say, boys?'

'Sure thing, boss. Yee-hah!' cried the gang, cheering and slapping me good-naturedly on the back while firing their guns in the air. All except Gentleman Jim Silver, who stood a little way off, staring at me from the deep shadow cast by the brim of his black hat.

'What do you say, Jim?' asked Wild Bob.

'We don't have much choice, do we?' he said in a slow and lazy voice. 'Now he knows the whereabouts of Destiny. Because we all know what happens to outsiders who know where our hideout is, don't we?'

Nobody explained *what* happened to unwelcome visitors to Destiny, and I didn't really want to find out, so I was mighty glad to become a fully-fledged fugitive and swear the oath of allegiance to the Daredevil Desperados of Destiny.

The Oath of Allegiance to The Daredevil Desperados Of Destiny

I swear to uphold the ideals of
The Daredevil Desperados Of Destiny,
which are:

1) To make Horatio Ham's life a misery

2) To hound and harass Horatio Ham
at every turn

3) To make Horatio Ham look stupid in
front of everybody (not difficult!)

4) To defend any citizen against
Horatio Ham's nefarious (that means
wicked) activities

5) To remain a Daredevil Desperado
until Horatio Ham has been defeated

6) To keep the whereabouts of Destiny
a secret

Wild Bob ffrance

P.S. 7) To never complain about Cornelius Duff's
unchanging menu of bacon and beans!

Then I was taught the Desperados' secret handshake. It is done with the left hand in order to keep your shooting hand ready to draw at the first sign of trouble. This is the handshake, but please remember it is TOP SECRET and I will be in real trouble if any of the others find out I've written it down in here:

I *did* find out, when I was sneaking a look at this strange diary you're always writing in. I've crossed out your drawing of our secret handshake before any harm has been done, so we'll say no more about it. *Wild Bob*

It was a real honour to become a lifelong Daredevil Desperado, but somehow I will have to tell them that I need to be moving on as soon as possible; I really must continue my journey home, but now that I'm a life member, will they let me leave?

At lunchtime, as I sat by the campfire, I told my new pals about my incredible journey. I told them everything: about leaving home and getting washed away on my raft; about the crocodile and the jungle; Thrak; the Perfumed Pirates and finally the evil Puppet Master.

I didn't think they would believe me, but the outlaws were amazed by my adventures and said I was the bravest Desperado of them all. They promised to try and help me get back home if they could – just as soon as I had helped them defeat Horatio Ham!

Oh well, it looks like I've got a job to do before I can think about going home. I will have to prepare myself for the task and practise lassoing until I'm as good as everyone thinks I am! First, though, I really want to speak to my mum. Even if she does say exactly the same thing every time, it lets me know that everything is still all right at home. I wound up my phone charger and tapped in my home number on the mobile.

'Mum!' I said when I heard her voice.

'Charlie? Is that you? Is everything all right?'

'Yes, Mum. I'm safe . . . I've joined a gang of Desperate Desperados and I have to stay here until we've defeated a baddy called Horatio Ham!'

'Sounds wonderful, dear,' she replied. 'Just get home soon, Charlie. You're very late and your dinner's quite cold.'

'Mum?' I called, suddenly very worried. Surely that's not what she usually said. Has something happened; has something changed? 'Mum?' I cried again, but she had already hung up. I tried ringing back, but I couldn't get a signal. I hope everything is all right – but the sooner I get home, the better . . .

Later That Day

Wild Bob said he was going to be in a meeting most of the afternoon, planning the Desperados' next move against Horatio Ham.

'You'll have to amuse yourself for a bit,' he said. 'But be careful; we sometimes get the odd mountain bear or cougar wandering into camp, and they can be a bit of a handful.'

I didn't mind being left to my own devices. I knew what I wanted to do. I had watched Yellow

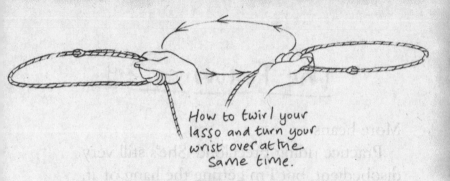

How to twirl your lasso and turn your wrist over at the same time.

Bill, one of the Desperados, practising with his lasso, and I noticed how he turned his wrist over as he twirled the loop above his head.

Well, it looks easy enough, I thought, and I went to practise with my own lasso, well out of the way of the others. I didn't want anyone to see that I wasn't quite as good as Wild Bob had led them to believe!

I spent most of the afternoon trying to get the rope flying through the air and landing on a target and, oh boy, it isn't easy. I think I lassoed myself a hundred times, and an innocent lizard once, before I somehow got the rope in a hopeless tangle and spent an hour untying all the knots! I'm never going to get the hang of this. Though at the end of the day, I did manage to lasso a stone about a metre in front of me. That's real progress!

The Following Day

More beans.

Practice riding Freecloud. She's still very disobedient, but I'm getting the hang of it.

More practice with my lasso. (I need it!)

Another singsong around the campfire (with bean supper).

The Next Day

Beans, followed by terrible tummy ache.

More practice on Freecloud. I think we know who the boss is now – *she* is, and since I've accepted that, things have been much better!

More practice with my lasso – getting better.

Multiple bottom explosions – tummy ache gone!

The Day After That

I carried on practising my lariat skills. I am not doing too badly; all my experience of swinging on vines through Gorilla City and climbing the rigging on the *Betty Mae* has given me a feel for handling ropes and I soon had the lariat plopping onto the little rocks that I used as targets.

As I practised, I noticed some really bizarre creatures living amongst the rocks, and although I am now a Desperado I'm still first and foremost an intrepid explorer, so I have jotted down a description of a couple of the weirdest animals and named them:

The Slam Dunk Toad
A harmless and comical creature, the Slam Dunk Toad can really make you jump as its flat, fat body lands with a loud slap on a rock right next to you!

The Slam Dunk
Toad.

The Galleon Lizard

The Galleon
Lizard's
body is the
shape of a
fat-hulled
galleon,
and its back
is crested
with spines and
fans, like sails
and rigging.
Don't be fooled
if you see one
lazily
basking in
the sun on
a rock; they can move very quickly and their
spines are deadly poisonous.

The
Galleon
Lizard

Staring Disaster In The Face!

HELP!

Please excuse my wobbly handwriting, but my hands are still shaking with fear. It was nearly all over for me today. I didn't know a lasso could get you into so much danger. If it hadn't been for some double-quick thinking on my part and some real fancy shooting from Gentleman Jim Silver, I would be just a memory by now!

After my usual morning chow-down (I'm picking up the Desperado lingo quite quickly) and checking the Desperado Notice Board for any new instructions, I took my lariat across to the practice area. I stood some stones on a large rock, took a hundred paces back and started to spin the lasso over my head. Once, twice, and throw. The rope snaked through the air and landed over the stone I had been aiming for. I tried again and succeeded again.

Now I did the same, but this time on the move. I threw my lasso whilst running; I threw it as I span round from low down, left-handed, right-handed; I threw the lasso from the back of a galloping Freecloud, and every time I hit my chosen target. I was good; I finally felt I might deserve the nickname of the Lariat Kid.

Feeling pleased with myself, I was just heading back towards the huts when a slight movement among the rocks caught my eye, and instinctively I turned and threw the rope. I thought it was a plant waving in the breeze, but as the loop of my lariat dropped over it and I pulled hard to tighten it, I realized there wasn't even a breeze in the air. So what was making the plant wave?

I gave the rope a yank, trying to pull the object out of the rock.

It looked like a funny plant!

Nothing happened so I yanked again, hard. Suddenly, and with a terrifying roar, a huge cougar leaped on top of the rock and I saw what I had done – I had lassoed its tail, which had been sticking up above the top of the boulder. BIG MISTAKE!

Any umbrellas?

Spitting and hissing, the cougar attacked, giving me little time to think. The animal launched itself at me with deadly claws extended and its huge fanged mouth open in a terrific and angry

roar. I did the first thing that
came into my head; reaching
over my shoulder, I pulled
the extending umbrella from
my rucksack. As the animal
dived towards me, I
dropped to my knees, avoiding its razor-like
talons, and thrust the umbrella into its gaping
jaw while pressing the release button.

I just managed to roll away as the lion landed
heavily on the ground and my umbrella
snapped open, forcing its mouth wider still. The
spokes of my brolly dug painfully into the roof
of its mouth; now the animal couldn't bite, and
in a mad frenzy the cougar ripped at the
contraption, shredding the cover and
pulverizing the wire frame. As I backed away
trying to find a place to hide, the cougar spat
out the remains of my umbrella, and with a
satisfied look started to creep towards me.

Now what? I was all out of umbrellas; I was
all out of Paterchak's mint humbugs and pirate
cutlasses. I was all out of ideas! Then, as I
stepped back against the volcano's sheer wall
and realized I had nowhere to run, the ground
in front of the cougar exploded in a puff of

dust and the sound of a pistol shot echoed around the bowl of the volcano.

Time For A Trim

I looked across to where the shot had come from and there, of all people, stood Gentleman Jim Silver, his hat pulled low over his eyes and one of his pearl-handled pistols smoking in his right hand. The angry cougar took another step towards me, and again a bullet ripped into the ground in front of it. Now the massive beast turned and with a roar, charged at Silver, streaking across the ground in a blur of furious yellow fur. In an instant, Silver dipped his left hand, drawing his other pistol, and with his two guns spitting lead he sprayed the ground in front of the charging beast, forcing it to turn away. A final shot cut across the animal's rump, singed its fur and sent it racing for the rocks.

The animal leaped across the boulders and without stopping, climbed the cliff face higher and higher, finally disappearing into the mouth of a cave that appeared as a tiny black dot high in the volcano's wall.

'Close call,' drawled Gentleman Jim, and with a chuckle he turned and headed back to the huts. Incredible! The silent, stand-offish gunman had come to my rescue.

'Thanks!' I called after him. Gentleman Jim pointed towards the ground where the cougar had charged. 'You can keep them as a souvenir,' he said as he disappeared inside his bunkhouse.

Keep what? I thought, and hurried over to where he had pointed. There, lying in the dust, were eight long cougar claws that he had neatly trimmed with his superb shooting. Excellent! These will be undeniable proof of my terrible encounter with a cantankerous cougar. Wait until I show my friends back at school!

A couple of my cougar claws!

Plans

This evening we all sat down to our supper of beans and bacon (I never thought I would say this, but I'm getting a bit tired of the Desperados' menu) and while we ate, Wild Bob told us the plans for tomorrow. He chalked a diagram of Trouble Town onto a painted board, and explained how we were going to rob Trouble Bank! I was appalled – surely we were supposed to be helping the people of Trouble, not taking their money!

'Calm down, partner,' said Wild Bob. 'You heard what the storekeeper said. Ham has taken over the bank and won't let the townsfolk have their own money. We're not going to steal the money, we're going to liberate it and give it back to the people who own it. That should set Ham's blood a-boiling!'

'Yee-hah!' cheered the Desperados.

'That's brilliant!' I cried. 'Just like Robin Hood.'

'I said we weren't robbin' anybody,' said Wild Bob. 'Now this ain't gonna be easy, so everyone must be on their best form. I don't want to have to go back for some straggler who's got themselves thrown in jail.' I don't know why, but I had the feeling that Wild Bob was looking at me when he said that!

Now I'm lying in bed, images of shootouts and chases flashing through my head as the sound of the Desperados' snores shake our flimsy wooden hut. I must try and get some sleep, though. Otherwise I will be too dozy to take part in tomorrow's raid. I will write more just as soon as I can.

The Following Day

OH NO! After all our planning and Wild Bob's warnings, I'm writing this part of my journal from inside Trouble County Jail! The only other prisoner is a young Indian brave, about my own age; but either he doesn't speak English, or he's not very friendly, because all he does is sit cross-legged on his bunk, silently staring into space.

Apparently I only have a few hours left, for at sunrise tomorrow Horatio Ham and Mad Marshal Mickey McKay have promised me a big surprise. I don't know what sort of surprise, but

I know it won't be nice; a while ago they got Nathaniel Slaughter, the town undertaker, to come and measure me for a coffin! Mad McKay has put extra guards on the jailhouse, but I do hope Wild Bob rescues me tonight. In the meantime I'll tell you all about our bank raid.

Six of us rode into town: Wild Bob; Gentleman Jim; Sneaky Pete; Jake 'Pint-size' Penley, Yellow Bill, who shook like a leaf at the first sign of trouble but was really as brave as a lion; and finally myself, the Lariat Kid.

Some of the other Desperados were waiting outside town as extra cover, in case we had to retreat, and the rest were back at Destiny guarding the hideout. My heart was pounding as we rode quietly down Main Street. I had never robbed a bank before, and I knew that Horatio Ham would not let us take the money without a fight. But I had sworn to uphold the Desperado creed and I was determined to do my best.

It was early
Morning when we
rode into Trouble Town.

The Lariat Kid Strikes

There were only a few early risers about and the town seemed calm and peaceful. There was no sign of Ham, but all of a sudden a lone cowboy spotted us and raced down the sidewalk.

'That's one of Ham's men. Take him, Kid,' said Wild Bob, and I unhooked my lariat and in one fluid movement had it spinning over my head; with a flick of the wrist I sent it arcing through the air, falling over the man's shoulders and slipping down to tighten around his ankles. I yanked and he came crashing down onto the wooden sidewalk. Brilliant, it worked! All my practising had paid off.

'That was real sweet, Kid,' said Wild Bob, and I beamed with pride.

Sneaky Pete ran over to the floored man. With a thin cord he tied the man's hands and feet and put a gag around his mouth. None of the townsfolk tried to stop us. They were firmly on our side, but they knew there might be trouble and started to head back home.

'Good morning, Bob,' said a lady in a bright crimson dress, smiling winningly. Her face was painted like a china doll's and she fluttered her long eyelashes. 'When are you going to come and see me, you big Daredevil Desperado, you?'

Bob's face blushed as red as the lady's dress.

'Well I . . . we're here on business. Excuse me, ma'am,' he stuttered.

'Who's that?' I asked as she winked at Bob and hurried away.

'Oh, er . . . local schoolmistress,' said Bob, and I heard Sneaky Pete give a loud snort. Schoolmistress! I thought. She's certainly not like any of the teachers at St Beckham's.

We carried on towards the bank where we loosely tied up our horses, ready for a quick getaway.

The Biggest Bullion Raid In Trouble's Troubled History – NOT!

'OK, this is it!' said Wild Bob in a serious voice, and I pulled my neckerchief over my face for a mask, as I'd seen cowboys do on the telly.

'There's no point in that, Kid,' smiled Gentleman Jim. 'Everyone knows who we are!'

'Is everybody ready?' asked Bob. 'Let's go. Victory to the Daredevil Desperados of Destiny!'

'Yee-hah!' we all shouted, and with Wild Bob leading, we crashed through the doors of the bank, Bob and Gentleman Jim firing their pistols into the ceiling for effect. My heart pounded with excitement and fear, but feeling more confident after the success with my lariat, I raced in . . . and promptly fell flat on my face!

'Mind the step,' said a lone voice from behind a long counter. I scrambled to my feet with as much dignity as I could muster.

'Nobody move. This is a hold-up!' yelled Wild Bob scanning the room with his pistol; but he needn't have bothered because the bank was empty. All except for the dusty old bank teller who had told me to mind my step, and was looking at us over his half-moon spectacles as calmly as though he dealt with bank robbers every working day.

'I'm sorry, Bob, you're too late; the money's already been stolen!' said the elderly man.

The Old Bank Teller.

'Ham guessed you might be planning something like this and he took all the cash first thing this morning.' And the teller pointed to an iron safe at the back of the room. Its heavy door stood open and we could see he was telling the truth. The safe was as bare as old Mother Hubbard's cupboard.

'Where's he taken it?' asked Wild Bob.

'I've no idea, but wherever he is, he'll be laughing his socks off. He thinks he's got the better of you.'

'We'll soon see about that,' said Bob, his hackles rising. 'He won't make a monkey out of me. Come on, boys!' And Wild Bob turned on his heels and marched towards the door.

'Good luck, Bob, but watch out. Ham's got his men everywhere.'

I don't think so, I thought. We only saw one, and I caught him. We opened the bank's door
... AND
WALKED
STRAIGHT
INTO
A HAIL OF
GUNFIRE!

BANG!

CRACK!

PEEOW!

Mayhem In Main Street

'Down!' yelled Wild Bob, and we hit the deck and rolled behind any cover we could find. Bob and I crouched behind a wagon tied up outside. Gentleman Jim and Sneaky dived behind a stone water trough; Pint-pot and Yellow Bill had rolled back inside the bank and were at an open window, pistols at the ready.

'There they are,' said Wild Bob, pointing up at the rooftops opposite the bank. 'They must have been hiding there all the time, waiting for us to make our move.' The rest of the street was now deserted. Wild Bob poked his head around the side of the wagon, and another swarm of bullets ricocheted all around us, sending great splinters of wood flying through the air like deadly darts. Yikes, what had I got myself into?

A whistle sounded from Gentleman Jim

behind the water trough. He was pointing to a porch above the barber's, where three of Ham's men were crouched underneath its large painted sign. Wild Bob nodded, and as the gunfire lulled, both men rolled out into the open, crouched on one knee for an instant as they sent a spray of bullets zinging through the air, shooting away the brackets that held up the signboard. Then they continued their roll until they had changed places; Bob was now hidden behind the water trough and Gentleman Jim was with me behind the wagon.

At the same time, CRASH!, the signboard dropped from its brackets onto the heads of the hapless hard nuts below, knocking them clean out!

'Sweet,' I said and Gentleman Jim grinned. Then, 'Watch out!' I cried, as two men came running across the sloping roof outside the saddler's, guns cocked and ready to fire.

'They're mine,' called Sneaky Pete and he raised his buffalo rifle and fired. BOOM! The powerful rifle shot one of the supporting pillars clean away and the roof started to collapse.

'Aaargh!' the men cried as they slid down the disintegrating tiles. *Boof!* One man landed with a heavy thud on the ground below. *Splash!* The other fell head-first into a smelly waterbutt. They lay motionless, knocked cold, and Sneaky Pete snorted in amusement though his face was still as mournful as a sad-faced clown's.

A Tornado Of Bullets!

Ham's men started firing at once, and within seconds it was complete chaos. They crouched on every rooftop and behind every sign; their guns spitting lead and sending out orange tongues of fire.

We ducked our heads as the air filled with the roar of gunfire. We've had it! I thought as the wagon in front of us started to collapse under a hail of bullets. Surely we were beaten; there were just too many of them. Then, with a banshee yell, Pint-pot launched himself through the bank window.

'Cover me!' he called and stormed into the middle of the road. As the Desperados started up a barrage of their own, Pint-pot planted his wooden leg in the mud and with a kick, started to spin round like a top.

Jake 'Pint-pot' Penley springs into action!

Rrrratatatatatat! With the destructive power of a tornado, Pint-pot fired in a furious frenzy while spinning round and round; he was as fast as a machine gun, quickly pulling one pair of pistols after another from the belts across his chest. *Whizz! Ptang!* Bullets ricocheted off signboards and rooftops and chimney pots, and, overwhelmed by the ferocity of the attack and in complete panic, Ham's men threw down their weapons and scattered.

'Yeehah!' crowed Wild Bob, walking out to congratulate Pint-pot. It was then that I heard a noise and looking up saw one lone gunman crouched on the portico behind us. He must have worked his way round the back during the gunfight and was just about to bring his rifle up to aim at Wild Bob Ffrance. I didn't have time to think, but acted on instinct. I ran along the curb, unfurling my lariat at the same time. I span the rope, once, twice, and let it fly.

The lasso tightened around a beam protruding from the porch roof, and as I grabbed the rope tight, I kicked against the sidewalk and went soaring upwards. Grip and Grapple would have been proud of me; as the rifleman cocked his weapon, I swung up above

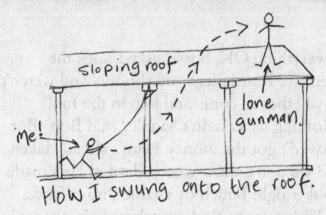

sloping roof ↗

me! →

lone gunman.

How I swung onto the roof.

the roof and let go. Sailing silently through the air – *CRASH!* – I landed on the man, knocking him and his rifle to the street below.

'Yippee-yi-oh!' I cried in relief, jumping down from the portico. My heart was racing and my hands were shaking, but the bank raid was over, and although we hadn't got any money, I was still in one piece!

'Well done, Lariat Kid!' said Wild Bob. 'Now let's get out of here.'

The Schoolmistress Comes To Our Aid

We rode out of town to meet up with the other Desperados, and as we approached the copse, I heard them cock their rifles.

'It's only us,' cried Wild Bob as we galloped amongst the trees.

'Everything OK, boss?' asked Mick the Miner. 'We heard plenty of shootin' and weren't sure whether to come and join in the fun!'

'Nothing we couldn't handle,' said Bob. 'But we haven't got the money. Ham's already taken it and we don't know where, darn it! He's made us look a right bunch of charlies, no offence, Kid. We've got to find out where he's taken it.'

Just then, I spotted a small dot on the horizon. 'Someone's coming,' I yelled, and immediately the Desperados drew their weapons.

'Who is it, Kid?' asked Bob.

'I'm not sure, just a minute,' I said, taking the telescope from my rucksack and training it on the approaching figure. 'It's that schoolmistress you were talking to. She's riding out in a little buggy.'

Soon the schoolmistress had steered her buggy into the copse and brought it to a halt.

'I thought I might find you here, Bob,' she said, fluttering her long eyelashes.

'What do you want, Susie?' asked Wild Bob, immediately starting to go red with embarassment.

'I bet you'd just love to know where Horatio Ham is, wouldn't you?' said Susie coyly, giving Bob the sweetest of smiles.

'Well, sure,' said Bob, getting a little flustered under her lingering gaze. 'Do you know where he is?'

'Oh, sure I do,' said Susie, lazily. 'But I can't give away information like that for nothing. Why, who knows what Ham would do if he ever found out I'd given him away.'

'Of course, Susie,' said Wild Bob, feeling in his pockets for some money. 'How much do you want?'

'Oh, I don't want money, Bob,' said Susie.

'You don't?' said Bob, gulping loudly.

'No Bob, I want a kiss. A long, lingering smacker of a kiss.'

'Yee-hah!' cried the rest of the Desperados. 'Go on, boss, give her a kiss!'

Bob went redder than ever and, closing his eyes, he leaned from his saddle to where Susie sat in her buggy, face raised and lips puckered.

Bob gave Susie the slightest of pecks but Susie's arm snaked around the back of his neck and pulled him onto her lips again.

They kissed . . . and kissed . . . and kissed (eugh!) and the Desperados cheered until, finally, Susie let Bob go. He didn't look quite such a wild Desperado anymore; he had a stunned look on his face and his mouth was smeared with lipstick.

'Now, that wasn't so bad, was it?' said Susie, with a smile.

'No,' croaked Wild Bob. 'Now, where's Horatio Ham?'

'You'll find him at the Pink Elephant Saloon, and he's got the money with him.'

'Sweet,' smiled Wild Bob, looking more himself all of a sudden. 'Well, boys, it looks like our trip might not be wasted after all. Thank you, Susie, you're a pal.'

'It was a pleasure,' said Susie. 'And you might need my help again. Ham thinks you've left town with your tail between your legs, even though you managed to scare off most of his men; now he's feeling safe, but he's still got one guard posted outside the saloon, who is armed to the teeth. I'm sure I can get rid of him quietly, if you want to take Ham by surprise.'

Bob sat thinking a while and then said, 'OK, Susie, if you're sure. Kid, you and Mick the Miner, come with me. The rest of you, position yourselves around the town and keep an eye out in case Ham's gunfighters return.'

Changing The Guard

Main Street was still deserted as Wild Bob, Mick the Miner and I followed the schoolmistress in her buggy. The rest of the Desperados fanned out to position themselves around town. As we approached the saloon, the three of us dismounted and led our horses up a narrow alleyway, where we watched as Susie stopped her buggy outside the saloon.

I could see her whispering something to the guard who was armed with an array of pistols and rifles. He looked over his shoulder towards the saloon and then shrugged his shoulders and nodded. The next minute, the two of them were walking towards the alleyway, the guard still looking nervously over his shoulder.

'Get back and keep quiet,' whispered Bob, flattening himself against the wall. Mick the Miner positioned himself close to the corner, and as soon as Susie and the guard turned into the alley, he raised one of his massive fists and bopped the guard on top of his head. The guard crumpled to the floor without a sound.

'Sweet! Thanks again, Susie; now, you get back home before you get into trouble,' said Bob.

'It was nothing,' Susie said as she went to leave. 'Now you come up and see me sometime, you hear?'

Showdown At The Pink Elephant Saloon

We led our horses into the street, and crept cautiously down to the saloon. I tied Freecloud to the hitching rail and held on to Fortune as

Bob tiptoed up to the saloon doors, peered inside, and then trotted back to us.

'Ham's in there,' he said. 'He's sat at a long table with Mad Mickey and three others. The table is stacked full of money and they're busy counting it.'

'Shall we storm the place together, boss?' asked Mick the Miner.

'No, I mean to have some fun,' said Wild Bob, smiling and mounting his horse. 'You stay out here as backup, until I call you. You, Kid, you're coming with me,' and he leaned down and pulled me up onto the saddle behind him.

'Ready, Kid?' he asked with a grin, and before I had time to answer he sent Fortune crashing through the swing doors and galloping across the polished wooden floor of the saloon. We skirted around the side of the long, fancy table and skidded to a stop in front of an astonished Horatio Ham. The horse reared onto its hind legs and let out an ear-splitting whinny.

Mad Mickey McKay went for his gun, sending a stack of coins crashing down, rolling and spinning across the floor. Faster than a rattlesnake's strike, Wild Bob's own gun appeared in his hand, cocked and pointing straight at the Marshal.

'Guns on the table, boys, and no funny business,' said Bob, and the four men sat at the table did as they were told. 'Looks like you've been caught with your fingers in the till, Ham,' said Wild Bob.

'How dare you,' interrupted Marshal McKay, spluttering and turning puce with anger. I can see why they call him Mad Mickey McKay now; he was absolutely fuming! 'I'll see you get ten years for this, you no-good, low-down farm boy.'

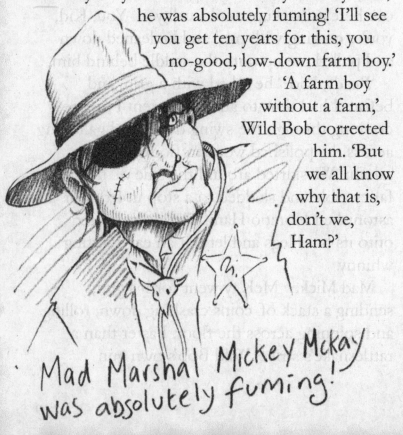

'A farm boy without a farm,' Wild Bob corrected him. 'But we all know why that is, don't we, Ham?'

Mad Marshal Mickey McKay was absolutely fuming!

Ham shrugged. 'All is fair in business and war,' he sneered. Then, looking closer at Bob, he said, 'Are you wearing lipstick?'

'No, I'm not,' said Bob, angrily wiping a sleeve across his mouth. 'Don't try and change the subject. I suppose you think it's fair to commandeer all the money from Trouble Bank?' he asked, through gritted teeth.

'I own the bank; by my reckoning I can do what I like with the money,' smiled the oily Ham. 'I'm going to use it to build a marvellous parade of new shops and casinos, saloons and theatres. It's for the town's own good.'

'Shops that you will own, but paid for by the people; you'll bleed the town dry,' said Wild Bob accusingly.

'Oh no, not completely dry. I have to leave them some money to spend in my shops. It's called business,' said Horatio Ham with a face as innocent as a baby's. 'I'm a businessman. What would you have me do?'

'Give the people back their money,' demanded Wild Bob.

'I can't do that, Ffrance.'

'Well I can,' said Bob. 'Kid, gather up all the money and dump it back in that trunk.'

Clearing The Table

I jumped down from Wild Bob's horse and landed with a thump on the floor. Then, under the unwavering stares of Ham, Marshal McKay and the two other men, I gathered stack after stack of banknotes and armfuls of cash and dropped them into the massive metal trunk that stood by the table.

'I don't know how you think you're going to shift that trunk, Ffrance,' said Ham with a smirk. 'It took four of us to lift it onto a wagon and then two strong horses to pull the wagon here. I hope you've got a carthorse handy.'

'Something like that,' smiled Wild Bob. 'Mick,' he called. 'Come in here a minute.' The saloon doors burst open and in walked Mick the Miner, his legs as thick as tree trunks and his chest as wide as an ox. 'Just lift that trunk up, would you, Mick?' asked Bob.

Horatio Ham snorted in derision, but Mick walked around the trunk, inspecting it from every side. He got down on his haunches and carefully tested its weight; satisfied, he heaved the trunk onto his back without a second's hesitation.

'What do you want me to do with it, boss?' his deep voice rumbled.

'Take it to Rafferty's store and tell him to make sure everyone in town gets what they are owed,' Wild Bob replied, and as if he were carrying nothing heavier than a blanket roll, Mick the Miner strolled out of the Pink Elephant Saloon.

'Kid, use your rope skills and tie them up good and tight,' said Wild Bob, throwing down a long length of rope he had looped over the pommel of his saddle. I fished the hunting knife out of my rucksack, cut the rope into four equal lengths and started to loop one around Ham, tying him tight to his chair.

'You won't get away with this, Wild Bob,' said Horatio Ham, spitting with anger. 'Anyway, I'll just take the money back again.'

'That would be a big mistake,' said Wild Bob,

suddenly looking very dangerous and levelling his gun at Ham's head. 'I won't be as lenient a second time. So, you've got to ask yourself, punk – is it worth the risk. Well, is it, Ham?'

Horatio Ham stared back at Bob, his face livid and running with sweat, but he didn't say a word. Then, from down the road, we heard the sound of gunfire. Some of Ham's men had returned and were starting to make a nuisance of themselves.

'Time to go, Kid,' said Bob. 'Go outside and mount up.'

Stopped In My Tracks

'You'll pay for this, boy, you just see if you don't,' yelled Ham, straining at the ropes that bound him.

I don't think so, I thought as I ran outside and jumped onto the back of Freecloud; we're out of here! Oh, but if only I had looked more closely at my saddle, I might not have been so confident.

Looking back inside the saloon I saw Wild Bob have a few parting words with Ham and then, just for the fun of it and in true Daredevil style, he launched his horse into a mighty leap. With an ear-shattering whinny and a wild look in his eye, the horse cleared the great oak table, his hooves missing the top of Ham's head by centimetres, and came clattering out through the swing doors.

'Let's go, Kid,' yelled Bob and galloped away down Main Street. I kicked Freecloud and she streaked away at top speed. Bob was some way ahead of me and the other Desperados were on their steeds and firing a few parting shots at Ham's regrouped forces.

All of a sudden, I came to a juddering halt and found myself hanging in mid-air still astride my saddle, as Freecloud galloped away from under me. I came crashing down in a cloud of dust, and as the dust cleared I saw that the street ahead of me was deserted. The Desperados hadn't realized I was no longer on

Me →

← /get left behind!

rope tied to saddle

Saddle

Freecloud carries on!

weakened girth strap snaps.

the back of Freecloud, and the whole gang were disappearing back towards Destiny.

Looking down at my saddle, I could see what had happened. Someone had anchored one end of my lasso to a hitching post and the other end to my saddle. Then, by cutting part way through the girth straps, they had guaranteed I wouldn't be going anywhere. But who could have done it?

'Well, if it isn't the Lariat Kid,' said a voice, and turning round, I met the smug smile of Silas Ham, Horatio's spoilt brat of a son. 'Not quite so cocky now, are you?'

Trouble County Jail

The slimy Silas Ham!

So that's how I have ended up here, waiting for the special surprise that Horatio Ham has promised me.

I was completely winded when Ham Junior yanked me off Freecloud's back, and it wasn't hard for him to wrap my own rope around me and lead me like a pet dog, back into the Pink Elephant Saloon. How embarrassing; the Lariat Kid caught with his own lariat!

Horatio Ham is a big bully

Inside, Silas Ham tied me to a table leg and went over to free his father and the others. 'Did I do good, Pa?' he asked.

'You did just fine, my boy,' said Horatio Ham as he shook himself free of the rope and limped towards me. I smiled when I saw that his foot was still giving him trouble. 'As for you, Master Lariat,' he continued, 'you didn't get very far did you, you pesky varmint. What's more, your beloved leader didn't hang around to save you either, did he? Some friend he is.'

I knew that wasn't fair and that Wild Bob wouldn't have known Freecloud was riderless as she thundered along in his wake. I was sure that as soon as he realized the truth he would organize a rescue party. In the meantime I had more pressing things to worry about.

Marshal McKay came marching over, his face still red with anger and his fingers twitching above the guns that hung at his sides.

'Want me to finish him now, boss?' he asked. 'It would be a real pleasure!'

'Oh no, not yet. He might just tempt

Ffrance back into town to try and rescue him, and then we'll be more than ready for him and his dumb Desperados. Anyway, I have a big surprise waiting for this pest, early tomorrow morning.'

Marshal McKay gasped. 'You don't mean . . .' he began.

'That's exactly what I do mean,' said Ham with a chuckle. 'We already have one hapless victim, and I'm sure a second won't be unwelcome. Now, get him out of my sight; take him over to the jail and put an extra guard on. No, put ten extra guards on!'

McKay frogmarched me straight to the jailhouse. Once inside, he unhooked a ring of large keys from the wall, pushed me into an empty cell and locked the door.

'Welcome to Trouble's premier bed and breakfast establishment,' he grinned. 'Except there's no bed, and you're gonna be the breakfast!'

'What are you on about?' I said nervously.

'You'll find out soon enough! Bye bye,' said McKay and closed the door that separated the cells from his office.

A Prisoner In Trouble

It's been a long, long night but I don't really want it to end, because as soon as dawn breaks, I know that Ham will give me the big surprise he's promised.

My first impressions of my temporary home were not good. The walls, although wooden, are thick, and the only window is heavily barred. I have a companion, however; the young Indian brave I mentioned earlier, and I thought that at least I'd have someone to talk to.

'Hi, I'm Charlie Small,' I said to the boy. 'What are you in for?' But my question was ignored. He didn't even look in my direction, or give any sign that I existed. He just sat cross-legged on the floor, staring up at the ceiling.

'We might as well be friends, seeing as we're both in the same boat,' I said. 'Do you know what's going to happen tomorrow morning – the great surprise?'

Again the boy didn't answer, continuing to stare into space. Perhaps he's in shock, or in some sort of trance, I thought. Or perhaps he's just really unfriendly, so I've given up trying to talk to him and now I'm looking for a way to break out.

I've been through my rucksack, hoping that something in my explorer's kit would give me an idea how to escape from this cell, but everything I've tried so far has been useless. I've tried gouging my way through the timber walls, first with my hunting knife and then with the crocodile's tooth, but the timbers are far too thick.

A pebble has just flown through the bars of the window and landed with a smack on my head. OUCH! Who would do such a stupid thing? Hold on, though, there's a piece of paper wrapped around the stone. It must be a message from Wild Bob. All my troubles are over! Wait a minute and I'll see what it says . . .

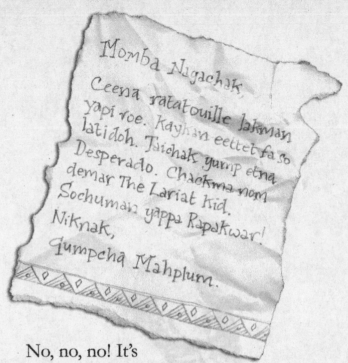

Momba Nagachak,
Ceena ratatouille Jakman
yapi roe. Kayhan eettet fa so
latidoh. Taichak yump etna
Desperado. Chackma nom
demar The Lariat Kid.
Sochuman yappa Rapakwar!
Niknak,
Gumpcha Mahplum.

No, no, no! It's
just a load of gobbledegook!
What am I going to do now? This *could* be
the last entry I ever make in my journal.

(If this is my last night, I'd just like to say
goodbye to my mum and dad, and thank you to
all the friends that have helped me on my
travels; Jakeman; Grip and Grapple; the Puffer
Fish Balloon; Jenny and her gran; the brave
Desperados. I would also like to say a big good
riddance to Thrak; the Perfumed Pirates; the
Puppet Master, and most of all Craik.)

Byeee!

Squashed Bug Alert!

Do not touch. This beetle can give you TERRIBLE diarrhoea. You have been Warned!

Oops, sorry about that. Those two pages were stuck together with an ugly bug from Trouble Jail. But I'm not out of trouble yet. Far from it: I'm in more trouble than ever!

Hanging Around In Space

Whoa! Both the young Rapakwar brave and I are now suspended from the top of a high cliff in a rusty old cage, and we're waiting for Ham's surprise; and it's much worse than I ever imagined. My stomach flips over every time I think about it. It seems we are going to be . . . No sorry, I can't bear to even think about it.

There is nothing we can do but wait and hope that someone comes to rescue us. Though, if there is going to be any sort of rescue attempt, it had better be SOON!

Meanwhile, although my life is in the greatest peril, all I can do is bring my journal up to date, and describe how we got here. It's so annoying because less than an hour ago, we were so close to freedom...

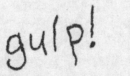

Nagachak

My heart had sunk when I read the note wrapped around the pebble that came whizzing into our cell. It was just a load of nonsense. But maybe the note wasn't meant for me at all. I pushed it through the bars into the adjoining cell.

'I think this might be for you,' I said to the boy. He turned round and for the first time looked me in the eye. Then, without saying a word he took the piece of paper and started to read. He remained silent for a very long time. Finally, he spoke.

'You are one of Wild Bob's Desperados? You are Lariat Kid?'

'Yes,' I replied.

'Then I must apologize,' said the boy. 'My name is Nagachak, son of the mighty Rapakwar chief, Sitting Pretty. I thought you were a spy, put here to try and learn the secrets of the great Rapakwar nation.'

'Not me,' I said. 'I'm in for bank robbery, and first thing tomorrow, Ham has promised me a big surprise. I don't think it's going to be a nice one!'

115

'I have been promised this surprise also,' said the boy, looking worried. 'It is not good, I know.'

'What do you know?'

'We are . . .' Nagachak hesitated. 'Have you ever heard of Mapwai?'

'Mapwai!' I cried. There was that name again, the name that had scared Wild Bob so much. 'What is Mapwai?'

'Mapwai is a giant, bloodthirsty, gut-guzzling voracious vulture, also known as the Great Bird Of Death. To hear of her is scary enough. To see her, they say, is enough to drive strong men mad . . . and we are to be sacrificed to Mapwai, at dawn tomorrow.'

'*Sacrificed?*' I asked desperately. 'What do you mean sacrificed?'

'We are to be given to the giant bird for breakfast,' said Nagachak mournfully. 'Ham is full of superstitions, and believes that if he gives gifts to this disgusting bird, luck will always be on his side.'

'What does the note say,' I stammered, starting to panic. There is no way I wanted to end up as a huge bird of prey's bowl of Cheerios! 'Are they coming to rescue us?'

'This note is from my father. He is a great friend of Wild Bob Ffrance. They have spoken, and they are coming to rescue us . . . some time tomorrow.'

Help!

Big bird's breakfast

'What time tomorrow?' I cried. 'We're being sacrificed at dawn!'

'I'm afraid they don't say,' said Nagachak, screwing up the note and throwing it on the floor. 'Kid, if we want to escape we have to do it by ourselves.'

Escape From Trouble Jail

I couldn't believe it. Things were going from bad to worse.

'I don't know how we're going to get out of here,' I said. 'The walls must be made of solid tree trunks.'

'I know, but I have been studying this building,' said Nagachak. 'I think the weak point is the roof.'

I looked up into the gloomy roof-space, and noticed that although the rest of the building was solid and strong, the roof itself was made of a thick thatch – dried reeds that were laid over bare rafters.

'You're right. That's a bit of an oversight!' I said. 'So that's what you've been gazing at; I thought you were just staring into space.'

'If there is nothing other than the thatch, we might be able to squeeze through onto the roof,' said Nagachak.

'Brilliant,' I replied. 'But how do we get up there? It's mighty high.'

We tried running and jumping, but we were nowhere near reaching the roof. I put my hands through the bars and gave Nagachak a leg up, but he was still someway short of the beams. The bars themselves, although they went all the way up to the roof, were just too slippery to shin up. Then, looking through my rucksack once more, I thought I might have the answer.

I took out the ball of string and the glue pen. Turning the glue pen over, I read the blurb.

SUPER-STRONG, SUPER-FAST, SUPER-GRIP GLUE.

STICKS ANYTHING
TO ANYTHING.
YOU'LL BE
AMAZED!

Right, I thought. Let's see if you're as good as you say! Starting about half a metre from the floor, I tied the loose end of the string to one of the bars with a special pirate knot, having first squirted the spot with a generous dab of glue. Then, unravelling the string, I knotted it tightly around the adjacent bar, which again I dabbed with the glue pen. Taking the string diagonally back to the first bar, I repeated the process, and continued zigzagging from one bar to the other as high up as I could reach. Like this:

How I built my rope ladder up the jail bars.

119

Standing back, I looked at my handiwork. Excellent! I had made a rope ladder, and if the glue would hold, we should be able to climb up high enough to grab one of the rafters and squeeze through the thatch!

'Ready to give it a try?' I asked Nagachak.

'After you,' he said with a grin.

I put my foot on the lowest rung and gently applied my weight. The string was thin but strong, and although the knot slipped a bit, it soon gripped tight and I lifted myself off the floor. Carefully, I placed my other foot on the next bit of string. Again it held. It was going to work! Soon I had reached the top rung, my hands gripping the two bars in front of me.

Then, stretching up, I grabbed hold of one of the beams. I swung my feet back and then up, my legs bursting through the thatch of reeds. Letting go of the beam with one hand, I forced through the reeds and dragged the rest of me up and out onto

Beams

hole!

underside of thatch

me

I swing up and punch my legs through the roof

the rooftop. I immediately spread my weight over the thatch to stop falling back into the cell below, and parting some of the reeds, I looked down at Nagachak.

'It's easy,' I whispered. 'Come on!'

A few minutes later, Nagachak was beside me on the roof, and we were looking down onto a courtyard bathed in moonlight. In the courtyard were two guards, both with rifles. I put my finger to my lips and we set off silently along the roof towards freedom.

I Kick The Bucket

As quietly as mice we crawled along the rooftop and onto the next roof. The courtyard was on one side of us, where the two guards were talking in low voices; smoke drifted up from their disgusting cheroots. On the other side of the roof was a dark narrow alley, which we dropped down into as silently as shadows.

We ran to the end of the alley and looked out onto Main Street. The town was asleep, but outside the front of the jail stood a gang of guards. Nagachak and I looked at each other,

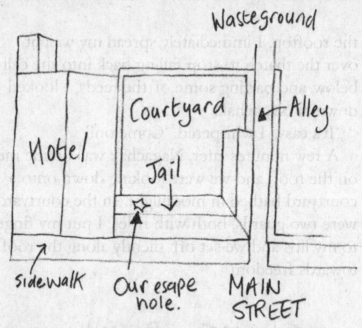

Wasteground

Courtyard → Alley

Hotel

Jail

sidewalk

Our esape hole.

MAIN STREET

shook our heads and scuttled back along the alley to the other end. This led onto a piece of wasteland on which stood a couple of run-down huts; beyond these was open country.

'Let's go,' said Nagachak and darted out into the moonlight and across the wasteland. His feet didn't make a sound in the dusty earth, and soon he was standing in the shadow of one of the huts. He gave a thin whistle for me to follow and I scurried out myself, feeling very exposed in the bright light of the moon. But nobody called; nobody challenged me, and I dived into the shadows alongside Nagachak, my nervous breath sounding loud in the still night air. We smiled at each other; we were going to do it! Carefully we crept along the side of the hut, invisible in the deep black shadow.

I still think it was a stupid place to leave a tin bucket! Right there, in the middle of the porch that ran down the side of the house. Anybody could trip over it in the dark, and somebody did. Me!

The bucket clattered and rang as it rolled across the wooden boards of the porch and immediately set the town dogs barking and howling. Nagachak and I were rooted to the spot, holding our breath and praying that no one would bother to investigate the noise. It was a forlorn hope, because a light came on in the hut straightaway and we heard a voice call out.

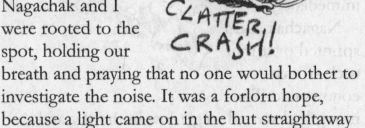

'Who the dang-devil is out there, disturbin' of the peace? Where's my blunderbuss? You better watch out, you pesky prowlers. I'll blow you to kingdom come!' And the wall next to us was peppered with tiny holes as a mighty bang shook the hut.

'Run for your life!' yelled Nagachak as the door opened and a shaft of light fell across the porch steps. We ran.

'Hee, hee,' we heard the man cackle. 'I'm a comin' to get ya! This is better than a raccoon hunt.' The strange man wasn't the only one to come after us. We heard a yell go up amongst the guards at the jail, and we knew that they would be on our trail immediately.

Nagachak and I sprinted over the rock-strewn countryside. The moon had started to get low in the sky and soon it would begin to lighten with the dawn. 'We need a place to hide,' panted Nagachak. 'We'll be sitting ducks out here!'

I looked around frantically, not seeing any possible hiding place in the featureless, flat

I'm comin' to get ya!

landscape. The rocks were too small to hide behind and there were no trees to climb or caves to conceal us.

'It's no good,' I said. 'There's nowhere to hide. Oh, wait a tick!' I noticed a large, flat slab of rock sticking out where the ground rose in a deep step. Like this:

We crawled right to the back of the rocky overhang.

A Rattling Fun Time!

There was just enough room to crawl underneath the rock and hide in the deep shadows. We only just made it; as we scrambled back to where the rock met the earth, we heard the sound of men approaching. We were completely out of breath, and it took all our concentration to calm down and try to breathe quietly.

'They've got to be somewhere around here,'

said one voice. 'Bring the light over.' A man ran over with a flaming torch and they held it high and surveyed the landscape as they walked up and down. 'Nothin',' said the voice, and then louder he called, 'They're nowhere to be seen.'

'They can't have disappeared into thin air,' came a new voice and I recognized it at once.

'Horatio Ham,' I whispered. 'Now we're in trouble.'

'I want this whole area searched. We'll smoke 'em out if we have to. It'll soon be dawn and I need them for the great sacrifice.'

We waited in silence, a nervous sweat dripping down our faces as we heard the men start to search the area, kicking over stones and pulling up thin scrubby bushes. Then, as the sky started to turn silver in the approaching dawn, we heard Ham say, 'There, under that slab. Have you looked under there?'

'No, boss. It's too low for me to get under.'

'Then have a good feel around. They've got to be here somewhere.'

'But, boss, it's just the sort of place a rattler might hang out.'

'Do it!' said Ham, and I heard the sound of him drawing back the hammer on his pistol.

The next minute, a man's arm was nervously feeling about under the rock, and Nagachak and I held our breath as he felt the stones and twigs all around us. Then he grabbed my knee!

'I've got something, boss,' he cried as I quickly opened my rucksack and pulled out the bag of marbles I had bought in Granny Green's village.

'What is it?' demanded Ham.

'Not sure yet, boss, but it ain't no stone,' he said, squeezing my knee so hard I nearly cried out. Instead I lifted the bag of marbles and shook them hard. They rattled loudly.

'Oh no!' cried the man. 'It's a . . .' And at the same time Nagachak picked up a forked twig from the floor and jabbed it into the back of his hand. The hand was whipped away with a cry.

'I've been bitten! A rattlesnake has bitten me!
I'm done for, boss.'

'Oh stop your whingeing and get yourself
back into town.'

'I need to see the doc, boss. I need to see him
quickly.'

'Do you think I'm made of money? I haven't
got money to waste on doctors. What a lot of
fuss over a little nip!'

We heard the man wander off, whimpering
softly to himself, and as Ham and his men
wandered away to continue their search
elsewhere, Nagachak and I congratulated
ourselves on our quick thinking.

A Rattling Bad Time

A rattling noise sounded again.

'It's OK, they've gone,' said Nagachak. 'You
can put your marbles away now.'

'That wasn't my marbles,' I gasped and we
both looked around in fear. We had celebrated
too soon, for sliding through a small crack at
the back of our hidey-hole, was a real
rattlesnake! It was fat and angry, and it coiled

up in front of us, its yellow eyes blazing and its tail rattling out an angry staccato.

Nagachak and I started to crawl slowly backwards out from under the rock, but the snake slithered round to cut off our escape. What now?

'How are we going to get out of this?' whispered Nagachak.

'I have no idea,' I replied. But even as I spoke I was gently searching through my rucksack again, trying not to make a sudden movement. My hand closed on the plastic lemon that I often used in my cooking, and just as I pulled it from the bag the rattler coiled back, ready to strike. I only just managed to unscrew the top when it struck at Nagachak. I squirted a stream of lemon juice straight at the snake's eyes

lemon juice!

and boy it must have stung, for the rattler coiled and writhed in pain. With an angry hiss, it quickly slithered away.

'Yahoo!' I cried.

'Shhh!' warned Nagachak, grasping my hand in thanks. 'Ham might still be around.'

'Sorry,' I whispered. 'Let's get out of here before the snake decides to come back.'

'Which one?' sniggered Nagachak as we backed out from under the rock, our eyes peeled for any further sign of the rattler. We both gave a huge sigh of relief as we emerged into the silver light of a beautiful dawn, but it froze in our chests as we turned around to see Horatio Ham and a line of his men, all armed and waiting for us.

'Well, look what just crawled out from under a rock,' said Ham with a sneer. 'And just in time for their special surprise. Grab 'em, men.'

Within seconds our hands were cuffed behind our backs and we were marched over to a covered wagon and hoisted on board. Half a dozen of Ham's men got into the back of the wagon to guard us, and the wagon started to move over the bumpy ground.

Caged!

Nagachak and I were driven fast across the countryside to the top of a high cliff looking out over a wide, sunken valley. Further along the cliff top we could just make out a tall rock, shaped like a crooked finger, pointing up into the sky.

'That's where Mapwai has his nest,' whispered Nagachak nervously.

Nearby, a big metal gantry hung out over the

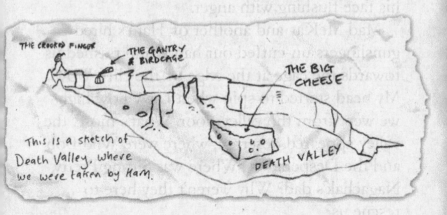

THE CROOKED FINGER

THE GANTRY & BIRDCAGE

THE BIG CHEESE

This is a sketch of Death Valley, where we were taken by Ham.

DEATH VALLEY

edge of the cliff and, from the end, a chain disappeared over the side. Mad McKay went over and started to turn a hand crank and, amidst much clanking and squealing of rusty wheels, a large and ornate metal cage rose into view.

'What do you think of my beautiful bird cage, Kid?' asked the unctuous Ham.

'Well, it's very rusty and there is no bird in it,' I replied, 'but apart from that, it's very pretty.'

'*You* go inside the birdcage, you dolt: you and this so-called son of a chief. Then the bird will come to you. And, for your information, that isn't rust all over the cage; it's dried blood. Ha ha ha ha!' Mean, vicious and downright bad, Ham started to laugh uncontrollably. 'Now get your sorry carcasses inside the cage,' he yelled, his face flushing with anger.

Mad McKay and another of Ham's hired gunslingers un-cuffed our hands and pushed us towards the cage at the edge of the cliff. Wow! My head started to spin when I saw how high we were from the valley floor. What's more, the valley appeared deserted; where were Wild Bob and the Desperados? Where was Sitting Pretty, Nagachak's dad? Why weren't they here to rescue us?

We were forced into the cage through a narrow doorway, which was locked securely behind us. Then McKay kicked the cage away from the cliff edge and we swung out over the void below. Again, with much squealing, the cage was lowered below the cliff ledge for about twenty metres.

The cage stopped and everything went silent. Nagachak and I sat on the barred floor of the cage, swaying high above the ground in the bright morning sunlight.

'What now?' I asked, but before Nagachak could answer, a cry came from the top of the cliff. It was Horatio Ham and he had started to chant:

Oh come great bird and accept this offering,
Oh come and feast on blood, guts and gore,
Two tender morsels I am offering,
With innards and entrails and claret galore.

A Quick History Lesson!

'What's he doing?' I asked.

'It's an old Rapakwar chant,' said Nagachak. 'In the old days my people thought the great bird represented both good luck and bad luck. I don't know why; perhaps because it has two heads.'

'Two heads!' I cried as a shudder of nerves went through my body. 'Nobody's mentioned two heads before.'

'Well, anyway,' continued Nagachak. 'They thought if they sacrificed a nice fat bison, Mapwai would bring them good luck instead of bad. It looks like Ham has gone one better and is offering human sacrifices.'

'But why should Ham care about the bird? He's not a Rapakwar.'

But to my great surprise, Nagachak replied, 'Well actually, he is. Sort of. Horatio Ham is my uncle.'

'Your uncle! And he's dangling you over a cliff as a treat for a monster two-headed bird? I don't understand. He doesn't look anything like a Rapakwar brave.'

'His father was not a Rapakwar. His name was Uriah Ham, a snake-oil merchant and scoundrel from back east, but he married the first daughter of Rolling Thunder, the old chief of the Rapakwar nation.

One day, Uriah was caught stealing diamonds that came from the Rapakwar mines, and they were both banished along with

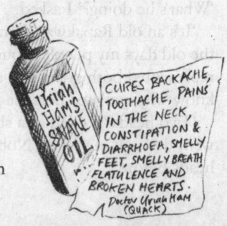

CURES BACKACHE, TOOTHACHE, PAINS IN THE NECK, CONSTIPATION & DIARRHOEA, SMELLY FEET, SMELLY BREATH FLATULENCE AND BROKEN HEARTS.
Doctor Uriah Ham (QUACK)

Horatio, their newborn child.'

'You've got diamond mines?' I interrupted.

'Yes,' said Nagachak modestly. 'The Rapakwar have mined diamonds for centuries. We only use the stones for ceremonial purposes, and only we know the exact location of the mine entrance.'

'Wow! Oh, sorry, please carry on.'

'Well, Rolling Thunder had another daughter, my mum, and when she married Sitting Pretty, my father, he became chief of all the Rapakwar lands; Ham has been busy stealing them back ever since. But we still own the diamond mines and of course that is what Ham wants more than anything; the trouble is he doesn't know where they are. So he captured me and tried to make me give up our ancient Rapakwar secrets; but I didn't and that's why I am here now.'

'Rolling Thunder . . . diamond mines . . . banished?' I said. This was all too much and I was very confused. 'Why didn't you tell me all this before?'

'We were too busy escaping,' said Nagachak.

Even now that I've written it all down, it's hard to take in. Ham is Nagachak's uncle! Not only does he want to run Trouble County, he also wants the Rapakwar Indian diamond mines.

What's more, he's prepared to sacrifice his nephew, and me, to get them! Is there no end to his greed?

Now my journal is up to date and Nagachak and I are waiting for the arrival of the Great Bird of Death. I have no idea what to expect next. Will I end up as a piece of cuttlefish for an overgrown, two-headed budgie? How the heck are we going to escape from this?

Just now we heard an ear-splitting screech echo around the valley. 'Mapwai is coming,' Nagachak said.

Help! I don't know if I shall ever make another entry in my journal.

Help!

Ham the horrid!
Help!
Home sweet home!
Oh
Ouch!
If someone sent me a cake with a file in it, I could escape!
That hurts.

Come back Thrak, all is forgiven!

AAARGH!

NO!

Tweet tweet

Is this what the great bird of death looks like?

Ceepers — Creepers

Marshal McKay is a nutter!

Wild Bob where are yooooul!?

The Great Escape

PHEW, we made it. Just!

The screech echoed across the valley as Nagachak and I span helplessly in the metal birdcage, high above the valley floor. Again the screech came, and then a terrifying sound that reminded me of the sails of a pirate galleon thrashing to and fro in a full-blown gale. The next minute I saw Mapwai for the first time, and it is one of the scariest things I've ever seen. Nothing had prepared me for the horror that came spiralling out of the sky towards us.

The vulture was as big as a bus, its powerful body covered in tatty black and white feathers. Her legs were as thick as drainpipes and her feet tipped with twenty-centimetre-long talons. But the scariest things about the bird were the two viciously-beaked heads that were attached to the ends of her scabby pink necks.

(Now that I have time, I've looked through my animal collectors cards and, lo and behold, here is a card all about the Mapwai.)

THE MAPWAI

The Mapwai, or Great Bird Of Death, is a giant two-headed, vicious and bloodthirsty vulture from Rapakwar Indian mythology. Anyone who sees the Mapwai, usually ends up as her next meal. According to legend, the Mapwai was so greedy that she grew an extra head in order to eat even more. As a consequence, she has grown to an enormous size. Chance of escape: Nil.

WILD ANIMAL COLLECTORS CARDS

Bird Food!

The bird dropped from the sky as fast as a stone. Not braking or checking her flight in any

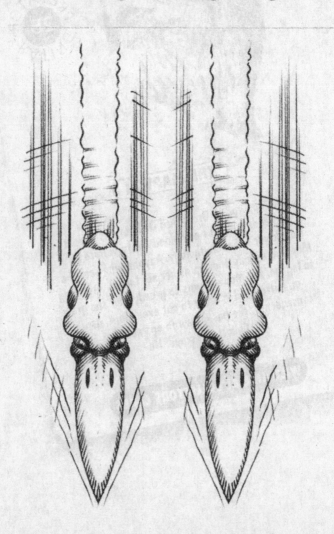

way, she slammed her feet into our cage, sending the whole crate rocking wildly on the end of its chain and we banged against the cliff wall. No sooner had we regained our shattered senses than the bird attacked again. The crowd of Ham's men cheered from the top of the cliff as we crashed and thrashed about.

'So long, Nagachak. We're leaving before the bird mistakes us for part of its treat. You should've told me where the diamond mines are, you silly boy,' shouted Ham, peering over the cliff edge. 'Oh, and good riddance to the Lariat Kid.' With this parting message, Ham pulled a lever and, with the sound of squeaking metal, the floor of our cage fell open on two rusty hinges.

YIKES!

My stomach flipped as I dropped out of the cage! At the last second I managed to grab the bottom bar, leaving me dangling by one arm, hundred of metres from the ground with the vulture swooping in for another attack.

I twisted around. Nagachak had grabbed the cage floor as he fell and was able to use it as a ladder and climb back into the cage to stand precariously on the frame.

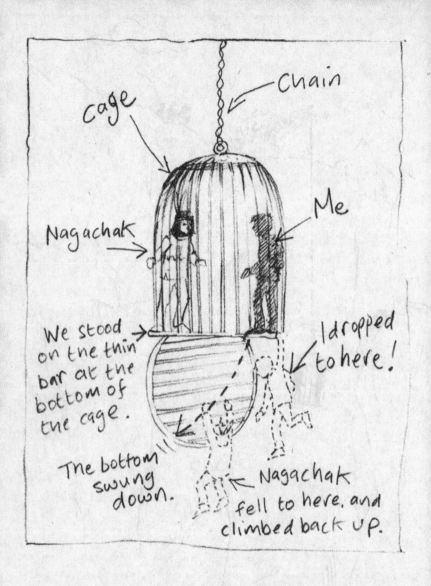

'Help, Nagachak,' I yelled, wriggling in mid-air like a worm on the end of a hook.

Nagachak leaped across the empty gap at the bottom of the cage and grabbed hold of my wrist. Just in time, I flipped myself back into the cage and stood alongside my friend as, *BANG!* The vulture hit us again, sending the cage dancing and spinning above the mighty abyss.

Twice more she attacked, bending the cage's bars and leaving gaps big enough to force her two deadly beaks through. Battered and bruised and breathing hard, Nagachak and I had hardly enough strength left to hold on. Now the great bird landed on an outcrop of rock about eight metres below us, stretched her necks, and darted her vicious orange beaks one by one up into the cage.

Nagachak and I both leaped for the top bars of the cage, quickly pulling our legs clear of the clattering beaks; but my jeans were ripped and my shin pouring blood from where the vulture scored a hit. Our arms started to burn with exhaustion as we hung on for dear life, our feet just out of reach of the bird's scything pecks.

'I'm going to drop any minute,' I yelled to Nagachak. 'I just can't hold on.'

A Stone's Throw

The vulture struck again, but as she forced her beak into the cage a large stone whizzed through the air and, – *Whack!* – it hit the bird hard on the side of one of her heads.

KWAAK!

Kwaak! The bird screamed, withdrawing her beak and gazing down into the valley below. Another stone sailed through the air, hitting the vulture on her other head. *Kwaak!* The huge vulture scanned the valley with her cruel eyes and, spotting something, spread her wings and silently glided away from the rock.

Nagachak and I lowered ourselves until we stood on the frame of the cage once again, shaking with relief.

'We've got to get down from here, before the vulture comes back,' said Nagachak. I looked at the void below our feet, all the way down to the valley floor.

'Any ideas?' I asked. Just then, an arrow whipped past my ear and clattered through the bars. 'Oh brilliant, now someone's shooting at us as well!'

A Leap Of Faith

'It's my father's arrow,' gasped Nagachak, squatting down and picking up the missile. A rope was tied to the shaft of the arrow and it passed back through the bars all the way down

149

to the valley floor below. 'What are we supposed to do with it?'

'Look!' I cried, 'there's a note wrapped around the arrow.' With one hand holding the bars, I squatted down and tore the paper away.

But the message was written in Rapakwarian again.

'You'd better tell me,' I said.

Nagachak took the note and started to read.

'"Boys"' he read aloud. '"You must trust me. Tie the rope to your waists, cling together and JUMP!"'

'Jump!' I cried. 'Is he barmy? Can't we just tie the rope to the cage and climb down?'

'"You can't climb down,"' Nagachak continued reading. '"It is too slow and the Great Bird Of Death will pick you off like caterpillars on a cabbage stalk. Trust me, and jump. Love, Dad (Sitting Pretty, Chief.) PS Make sure the rope has passed over the frame of the cage before you leap!"'

'Let's do it!' cried Nagachak, and started to wind the end of the rope around his waist. It wasn't easy, balancing on the narrow bar of the cage and tying the rope at the same time. He wobbled and slipped and at one point I thought he was a goner, but at last he succeeded. As soon as he had finished, I took the excess that hung from his waist and wrapped it around me, tying it off with a double heave-ho knot, taught to me by the pirate Rawcliffe Annie.

'Ready?' he asked. I checked the rope at our feet, making double sure that it had passed through the bottom rung of the cage's frame.

'Ready,' I stammered, feeling anything but ready as we clung together.

'JUMP!' yelled Nagachak, and we jumped off the cage and out into thin air.

'*Aaaaaaaaaaaaaagh!*' We dropped like stones and I immediately wished I had not put my trust in Big Chief Sitting Pretty. I hadn't even met him and here I was jumping from a cage at the top of a cliff, just because he'd told me to. Next I'd be sticking my head in an oven for him!

Then, about halfway down, the rope tightened and our descent started to slow! How was that happening? And then I saw: Nagachak's dad had tied a boulder to the other end of the rope, one just a bit lighter than Nagachak and I together, and it acted as a perfect counter-weight to us. We glided down to the ground as sedately as if we were on an escalator. Brilliant!

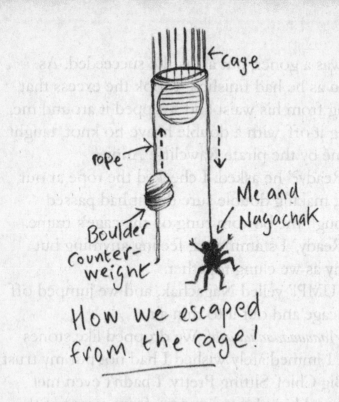

How we escaped from the cage!

The Great Chase

As soon as we touched down, Sitting Pretty ran over to us and cut us free with a slice of his knife. He was reassuringly calm, seemed very strong and looked both fierce and kind at the same time.

'Quick boys, follow me,' he said and led us through a maze of rocks until we were standing at the edge of the vast valley floor. Galloping towards us at breakneck speed on his beautiful black stallion was Wild Bob Ffrance. With one hand he was leading a snorting, wide-eyed pinto pony, and in the other he was spinning a slingshot. Racing up the valley behind him and no more than five metres from the ground, was Mapwai. Even as we watched, Wild Bob loosed the slingshot and sent a large stone whizzing through the air, to crash against the mighty bird's skull.

The vulture shrieked and turned away, dazed. Now Bob was upon us.

'Quick, mount up,' he yelled. 'We've only got a matter of seconds.' He was right. I leaped into the saddle behind him; Sitting Pretty and Nagachak mounted the pinto and we galloped off, just as Mapwai regained her senses and took up the chase once again.

Then I saw our horses were each dragging the bloody carcass of an old steer as extra bait for the vulture.

'Is that wise?' I shouted at Wild Bob as we thundered over the rocky ground. 'Isn't that just encouraging it?'

'Sure thing, Kid,' Bob yelled back. 'But don't worry. The Chief and I have a plan, and it's real sweet! Just sit back and enjoy. Yee-hah!'

We galloped away, around a curve in the cliff wall and out across the open valley floor. I could hear the great scything beats of the vulture's wings as she powered through the air behind us.

'Faster,' I yelled, urging Fortune on. 'Faster, or it's curtains for us all!'

The black stallion's hooves drummed on the hard mud, sending great billowing clouds of dust into the air. In front of me sat Wild Bob Ffrance, eyes wide with excitement. To our side raced Sitting Pretty and Nagachak. Behind each horse, the old cattle carcasses bounced and bucked in our wake.

'Not much further now, Kid,' yelled Wild Bob over the din of pounding hooves.

I do hope not, I thought, as I looked behind me. Mapwai was right on our tail. Her two heads rolled from side to side as she swooped over the rust-coloured earth and I heard the clack of her beaks as she lunged at the bloody bait we dragged behind us. All of a sudden Fortune reared as the vulture grabbed the carcass we were dragging, bringing us to a juddering halt.

'Come on!' cried Wild Bob, kicking the stallion back into a full gallop and snatching the meat out of the vulture's beak. 'Don't give up now!'

We raced away, and there directly in front of us was the great wedge of rock known as the Big Cheese. The rock rose sheer and high from the valley floor and tapered to a viciously sharp edge – and we were racing straight towards it. Again I heard the hollow clack of the vulture's beaks right behind us and, as the bird let out an ear-splitting screech, I nearly fell from the horse in fright.

I really didn't think we were going to make it!

Divide And Rule

We galloped towards the knife-edge corner of the Big Cheese. One head of the vulture snapped at the carcass Bob and I were dragging; its other head snapped at the carcass dragged by Sitting Pretty's pinto. Still we galloped on, straight towards the huge rock.

'Turn, Bob. Turn!' I yelled. Surely we were going to be dashed against the lethal rocks that littered the ground around the base of the Big Cheese! 'Help!' But Bob didn't turn and we raced on towards a certain and sticky end!

Then at the very last second, when the black stallion was already stumbling over a fall of loose stones and the Big Cheese loomed massive in front of us, Wild Bob yanked on the reins and our faithful steed turned and galloped madly along the side of the colossal outcrop. As we turned to the right, Chief Sitting Pretty turned to the left and hurtled along the other side of the rock. The monster vulture tried to follow both of us! Her right head, snapping at the steer that Bob was dragging, followed us to the right; the bird's left head followed Sitting

Pretty's steer to the left, and at full speed the vile vulture hit the knife-sharp edge of the Big Cheese!

With an awful *Kreeeeeeech*, the bird was rent asunder, splitting right down the middle, and her two halves dropped heavily to the ground on either side of the rock. There was a sudden silence except for our gasping breath. It was over! We were saved! Bob pulled his sweating, snorting stallion to a halt.

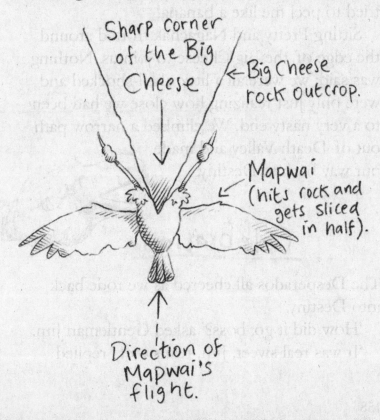

Sharp corner of the Big Cheese

← Big Cheese rock outcrop.

Mapwai (hits rock and gets sliced in half).

↑ Direction of Mapwai's flight.

'Ooee, that must have stung,' said Bob grinning, but strangely I couldn't help feeling sorry for the creature. Yes, she had tried to kill me; she had tried to strip the flesh from my bones, but that's only what vultures do, isn't it? It wasn't her fault. Then as we trotted alongside the remains of the monster and I saw her massive curved beak and her pitiless, wicked eye, I breathed a huge sigh of relief. No, I wasn't sorry at all; hot-diggity-dog – she had tried to peel me like a banana!

Sitting Pretty and Nagachak trotted around the edge of the Big Cheese to join us. Nothing was said; we were all a little shell-shocked and were only just realizing how close we had been to a very nasty end. We climbed a narrow path out of Death Valley and made our way back to Destiny.

Celebration

The Desperados all cheered as we rode back into Destiny.

'How did it go, boss?' asked Gentleman Jim.

'It was real sweet, Jim, real sweet,' replied

Wild Bob. 'Horatio Ham has been foiled again and what's more, Mapwai, the Great Bird Of Death, has been slain!'

The Desperados cheered even louder, whooping and hollering and firing off their pistols.

'This calls for a feast,' declared Cornelius Duff, who already had an extra large pot of baked beans bubbling on the campfire. Soon, with the help of a large bottle of firewater, the Desperados and Chief Sitting Pretty were dancing a Rapakwar victory dance around the roaring campfire, waving rifles and tomahawks, and chanting 'The Mapwai is dead, the Mapwai is dead, Ee-I-Adio the Mapwai is dead!' Then, when they were too tired to dance anymore, Cornelius Duff dished out the beans and, as a special treat, a big bowl of cactus soup (yum yum, I don't think!).

We had speeches and songs and Chief Sitting Pretty told the whole saga of our fight with Mapwai (which was a bit boring as he spoke in Rapakwar, and I didn't understand a word!). Then the pipe of peace was passed around, to strengthen the friendship between the Desperados and the Rapakwar nation.

'No thanks,' I said when the pipe was passed to me. 'I don't smoke.'

'You must,' whispered Wild Bob. 'Otherwise the Rapakwar will take it as a great insult. Just take a little puff.'

Really disgusting pipe of peace!

I put the pipe to my lips and as the disgusting green smoke floated around my head, I sucked. The evil-smelling smoke hit the back of my throat. It was disgusting – hot, rough and sour – and I instantly collapsed in a fit of uncontrollable coughing. The Desperados roared with laughter but as my head cleared and I could see their friendly faces through my watery eyes, I laughed too; it felt so good to be a Daredevil Desperado!

All too soon though, it was time for Nagachak and his dad to go. Chief Sitting Pretty, the proud and implacable warrior chief who looked as if he had been carved out of solid rock, put his hand on my shoulder.

chief sitting Pretty

'Nagachak has told me how you helped him to escape, Kid Lariat. You have proved yourself a worthy friend and I now make you an honorary Rapakwar Brave.' With this, he took one of his many bead necklaces and placed it around my neck. 'Good luck, brother. If you ever need my help, send a message and I will come.'

'Wow! Thank you,' I said, beaming with pleasure at this unexpected honour.

'Goodbye, Kid,' said Nagachak with a smile, and shook my hand. They mounted their horse; Chief Sitting Pretty flicked the reins, and amidst much cheering, the pinto raced out of Destiny.

As I watched them go, I wondered how long it would be before *I* would be able to leave and continue my journey home. We had escaped the Great Bird Of Death, but horrible Ham was still about, lording it over the poor people of Trouble County. Before I could go I had promised to help defeat him. To be honest, I was beginning to wonder if that would ever happen.

As I made my way back towards the bunkhouse, I glanced down at the necklace the

Chief had just given me, and gasped. It was made up of hundreds of brightly-coloured beads, but there in the middle, sparkling in the morning sun, was a diamond as big as a walnut!

Wow! Chief Sitting Pretty gave me a diamond as big as a walnut!

Sleep Glorious Sleep!

Now my journal is right up to date, and it's time for bed. I'm absolutely exhausted, and I ache all over. No one wake me up for a week!

zzZ²z²zᶻᶻᶻz!

Later

You'll never guess where I am now. No, really, you'll never, ever guess. I can hardly believe it myself. I'm deep down inside the bowels of the earth, looking through a crack in a rock at a scene illuminated by the glow of a thousand oil lamps!

First, though, I must tell you all about the big showdown between the Daredevil Desperados and Horatio Ham's Hired Honchos! All about my meeting with . . . No, let me continue from where I left off.

Invitation To A Fight

'Kid! Kid Lariat, wake up.'

'Wha . . . ?'

'Wake up, Kid. It's time to go.' It was Wild Bob Ffrance.

'Time to go where? I've only just this minute dropped off to sleep,' I complained.

'You've been asleep for two days, Kid,' chuckled Bob. 'Now get up. We've got an appointment to keep.'

'What appointment?' I asked, still very fuzzy

in the head. I hadn't made any appointments.

'Shake a leg and I'll tell you all about it while you're getting dressed,' said Wild Bob.

I stumbled out of my bunk and pulled on my jeans. The hut was deserted and I could see through the windows that the sun was already high in the sky. 'What's going on?' I asked.

'When we got back from Death Valley, I held a meeting with the rest of the Desperados,' said Wild Bob. 'They were horrified when they learned what Ham had tried to do to you and Nagachak and we decided that enough is enough! Our little raids have had no effect whatsoever. We must try and destroy Ham's power base once and for all. To that end, I sent Ham an invitation, an invitation I'm glad to say he has accepted.' With these words, Wild Bob handed me this scrap of paper:

Let's get ready to rumble!

TO HORATIO HAM,

THIS FEUD HAS RUMBLED ON LONG ENOUGH.
LET'S GET IT SORTED.

You are cordially invited to a once-and-for-all showdown between you and the Desperados.

Time: 17th of the month at 12 Noon.

Place: The Wasteland. Prize: Winner takes all.

RSVP.

BRING YOUR OWN GUNS.

'Wow!' I cried. 'A final showdown. That's a bit drastic. What happens if you lose?'

'Losing is not an option,' said Wild Bob, somewhat grim-faced. 'But we've got to face the fact that we might well lose. Sneaky Pete has been out sneakin' around, and has just reported back that Ham has a gang of hired gunslingers over five hundred strong.'

I whistled. 'That's one heck of a lot of men. How many do you have on your side?'

'Well, all in all, counting you, about twenty,' said Bob.

'Twenty!' I cried. 'We'll be driven out of this state and into the middle of next week!'

'We might be driven out of this life altogether,' said Bob. 'So I just want to say, you've been a real pal and I've no right to ask you to fight my battles for me. If you want to get going on your journey, no one will hold it against you.'

But I didn't even need to think about it. 'You saved my life, and there's no way I'm going to let you and the rest of my pals face Horatio Ham without me,' I said, and immediately thought, whoops, that was a bit hasty!

'Good lad, I knew we could count on you,'

said Wild Bob, smiling broadly. 'Now, you'd better get ready.'

'How many days until the seventeenth?' I asked, wondering how long I had got to hone my lariat skills.

'Erm,' said Bob. 'Today is the seventeenth!'

'Today!' I cried. Hot-diggity-dog! 'And what's the time now?'

'It's eleven o'clock,' said Bob, standing up to leave. 'We've got one hour until showtime! I'll let you finish getting ready. I've got some last minute things to deal with.'

I said who keeps shooting my Journal?! →

Sending Signals

One hour? ONE HOUR! What on earth was I going to do? I hadn't come all this way to be blasted into eternity by a power-crazed son of a snake-oil merchant; but I had also given Wild Bob my word that I would stay and fight. We needed help. We needed reinforcements, but how on earth was I going to get any? Then I remembered Chief Sitting Pretty's promise. He would help; he said he would. All I had to do was send him a message . . .

I staggered bleary-eyed into the sunshine, and the first thing I saw was the campfire in the middle of the compound sending a plume of smoke into the sky. That's it, I thought. A smoke signal – I'll send a smoke signal. Hold on, though. I don't know how to do it! Never mind, I thought, I'll have to use Morse code instead and just hope the Rapakwar warriors understand and come running! I ran back into the bunkhouse for my blanket and dampened it under the camp pump. Now, I thought, let's see if this works.

'Could you give me a hand, Mr Duff?' I asked.

'Of course, my dear,' said the kindly corpulent cook, putting down his tea-towel and waddling over.

'If you just stand on one side of the fire and hold the corners of this blanket, I'll do the rest,' I said. Holding the blanket low over the smouldering cinders, we lifted it once, twice, three times. Each time, a separate puff of smoke drifted up into the air, higher and higher until it passed through the mouth of the volcano. We did three small puffs, three large puffs and then another three small ones.

My smoke signal.

Dot-dot-dot. Dash-dash-dash. Dot-dot-dot. SOS!

Oh, I hope the Rapakwar receive the signal . . . and understand it!

'Are you ready, Kid?' shouted Wild Bob from over by the corral. 'It's time to go.'

An Appointment With Fear

The Daredevil Desperados were all waiting for me, so I slung my rucksack on my back and mounted Freecloud, who had followed Wild Bob all the way home after dumping me in the Main Street of Trouble town.

I grabbed one of the bacon sarnies that Cornelius Duff was handing out, and wolfed it down. I was starving, but either the bacon had gone off or I was getting really scared, because my tummy started to burble like a pan of his bubbling baked beans!

Solemnly we rode two abreast up the steep path, through the tunnel and down the hidden track to the outside of Destiny volcano. The Desperados were armed to the teeth with rifles and pistols and slingshots and blunderbusses, but they knew it would never be enough against Ham's hordes. The Daredevils were going to fight a losing battle, but they had a job to do and would do it to the best of their ability. My knees were knocking against Freecloud's side as we kicked our horses into a gallop and rode off towards the wasteland.

Ham's Hordes

The blood froze in my veins when we arrived at the wasteland, a huge and rocky open area. Silhouetted against the skyline, on the other side were Horatio Ham's henchmen, all five hundred of them. Our little band of Desperados looked pathetic in comparison. How on earth were we going to escape from this deadly confrontation? Where were the Rapakwar Indians; had Chief Sitting Pretty understood my message?

I looked at Wild Bob Ffrance. Had he any ideas? When I saw his face, I could see that he hadn't. He caught my questioning look.

'Don't worry, Kid, something always turns up when you least expect it.'

'Like the Rapakwar Indians?' I asked.

'How do you mean?'

'I sent them a message, but they don't seem to have received it.'

'Never mind, I don't think they would be the answer,' Bob said, smiling.

'Why, I thought a tribe of warrior braves would be just the thing!' I said, feeling a bit put-out. Then, as a bloodthirsty call sounded

171

from the low ridge to our left, I saw what Wild Bob meant. There, on the backs of their war-painted ponies, longbows over their shoulders and tomahawks in hand, were the Rapakwar braves. All twelve of them, and apart from Sitting Pretty and Nagachak, the rest were as skinny and stooped as their longbows and as toothless as toads. They were wrinkly old granddads!

'Is that it; is that all they sent?' I gasped.

'That, I'm afraid, Kid, is the entire male population of the Rapakwar nation. And that's why I didn't bother asking for their help!'

Brilliant, now we're really done for!

Parley

I thought to myself: I've got to try and stop this madness before the obnoxious Ham defeats the brave Daredevil Desperados. I would put a stop to it, right now: I would demand a pow-wow! Surely this situation could be resolved by talking it through? I quickly opened my rucksack and felt around inside until I found my white scarf (well, white and blue, really). Then carefully and quietly, I leaned over and withdrew the rifle from the holster on Gentleman Jim's saddle. I tied the scarf of truce to the end, and holding it high in the air, I gave Freecloud a kick and sent her galloping into the middle of the wasteland.

My flag of truce.

'Come back, Kid,' yelled Wild Bob. 'It's no good, they won't listen.'

'I've got to try,' I shouted over my shoulder as I brought Freecloud to a halt in the middle of the arena, facing Ham's army of thugs. My heart was pounding against my ribcage, and my hands were clammy with fear. Now it was up to Ham to send a negotiator out to talk to me. Already, I could see Ham talking to a group of his men. Perhaps this was going to work. Then, quite unexpectedly, I heard a low rumble of thunder. That's strange, I thought, looking at the sky, there isn't a cloud to be seen.

The rumble grew louder and louder as one of Ham's men galloped out to meet me. This is more like it, I thought. Now we're getting somewhere. Imagine my surprise then, as the rider swung his rifle out of its holster, and at full gallop, aimed and fired, blasting a huge hole in my scarf of truce! Yikes, Bob was right. These men weren't prepared to talk. It's time to get out of here. Now!

I turned Freecloud around, ready to scarper, but as I did so the rumble of thunder became deafening and the ground beneath our feet started to shake violently. Over to my right, a huge dust cloud hung in the air. What was it; an earthquake; a vast army of tanks? I started to shake as violently as the ground – this was terrifying!

The rifleman seemed just as frightened, made a U-turn and retreated into the distance. The dust cloud grew closer and closer and the ground started to shake even more. It was getting hard to stay on Freecloud. What the heck was going on – had Destiny erupted?

Ham's man had had the right idea; it was time to go. I gave Freecloud a kick, but now the ground was shaking so much I couldn't hold on, and as Freecloud galloped off towards the Desperados, I was shaken out of the saddle and landed with a thump on the ground. Again!

I got to my feet quickly. The cloud of dust was now only a couple of hundred metres away and closing fast. Then, as a breeze parted the billowing clouds for a second, I could see what was hurtling towards me. Bison, a hundred thousand strong! I was rooted to the spot in the path of a gigantic bison stampede. HELP!

The dust cloud parted...

Swallowed Up In A Bison Stampede

There was nothing I could do. Even if I ran I couldn't reach the end of the humungous herd before it was upon me. I was going to be trampled as flat as a piece of paper.

'Kid!' I heard Wild Bob cry above the cacophony of half a million thumping hooves, but then I was swallowed up in the great, swirling fog. The dust filled my nose, the noise filled my ears and the last thing I saw before I closed my eyes, was the massive leader of the herd dip its head, ready to strike. His woolly head was as broad as an armchair, his horns as thick as Thrak's mighty arms. I squeezed my eyes shut and braced myself for the collision. Aaargh, here goes!

But the strangest thing happened. I felt the lightest of bumps from the great bull's head as it gently scooped me from the floor with its horns. With a toss of its head I was sent spinning through the air. I braced myself for the crushing thump as I bounced off the bison's back and fell under the herd's pounding hooves . . . but the next minute I found myself sitting on a stool next to a very strange little man indeed!

What on earth was going on?

Jakeman's Patented Hydraulic Bison

I looked round in disbelief. The man next to me was very short, hardly any taller than me, and had an enormous peppery brown moustache sprouting from under his bulbous nose. On his head he sported an old flying cap and a pair of oily goggles.

This was totally bizarre: who was he, and how did I get here? One minute I had been stuck in the path of a bison stampede in the middle of the dusty wasteland, and the next it was as if I had been suddenly plucked from the earth by a passing spaceship. Maybe I had! I started to panic.

I was sat next to a very strange little Man.

'What's going on?' I cried above the noise of thumping pistons and hissing airbrakes. 'Where am I?'

'Just a minute, Charlie!' said the strange man, frantically pressing buttons and pulling levers.

Hold on! How did he know my name? This was getting weirder by the minute!

'Ah, that's better. So glad you could drop in, Charlie! I've been looking all over the place for you.'

'You have?' I asked in amazement. 'But who are you and how do you know my name; are you some sort of alien who's beamed me up into their flying saucer?'

'No, I'm not an alien and you're not in a spaceship,' chuckled the little man, adjusting his goggles. 'You're . . . yikes! That was a close one.' He twisted the throttle grip on a pair of cow-horn handlebars and with a smart double-declutch, he changed gear and our mysterious craft accelerated away to the sound of screaming machinery.

The man reached under his seat and pulled out a sheet of paper. 'This might explain where you are,' he said.

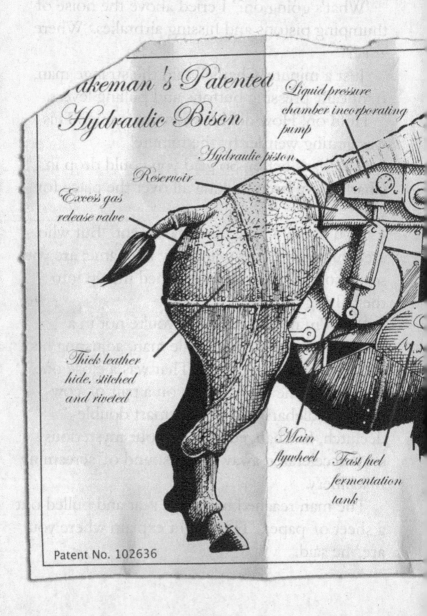

akeman's Patented
Hydraulic Bison

Liquid pressure
chamber incorporating
pump

Hydraulic piston

Reservoir

Excess gas
release valve

Thick leather
hide, stitched
and riveted

Main
flywheel

Fast fuel
fermentation
tank

Patent No. 102636

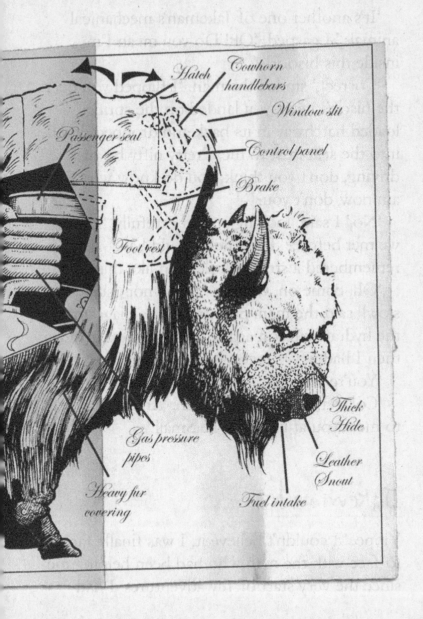

Hatch

Cowhorn handlebars

Window slit

Control panel

Brake

Passenger seat

Foot rest

Thick Hide

Leather Snout

Gas pressure pipes

Heavy fur covering

Fuel intake

'It's another one of Jakeman's mechanical animals,' I gasped. 'Oh! Do you mean I'm inside this bison?'

'Correct,' smiled the man. 'I flipped you over the bison's head, you landed on the spring-loaded hatchway in its back and dropped down into the seat next to me. Pretty nifty bit of driving, don't you think; you do know who I am now, don't you?'

'No,' I said, looking at him carefully. 'Have we met before?' I'm sure I would have remembered a strange little man like this.

'Oh, come on, Charlie. You're not usually so slow!' said the man, pointing at the diagram of the hydraulic bison again. 'Have a guess.' And then I had it. Of *course*, it was obvious!

'You're Jakeman!' I cried.

'Correct,' chuckled the man. 'And it's so nice to meet you at last, Charlie Small.'

Jakeman!

Yippee! I couldn't believe it. I was finally face-to-face with the man who had been helping me since the very start of my adventures. I had

182

ridden his steam-powered rhinoceros across the endless plains towards the gorillas' jungle; driven his jet-propelled swordfish through stormy seas; sunk an enemy ship with his clockwork limpets and been saved from certain death by the monstrous hydro-electric submawhale. And here was the man who had invented all those wonderful machines.

'This is brilliant! I've been desperate to meet you,' I cried, and all the questions that I had been bottling up inside for so long, came pouring out. 'How come you keep helping me, Mr Jakeman; do you know how I ended up in this strange world; can you tell me how to get home?'

'Slow down, slow down, Charlie my boy. Yes, I can answer all of your questions . . . but later. First we've got a job to finish.'

'We have?' I asked. In all the excitement of meeting Jakeman, my mind had become a jumble, and I had no idea what I was supposed to be doing.

'Of course, you haven't forgotten Horatio Ham have you? Look!' Jakeman pointed out of the small slit of a window in front of us and I could see we were charging straight towards

Ham and his horde of hired guns. 'I'm the lead bison in this stampede,' he added. 'And wherever I go, the herd will follow.'

He throttled the bison up and we powered forward even faster, and from the noise coming from behind us, I knew that the rest of the huge herd was following.

Operation Demolition

'Just a minute, the view's a bit restricted in here,' said Jakeman and with a flick of a switch the hatch doors swung open, our seat was raised, and we could peer out over the top of the hydraulic bison's powerful shoulders. Brilliant!

Ham's men were panic-stricken. Some were mounting their horses to escape, some just running away on foot, and in the middle of them all, Horatio Ham stood stock-still with a look of complete disbelief on his face.

'Run, Ham, run!' I yelled, standing up so that the top half of my body was sticking out of the bison. Goodness knows what Ham was thinking. Perhaps his mind was a complete blank. I'm not exactly sure what happened next, but as we galloped straight at Ham, I heard a whoop and a yell from behind us. I turned to see Wild Bob Ffrance, the Daredevil Desperados and the Rapakwar warriors joining the back of our stampede.

'Come on, Bob. They're on the run!' I yelled, but when I turned forwards again, we had passed right over the spot where Ham had been standing and I could see neither hide nor hair of him. Whoops! Had we pummelled him as flat as a very flat pancake?

I had no time to think, for Jakeman turned the bison stampede straight towards Ham's ranch, Two-Eyes. It must have changed a great deal since Wild Bob's parents had owned it, because now a huge and gaudy mansion stood on the land. But not for long!

'Heads down, closing hatchway,' called

Jakeman and I sat back down as the seat lowered and the hatch closed. 'Hold on tight, this is going to be a rocky ride,' he chuckled.

We hit the wooden homestead at full pelt, the rest of the bellowing buffaloes right on our heels. To the thunderous sound of splintering wood and crashing furniture, we ploughed right through the mansion. Ham's headquarters were history.

Mission accomplished!

So Long To The Desperados

It takes a long time to stop a bison stampede, and when Jakeman finally brought the huge herd to a standstill, we were a good half kilometre beyond Two-Eyes. As the snorting, panting bison herd lowered their heads to feed on Ham's lush pasture, Wild Bob and his men rode up.

'Yippee! I've never seen anything like it!' cried Wild Bob. 'Who's your pal, Charlie?'

'This is Jakeman,' I exclaimed. I was so thrilled at having met Jakeman, and by our battle with Horrible Ham, that my words came pouring out so fast they started tripping over one another in the rush. 'He's the man I told you about; theonewhobuiltallthosemarvellous mechanicalbeasts, he's . . .'

'Slow down, Kid,' said Bob with a smile. 'Where did you spring from, partner?' he asked Jakeman.

'Oh, a long way away,' said Jakeman quietly. 'Miles away; worlds away!'

'Well, I'm mighty pleased to meet you, sir,' said Bob. 'You were brilliant, both of you,' and as the Desperados cheered and threw their hats into the air in celebration, Chief Sitting Pretty, Nagachak and the small band of wrinkled warriors immediately went into their victory dance, whooping and chanting.

'Have we done it, then?' I asked Bob above the noise. 'Has he gone?'

'I should say so. I saw him run like a jackrabbit, just before you hit. He ran to the ridge and left in a wagon with his slimy son, Silas. Don't worry; we won't be seeing him again. He looked scared half to death! Yee-hah, we've won!' crowed Wild Bob and joined in the Rapakwar dance, stamping his feet and shouting at the sky.

'What now?' I asked when the celebrations had subsided. 'Are you going back to Destiny?'

'No need to, Kid. We've won. We can all go home. Well, I'll have to rebuild mine first, of course,' he said looking down the slope to the pile of shattered wood where the ranch used to be. 'That's no problem, though. I wouldn't

(Not so cocky now, are you Silas?)

want to live in
Ham's ghastly
palace; and I'd
be mighty
proud, Kid, if
you'd stay and help.'

'Oh, that won't be possible, I'm afraid,' said
Jakeman. 'I'm going to show Charlie . . . I mean
the Kid, how to get back to his own home.'

'Oh, wow! Do you mean it, Mr Jakeman;
you're going to show me the way home?'

'Of course, Charlie my boy. Why do you
think I've come all this way – just to say "How
do you do?"'

'Oh, brilliant!' I cried, leaping up and down
in excitement. 'I'm going home!'

'Well, I'll miss you, Kid. You've been a real
pal and no mistake. We couldn't have done it
without you,' said Wild Bob, mounting Fortune
and leaning forward to shake my hand. 'Now
you take care, you hear? I hope you make it
home. So long, partner.'

With a wave Wild Bob led the others back
towards Two-Eyes.

Goodbye, Bob.

On My Way Home

Jakeman and I climbed back into the hydraulic bison, and as he set the machine in motion, I turned in my seat and waved as the Daredevil Desperados, and the Rapakwar Braves disappeared down the hill. I will miss them very much, they were all such good friends; but the best amongst them, and the one I'll miss the most is Wild Bob Ffrance.

Jakeman steered the bison at a trot across the open ground at the top of the hill, and soon we passed through a ravine and out across an arid stretch of ground that quickly turned into a desert. I was feeling sad about leaving my good friends behind, but I was also really, really excited about meeting the marvellous Jakeman. There was so much I needed to ask him.

'It's brilliant of you to help me like this,' I said, as soon as we were on our way.

'Think nothing of it, Charlie my boy,' he said with a smile.

'And you're sure you can help me get back to my mum and dad?'

'Yes indeed,' he said. 'It's the least I can do.'

'What do you mean?'

'Ah, well,' said the little man, coughing and turning a little red. 'You could say, I suppose, that it was, um . . . a little bit my fault you ended up here at all.'

'Your fault that I sailed down a crocodile-infested river and had to arm-wrestle a huge silverback gorilla? How on earth could that be your fault?'

'Well, let me explain. It all started when I was trying to re-set the huge clock that sits on top of my factory. I had just . . .'

Whirr, chung, clunk!

'Oh no, what's that?'

There was a terrible grinding noise from the bison and we came to an abrupt and squealing halt. Jakeman jumped down and started to unscrew various plates underneath the heavy coat of the magnificent machine.

'I thought so,' said Jakeman, sighing. 'He's got sand in his joints. There's nothing I can do about it now; I'll have to send Philly, my assistant, to come and repair it later.'

'Oh, that's great!' I cried in frustration. 'Now I'll never get back home.'

'Calm down, Charlie,' said Mr Jakeman. 'Of

course you will. We're just going to have to walk a bit, that's all.'

'Walk!' I gasped in astonishment. 'Exactly how far is it?'

'To your home, you mean? Oh, you can't measure that in kilometres, Charlie. I'll have to do some inventing to get you back there, which means we must go to my factory first . . . and that's only about three thousand kilometres or so.'

'Only three thousand kilometres!'

'That's right. Come on, Charlie; the sooner we get started, the sooner we'll arrive. And I can explain all about how you got here, on the way. Best foot forward!'

Speechless, I jumped down to join him.

A Not So Helpful Hand

We set out across the desert sands under a blistering sun. It was hot and thirsty work; almost too hot and tiring to talk, but there were lots of things I needed to know.

'Who are you, Mr Jakeman; are you some sort of magician?' I asked, panting for breath.

'Goodness me no, Charlie, nothing like that!' he puffed. 'I'm a scientist and an engineer. Although some people might think that amounts to the same thing!'

We carried on trudging through the deep sand. It was so hot it felt like my brain was starting to fry. I wish I had put some sun block in my explorer's kit.

'So how could it be your fault that I ended up in this strange place?' I managed to gasp.

My brain frying!

Who exactly is Jakeman?

'Yes, yes. It's high time you knew. *Phew!* Let's stop for a rest and I can explain, as far as I know, exactly what happened and how you got here.'

Brilliant, I thought, taking the water bottle from my rucksack and handing it to the funny little man. At last I'm going to learn the truth. Where I am; why Mum can't hear me when I phone her; why, when I've been away for hundreds of years, I still only look eight years old!

'Well,' said Jakeman, taking a swig of water. 'It was like this . . . Whoa, what's that?' he cried suddenly, dropping the bottle in terror. I looked down at his foot and gasped. A strong, hairy hand had emerged from the desert sands at our feet and had grabbed Jakeman by the ankle.

'Oh Charlie, help!' he cried, as the hand started to pull him down into the sand. He had already sunk up to his waist and I grabbed hold of his arms to try and pull him out. It was no good; whatever was on the other end of him was a lot stronger than me.

'I can't hold you, Mr Jakeman,' I yelled as he disappeared up to his shoulders.

'Charlie,' he cried. 'Remember this . . .' but with a final tug, the thing beneath the sands pulled Jakeman below the surface and he completely disappeared!

'Oh no! Come back, Mr Jakeman. Come back!' I yelled. I couldn't believe it; I was alone in the middle of a desert and the only man who could tell me how to get home, had just been swallowed up by the sands. I had to find him; I just HAD to find Jakeman!

I fell to my knees and dug my arms into the sand where he had been, then pushed aside with a swimming motion. There was nothing there. I dug deeper. Still there was nothing, so I took the crocodile's tooth from my rucksack and, using it as a trowel, dug deeper and deeper and deeper into the sand. Finally, I heard a clang as the tooth struck something hard.

Hurriedly, I brushed away the remaining sand, revealing a domed metal lid with a handle on one side, like this:

A domed metal lid

I crouched down and pulled with both hands. The lid opened easily, revealing the mouth of a tube that led straight down into the ground.

Down The Tubes

I lowered myself feet-first into the tube, hoping that I might feel a foothold, but the inside of the tube was completely smooth. So I placed one foot either side of the pipe and then eased my arms over the rim. Immediately, I started to

drop, but the braking
effect of my rubber-soled
trainers slowed my
descent just enough.
Soon though, my legs
started to ache like billy-o
as I continued to keep
them pressed against the
inside of the tube.

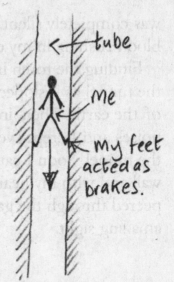

Down I dropped;
down, down, down
through the dark until I
lost all track of time. Then bright flares of light
started to pierce the darkness. They flashed and
changed colour, from white to red, then blue,
green and yellow. Faster and faster they
flickered until it felt as if I was falling through
the middle of a crazy rainbow. Then everything
went black again, and on a sudden updraft of
air, I started to slow down. By the time I
reached the bottom I was almost floating, and
landed on hard ground, amazingly without a
bump.

I was in a dark tunnel, carved from solid
bedrock. It was almost pitch black, and I
strained my ears to try and hear anything, but it

was completely silent. All I could hear was the blood rushing in my ears.

Finding the torch in my rucksack, I followed the tunnel as it sloped deeper into the bowels of the earth. Then, in the distance, I could hear noises and I crept even more carefully along the tunnel. Soon I came to a crack in the tunnel wall and with my heart beating fast with fear, I peered through the gap and saw the most amazing sight.

Oh my goodness!

Subterranean Denizens

By the light of a thousand oil lamps I could see a horde of creatures moving about, digging into the rock and carrying away piles of rubble in hand carts.

The creatures looked half-human and half-ape, with wide powerful shoulders and thick muscular arms matted with coarse hair. Their faces were fierce and heavy-browed and when they snarled in their efforts to smash the rocks with their crude instruments, they exposed a row of large and pointed teeth. I scanned the thronging mass, but couldn't see any sign of Jakeman.

It was incredible; these creatures looked almost like Neanderthal men. Perhaps I had discovered a lost stone-age tribe that everyone thought had been extinct for thousands of years. Big deal! I thought, for I hadn't discovered any sign of Jakeman. Oh, blooming heck, this was terrible! What was I going to do next?

I started to panic but knew I must calm down and get my thoughts in some sort of order. Looking around to make sure I was quite safe, I squatted at the back of a deep alcove and fished out my journal. Perhaps writing up my latest adventures would help me think more clearly.

Now that I'm finished, I feel a lot calmer, and I must continue to look for Jakeman. I've got to find him if I'm ever to discover my way home, and as long as I keep away from those scary-looking creatures I should be safe. Then, as I crawled out of the alcove, I felt something under my foot. Bending down, I picked up a pair of oily goggles. Jakeman's goggles. So he had been here! Perhaps he was in the next cave after all, and I had overlooked him in the crowd. I crept across the passage and pressed my face against the narrow crack, to check.

'RARRR!' All of a sudden a hideous face popped up on the other side of the crack in the wall. It was one of the Neanderthal ape-like things.

I'VE BEEN SPOTTED!

HELP! ~

```
PUBLISHER'S NOTE
This is where the fourth journal ends.
```

A Desperado Dictionary

Amigo – Friend.

Bangtail – Wild horse.

Bellyache – Complain.

Bushwhack – Ambush.

Chow – Food.

Chuck – Food!

Critter – Creature, or a
            no good person.

Dude – A city slicker.

Hooks – Spurs.

Hang fire – Wait.